Canyon Diablo

CANYON DIABLO

MAX McCOY

PINNACLE BOOKS
Kensington Publishing Corp.
www.kensingtonbooks.com

PINNACLE BOOKS are published by

Kensington Publishing Corp.
119 West 40th Street
New York, NY 10018

All Kensington titles, imprints, and distributed lines are available at special quantity discounts for bulk purchases for sales promotions, premiums, fund-raising, educational, or institutional use. Special book excerpts or customized printings can also be created to fit specific needs. For details, write or phone the office of the Kensington special sales manager: Kensington Publishing Corp., 119 West 40th Street, New York, NY 10018, attn: Special Sales Department; phone 1-800-221-2647.

PINNACLE BOOKS and the Pinnacle logo are Reg. U.S. Pat. & TM Off.

ISBN-13: 978-0-7860-3173-3
ISBN-10: 0-7860-3173-5

First printing: April 2012

10 9 8 7 6 5 4 3 2 1

Printed in the United States of America

For Gary Goldstein

Think not that I am come
to send peace on earth:
I came not to send peace,
but a sword.

> —Matthew 10:34

PROLOGUE

Arizona Territory, 1871

Royal Oatman sat down on a rock at the edge of the red canyon. His teeth were chattering from fear, and he drew his knees up to his chin.

The dread had started small, with just a thrill in his chest. He glimpsed shadows over the rim of the gorge moving toward him. When he saw a human figure crawling behind a creosote bush, not forty yards away, the fear became a fever in his head and chest, clouding his mind and making his hands tremble.

"Roy!" a woman's voice called sharply from behind.

Oatman hugged his shins. He closed his eyes tightly and pressed his forehead against his knees, stifling a sob. He hoped the Indians would kill him before they got to his wife and children. There was a capped and loaded Dragoon pistol in his belt, but Oatman had not the will to draw it.

"Roy!" the woman demanded. She was standing in the front of a wagon and her pinched face was shrouded by a billowy white bonnet. She was wearing a periwinkle dress and her hands were folded on top of her bulging stomach. "Do something!"

Oatman flung his head back and snatched the maroon fez with the gold tassle from his head, revealing an unruly crown of blond hair. He dropped the hat on the ground and clasped his hands together in prayer, and the lace on his cuffs fell back to reveal his bare forearms.

"Yea, though I walk through the valley of the shadow of death . . ."

The heavy wagon with the faded green sides and the broken rear axle was a few yards behind him. Its rear corner sagged heavily and the big red wheel tilted out of track, jammed against the box. The bottom of the grease bucket, which hung beneath the axle, was resting on the rocks. As the oxen shifted in their traces, moving the wagon a few inches back and then forward, the iron rim of the wheel screeched against the dry wood.

The wagon had been unloaded to make it lighter, and an improbable array of objects littered the wash: an elaborately carved headboard, a dressing table and mirror, an oak secretary, boxes of books, a pair of red velvet-covered chairs, a mantel clock (with the face in the belly of an elephant with real ivory tusks).

In addition to Royal's wife, the wagon held their three children—Lucas, who was thirteen, and his younger sisters Abigail and Adeline. All, like their parents, were disturbingly blond. When the axle had broken, the children were laughing and playing in the wagon, protected from the sun by the hoop of canvas. One of the games they played was "what if" they were being attacked by Indians.

Lucas said he would grab his father's rifle and fight them off. Abigail, who was eight, said she would run away. Adeline, who had just turned twelve, said she would kill herself with a butcher knife to keep from being taken captive.

There was another child in the box of the wagon, a brooding dark-haired eight-year-old boy who did not participate in the game. He had seen the shadows flitting along the rim of the canyon, but had kept silent. Long ago, he had learned that what he had to say did not matter.

The boy's name was Ishmael and his mother had died giving birth to him. He had been adopted as a yowling infant by a family of bakers named Sheets in Mineral Creek, Texas. But after two years, the family had grown weary of the boy's unhappy demeanor and nearly constant screaming and passed him on. By the age of seven, three other families had taken him until the Oatman family, in a fit of religious fervor, rescued him in the name of Jesus.

The Oatmans were followers of a minor messiah by the name of Jack Chappel, who was wanted in the state of Arkansas. He had held a lottery to sell a corner lot in Fort Smith that he did not own. In north Texas, Chappel declared he was God's representative on earth and founded the Sacerdotal Order of Melchizedek, with himself as high priest. After discovering a war surplus crate of fezzes that had once been the property of the Red River Zouaves, Chappel declared the fez to be the sacred male headgear of the order. He also declared that all priest holders should adorn the cuffs of their shirts and trousers with lace. He found a willing flock by preaching that a better world was coming for those who followed the true faith. That better world, God had told him, was along the banks of the Colorado River in California.

In June, he led a wagon train of twelve families out of Texas.

After weeks of hard traveling, the train found itself on the banks of the Sante Fe River in north central New Mexico. Here, Chappel declared that he had received a new communication from God. They were to stop and establish a colony. The Almighty had also shared a joyful new commandment: The men must share their wives with Chappel for marital relations, as a demonstration of faith. Jesus especially wanted Chappel to share this joy with the wives under the age of twenty-five years.

Six of the families remained with Chappel in New Mexico Territory, but five others discarded their fezzes and turned back in disgust for Texas. Royal Oatman prayed and fasted on the issue for three days, at the end of which he announced that he believed the Lord wanted them to continue on to California.

Rebekah Oatman was doubtful, but was nothing if not a dutiful wife.

Three weeks later, the Oatmans found themselves in Arizona Territory, crossing from one lonely village to another, begging a little food for themselves and their animals, but always pressing west. In a month, they had left the last village thirty miles behind, and Oatman attempted to follow the California-Santa Fe Trail, but became badly lost. He had been told to make Wolf's Crossing on the Little Colorado River, or risk being blocked by the deep red slash in the desert called Canyon Diablo.

They traveled at night, as a relief from the demon sun, and they continued even though their food was all but gone and the team of oxen was ribs and shoulders, dying slowly in their traces.

It was then that Oatman had driven the wagon to the rim of the canyon he had been warned about. They turned north, in hopes that they were not far away from Wolf's Crossing, Oatman walking beside the team. But the terrain was difficult and, during one stretch where the smoothest way was a rocky ledge not far from the canyon rim, one of the wagon's back wheels crashed from a high rock to the limestone slab below, shattering the axle. With no spare, and no amount of hardwood nearby from which to fashion another, Oatman was seized by despair.

It was now the first of August, and the sun turned the rocky landscape into an oven. They unloaded the wagon in an attempt to continue with the broken axle, but still the wheel was binding against the box. Their only choice was to walk to Wolf's Crossing, but Oatman didn't know if it was one mile or fifty. Because their water would soon be gone, Oatman contemplated the unpleasant task of slitting the oxen's throat in order to drink the blood.

That's when he glimpsed the shadows moving at the edge of his vision. An Apache warrior draped in a mangy wolf skin appeared twenty yards away, standing and watching. The fear became an unbearable pressure that drove thought from Oatman's mind and forced him down onto the rock, helpless. The old Dragoon pistol tucked in his belt offered no comfort.

"Roy," Rebekah called from beneath canvas. "What shall we do?"

But Royal could not summon the will to answer.

The warrior came forward, his long black hair swinging with each stride. The wolf's skull was still attached to the mangy cape, and the upper jaw with its yellow teeth jutted over the Apache's face like the bill of a forage cap. Yellow paint was daubed across his cheekbones and the bridge of his nose. Except for a breechclout and a pair of knee-high moccasins, he was bare beneath the wolfskin.

"*Nosotoros hambrientos,*" the warrior said.

But the Oatmans did not speak Spanish.

"Go away," Rebekah Oatman said. "Can't you see you're scaring us?"

But the warrior did not speak English.

He was thirty years old, an old man in Chiricahua Apache society, and was weary from a decade of war with the whites and, long before he was born, the Mexicans. He had lost his power two years ago, when a bullet from an Army Springfield had taken the tip of his trigger finger. Although the injury was slight, it was deeply symbolic, and he had lost confidence in his ability to wage war. Now, he was only suited to leading raiding parties of novices to steal food and livestock. None of the young men accompanying him had yet completed the sacred number of raids— four—in order to be recognized as warriors.

Desperation had forced them to range far from the Apache homeland to the southwestern fringe of the Navajo reservation, to an area all tribes knew as "the haunted lands." This region of deep canyon and painted desert was shunned by both tribes because of what the Navajo called *chindis*, the evil that is left behind after a human being dies. The Apache called the shadows that crept through draws and canyons in search of the blood of living persons *los Sanguinarios*. In folklore, the only defense against the bloodthirsty ones was a shard from a fallen star.

The warrior, Old Wolfskins, dared to cross the haunted lands only because he had a knife made from just such a star. Since losing the tip of his finger, he had been forbidden to touch firearms with his right hand. But he was no good at shooting with his left hand, so he eventually traded five stolen horses to an old white man for an old and curious black knife. The knife had been forged from one of the strangely heavy iron-rich rocks found around a great round depression in the desert known to the whites as Coon Butte, but which all Indians knew as the place where a star had once fallen to earth.

The knife had a handle made from a human thigh bone and a guard made of brass. The seven-inch blade was dark and had a curious mottled pattern, which resulted when the Mexican smith, a couple of centuries before, folded the iron into earthly steel, many thousands of times, with just the right amount of charcoal. The knife was just soft enough to be unbreakable and just brittle enough to hold a wicked edge.

He gripped the dark knife as he approached the family with the broken wagon, for he knew this spot near the canyon rim was full of power. The wagon and the whites might not even be real. Perhaps they were some trap set by the spirit of the place, or Coyote, or perhaps even the *Sanguinarios* themselves. Or, they might be ghosts. Broken things were a favorite of ghosts, and the things piled around the wagon looked otherworldly. The whites were strange, much stranger even than their cousins the Mexicans. It was difficult to tell in such situations. Since losing his power, Old Wolfskins had grown timid. He didn't even know if the language they spoke was the language of the whites, or the language of ghosts. But perhaps, he told himself, if he acted in the old way, some of his power would return.

"Go away!" Old Wolfskins shouted in his native Western Apache dialect, summoning up his best war voice and brandishing the knife. "Turn your faces from us and go away. Follow the sun to beneath the stone, where you belong!"

Rebekah and her children cringed at the outburst.

"What's he saying?" Lucas asked.

"Something in Hebrew," his mother said. "Roy, you know your verses. Say something to him. Tell him to go away."

But Royal Oatman began to pray silently.

Lucas edged closer to his father's old .50-caliber plains rifle, which was on the floor of the wagon box. Abigail and Adeline were peering over the tailgate at four other warriors, who had appeared from the scrub.

The Indians were threading their way through the Oatmans' household things, unsure if the weird objects were of this world or the next. The youngest of the warriors, a fifteen-year-old who wore a beaded necklace with a silver conch, paused at the dresser mirror to stare at his own image. He reached out and touched the glass with a tentative forefinger.

Lucas closed the fingers of his right hand around the stock of the rifle.

Old Wolfskins cupped one hand like a bowl and made an eating motion with the other.

"He's hungry," Ishmael said.

"We have no food to spare," Rebekah Oatman said.

Royal Oatman swallowed hard and tried to speak, but no words came out. He wanted to tell his wife to give the warriors some beans and bread, but he could force no sound from his throat.

At the back of the wagon, the fifteen-year-old warrior took a step forward and reached out with delicate brown fingers to touch Abigail's blonde hair. She screamed and scooted back.

Lucas brought the old gun clumsily up to his shoulder, cocked it, and pulled the trigger. The hammer fell on the percussion cap and there followed a thunderous noise.

The half-inch ball punched a hole in the bridge of the young Apache's nose and exited with a fist-sized mass of brain and bone from the back of his head. He fell dead, his hand still outstretched.

The other warriors stared in disbelief at their dead companion, then looked at the boy holding the mountain rifle. A thin rope of blue smoke curled upward from the muzzle.

Lucas dropped the rifle and jumped out of the wagon. He rolled on the ground and then came up and glanced at Old Wolfskins, then began running.

"Son!" Royal Oatman shouted.

A pair of warriors, war clubs in hand, bolted down the wash after Lucas.

Rebekah grabbed the hands of the two girls and pulled them behind her as she sought her husband's side for protection. Ishmael climbed slowly down after them. Royal Oatman, who had now managed to stand, pulled his wife and daughters to him.

"It was an accident," Royal Oatman said. "Don't hurt us. It was an accident."

Old Wolfskins' eyes burned with anger. He shook the dark blade at the girls.

"No," Royal Oatman said. "You cannot have the children."

"Papa," Adeline said, tears running down her cheeks. "Oh, Papa."

Frightened, Ishmael took a step backward, trying to join the huddled family.

Royal Oatman pushed the boy forward.

"Take this one," he said. "He's a bastard. Nobody will miss him."

"*Bastardo,*" the warrior said, recognizing the word.

Then Rebeka Oatman shrieked.

The two warriors were dragging the body of Lucas by its heels back toward the wagon. The arms trailed behind and the blond head was dripping blood.

"My God, my God," the woman cried. "Why hast Thou forsaken us?"

The woman jerked the revolver from her husband's belt, clumsily drew the hammer back, and pressed the muzzle against the back of her eldest daughter's head.

She jerked the trigger.

In a blossom of fire and pink mist, twelve-year-old Adeline fell dead at her feet. The shot echoed back from some far cliffs, and the puff of gun smoke drifted like a disembodied soul in the still air over the body of the girl.

Then Rebekah Oatman cocked the revolver again and pointed it at eight-year-old Abigail, who was backing away in horror. The girl tripped over her skirt and fell to the ground.

Old Wolfskins stepped forward, grasped the barrel of the revolver with his free hand, and wrenched it away. With his right hand, he brought the black knife up and thrust the blade into the base of her throat.

She fell to her knees, gurgling, hands clasped to her throat. Blood seeped from between her fingers. In a few moments she fell on her side, hunched around her bulging stomach, but she continued to make small noises.

Old Wolfskins knelt beside her and placed a hand on her stomach. Confused, he ran his hand up her skirt and pulled out a pillow. Angered by the ruse, he cut the pillow open and flung it. The pillow hemorrhaged goose down as it sailed through the air and landed, deflated, near the wagon.

Abigail got to her feet and ran into the brush along the canyon rim. None of the warriors followed. By this time, Rebekah Oatman was silent.

Royal Oatman fell to his knees, hands clasped.

"Help me, Jesus!"

Offended by the cowardice, Old Wolfskins turned the gun around in his left hand, cocked it, and at point-blank shot the man in the chest. With a look of relief, Royal Oatman fell on his back, his arms outstretched, a smoking hole the size of a thimble in his shirt. His dead eyes were open, looking up at the sky.

Old Wolfskins barked an order, and two of the young men climbed into the back of the wagon and found the family's food. There were some dry beans and a bit of salt. Bug-infested cornmeal. One warrior yelped when he found half a bottle of whiskey. Another found a blanket in which to wrap the body of their dead comrade. They would bury him, Old Wolfskins said, in the caves just below the rim of the canyon, and they would recall the events of his brief life and celebrate his warrior death.

"Do not look at his face," Old Wolfskins cautioned the novices. "To look upon the face of the dead is to invite their ghosts to linger among the living. Turn his face away and wrap the blanket tightly around him."

They would slaughter the oxen in their traces and hack away the best meat to carry back to camp. Then they would set the wagon on fire and leave the bodies where they fell for other whites to find. The man's body would be separated from his manhood, however, so that he would impotently wander the otherworld forever as punishment for his cowardice.

Old Wolfskins was glad the smallest child had run into the scrub, where she could die with the other animals. Then he looked at the boy, who was still standing defiantly on the spot where the man had pushed him.

The boy had wild dark hair and his nose was dripping snot and his hands were jammed into his pockets. The boy was big across the chest and long of limb and Old Wolfskins thought he would grow into a strong young man.

Old Wolfskins called to one of the warriors. He told him to tie the boy's hands and they would lead him back to camp and he would become a slave for the old woman who had lost her son that day.

But when the warrior reached out with a leather cord to bind the boy's hands, the boy pulled an old scratch awl from his pocket. He slashed out at the warrior, who jumped back just in time to keep the rusty point from piercing his stomach.

"I ain't afraid of you," the boy said. "I ain't afraid of nothing!"

Old Wolfskins rapped the back of the boy's head with the barrel of the revolver, and he went down. In Western Apache, he congratulated the barely unconscious boy on his courage, then scolded the warrior for being so careless.

When later they bound Ishmael's wrists with a six-foot leather strap and pulled him to his feet and back to consciousness, the body of the dead Apache youth had been wrapped in one of the blankets found in the wagon. Old Wolfskins instructed one of the novices to find a tree branch, wrap it with linen, and soak it in the wagon's grease bucket to make a torch. Then they hoisted the body on their shoulders and, pulling Ishmael along, followed Old Wolfskins as he led them along the edge of the canyon rim.

Soon, they found a natural vault over a deep fissure. Old Wolfskins stepped beneath the overhanging rock and peered into the darkness beyond. He could feel cool air on his face. He told the novices that here was a cave, and that it might be deep enough for burial. He led them beneath the overhanging arched rock and into a passage that was large enough for a man to ride a horse through. They knocked some dirt and gravel loose while climbing down, and a layer of powdery red dust swirled in a shaft of sunlight inside the mouth of the cave.

On the right side of the entrance was a lump of rock that, through a trick of light and geology, looked like the profile of an old man. As Old Wolfskins passed the stone, he touched his hand to the rock, feeling the jutting nose and chin, reassuring himself that it was indeed inanimate.

Old Wolfskins led them deeper into the cave. When they lost the daylight, he paused and used a flint and steel to ignite the torch. Holding the torch high in his right hand, he stepped forward and ran the three fingertips of his left hand along the cool limestone wall.

"Listen!" Old Wolfskin told the novices. "There is only one way to find your way out of a deep cave, and that is to follow the cave wall with one hand on the way in, and then to use the other hand against the same wall on the way out."

Ishmael didn't know what the crazy old Indian was saying, and he wished he would shut up. His head ached from the blow. He could feel his blood trickle, warm and sticky, beneath his collar. A sickening stench from somewhere deep in the cave stung his nostrils.

"Ain't afraid of nothing," Ishmael said softly. "Afraid of nothing."

Old Wolfskins led them deeper and deeper into the cave, explaining that the body of the youth must be well-hidden. The passage was narrow and twisting, and Ishmael banged his forehead against low-hanging rocks.

"God dammit," the boy said.

Recognizing the tone of an oath, the old Indian turned and scowled at the white boy. Failing to display respect during the burial would invite calamity.

Eventually the cave opened into a high-vaulted chamber that was as large as a cathedral. Old Wolfskins told the novices to be careful, because there might be a mountain lion or a bear lurking in the darkness.

Old Wolfskins held the torch high over his head.

Then he took a step forward into the chamber, and something snapped beneath his foot like a dry twig. Old Wolfskins glanced down and saw that he had placed his moccasin on a human arm bone.

And then he saw the bright splotches of fresh blood beside the old bone. Fear swelled in his chest as he attempted to back away, but he placed his heel in a dusty ribcage. He turned, swinging the torch, and the moving circle of firelight swept over the body of eight-year-old Abigail Oatman.

Old Wolfskins gave a cry of disbelief.

The little girl was splayed on the ground like so much bloody laundry, her pink intestines coiled beside her. Hunched over the body was a dark form, claw-like fingers dripping red, eyes shining in the torchlight.

Arizona, 1935

"So, what was it?" the woman asked, her tan forearm on the top of the green metal table, a yellow pencil clutched in her fist like a weapon. "One of those— what did you call it—a *sanguinario*?"

"Don't know," the old man said. "Old Wolfskins dropped the torch and drew the power knife and backed everybody out in a hurry. They buried the Apache boy elsewhere."

The woman sat up in the metal chair, her eyes narrowing.

"I'm not sure I believe a word of it," she said. "I've read about the Oatman Massacre in the history books, and it didn't happen like you describe."

The old man leaned back and laced his fingers across his stomach.

"Just because it's in print doesn't mean it is true," Jacob Gamble said, his blue eye squinting against the demon sun. His right eye was covered by a black patch. He was wearing dark trousers, a black vest, and a white shirt with no tie. His dark jacket was draped over the back of the metal chair, and the left pocket sagged with the weight of a pistol.

It was ten o'clock on a Friday morning in the middle of April and already the temperature was eighty degrees. They were sitting at a metal picnic table beneath the white stucco canopy of a gas station, hard beside a concrete bridge that carried Route 66 over a red rock canyon. Stretching along its rim were clusters of square rock buildings with exposed wooden beams meant to resemble pueblos. A road sign above the fake cliff dwellings beckoned travelers to tour the APACHE DEATH CAVE. Another message, in red block letters across the front of the gas station, commanded, FEED THE MOUNTAIN LIONS!

The woman sighed. Her name was Frankie Donovan, and she was twenty-six years old. She wore a gray pinstripe suit and a red silk tie, and her face had begun to dew with sweat.

"You old pirate," she said. "You're wasting my time."

"I rather think it is the other way around," the old man said. "You're the one who summoned me."

A family of Okies sputtered into the gas station in an old Model T truck. The father sat defiantly behind the wheel. His sad wife with limp dark hair and a thin printed dress was beside him, a crying toddler on her lap. In the bed of the truck were three more children, none older than ten, their hungry faces peering out from above the staked sides of the truck. The engine died with a clatter, then the radiator gurgled and began to hemorrhage steam and water.

The woman glanced away from the broken Okie truck.

"What do they call this place now?" the old man asked.

Frankie brushed her bangs from her eyes with the back of her hand.

"Two Guns," she said. "At least, that was the inspiration of the man who built the zoo and the fake ruins as a tourist trap. His name was Harry Miller, and he claimed to be a full-blooded Apache, but he was as white as you are. They tell me he ended up shooting his partner over a business deal gone bad, about ten years ago."

"The Navajo thought this place cursed—they said it was inhabited by the revenge-hungry ghosts of the dead," the old man said. Then he made a sound deep in his throat. "I would have scoffed when I was younger, but now I am eighty-five and feeling more and more like a ghost myself."

"You still seem very much among the living."

"I could give you the chance to find out," the old man said.

"Back to business," Frankie insisted.

"Reckon we could get a drink around here?"

"No," Frankie said. "It is mid-morning and there is work to do. You can drink when we're finished. Do you recognize this place?"

"None of this was here fifty years ago," he said. "No buildings, no highway bridge, nothing except the canyon. The railway bridge wasn't finished yet, and the only place to get across the canyon was at

Wolf's Crossing, along the Little Colorado, miles north of here. I don't know if this cave they talk about here was the same one or not—the one I recall had an arch over the entrance, a kind of natural bridge."

"There was an earthquake in 1886," Frankie said. "Shook things up pretty good, I understand. Could have made a jumble of the entrance."

"How the hell do you know so much?"

"I do my research," Frankie said.

"Then tell me about the town."

"Canyon Diablo is a ghost town now," she said. "Not much left except the abandoned Navajo trading post and some foundations. The steel railway bridge remains, of course. The Santa Fe seems to be quite proud of it. But, in a week, Canyon Diablo, the wickedest city in the West, will be reborn—or at least some version of it will."

"I thought they did all of that at the studio."

"Ordinarily they do, but you can't construct a bridge that is a tenth of a mile long and two hundred and fifty feet tall on a sound stage," Frankie said. "At least you can't do it and put a real locomotive on top. And since you can't tell this story without the bridge, Mister Huston wanted the real thing."

"Mister Huston," the old man scoffed. "What John Huston told about me in the last talking picture was lies and damned lies. About the only thing he got right was my name, Jacob Gamble."

"It's Hollywood, Jake," Frankie said.

"Nobody calls me Jake," the old man said. "Not anymore."

"Jacob, Huston wants to tell the story of what happened twenty years after that movie ended and, now that he knows you're alive, he wants your help to get it right."

"I would have liked more money for the story."

"You're not famous enough for more," Frankie said. "You're not Dillinger or Barrow. And times are tough, if you haven't noticed. There's precious little joy to go around."

From the rock-and-chicken-wire pens behind the gas station, one of the big cats growled. The Okie children had wandered back there while their father fought with the leaking Model T.

Gamble watched with disdain.

"That bother you?" Frankie asked.

"They shouldn't be allowed to put those panthers in cages," Gamble said. "It would be kinder to kill them."

"I meant the children being so close."

"Do you want to hear the rest of the story or not?"

"Only if we can get it right," Frankie said. "Do you think we can get it right, Jake?"

From behind came the unhappy cry of one of the mountain lions. The old man's blue eye blinked and then closed. He crooked a finger toward the sound and said, "Listen. The Apache said that sound was the harbinger of death."

"The boy," Frankie said. "Tell me more about the boy in the cave."

"Your first guess will be that I was the little bastard boy, but that would be wrong. By '71, I was a young man. Then you might think that I was there, somehow, but that's not the case, either. The truth is that I have told you about it just as it was told to me, and by-and-by you will understand."

"Jake," Frankie pleaded. "Let's stick with the boy."

"We'll come back to the boy," Gamble said sternly. "The things I'm going to talk about all happened a long time ago, and a helluva lot has changed since then. About the only thing that hasn't changed is that a Double Eagle still feels good in the palm of your hand."

The old man held out a gold coin.

On one side of the coin was a profile of Lady Liberty with thirteen six-pointed stars around her head. On the other side was the seal of the United States of America—an eagle holding an olive branch in one talon and a clutch of arrows in the other. The date below Liberty was 1850.

"Jacob, you're not supposed to have that."

"It's my lucky Double Eagle," he said. "Minted in the year I was born. It is made of damned near an ounce of gold and for most of my lifetime has been worth twenty dollars."

"The government has ordered all privately-held gold confiscated."

"Twenty dollars is a month's wages for a working man, so when you have a Double Eagle you know that nothing truly bad can happen," Gamble said. "You have the means to buy food and shelter, or whiskey, or medicine. If you're sick or just down on your luck, a Double Eagle will tide you over for thirty days, which is enough time for you to feel better or for your luck to change. If you're lonesome, a Double Eagle will buy you a woman for however many nights it takes to get over it. There are things, of course, that having an ounce of gold won't fix, but these are celestial concerns. Here on earth, the Double Eagle is a surefire solution to what ails you."

"You're crazy," she said. "Put that up before you get us both arrested—or robbed."

"This was minted before the war, so it lacks the 'In God We Trust' that the Yankees added to all their money to ease their consciences. This coin has weight, unlike the silver certificates and other paper the government makes people use now. But paper isn't real money, just a promise to pay. Only gold is real."

"Prison is real enough," she said. "You should know."

"Gold is worth what, thirty-five dollars an ounce?" the old man asked. "I have thirty-five bucks in the palm of my hand."

"Put that up and get back to the story, please?"

"This is the story," Gamble said. "The book says that love of money is the root of all evil, but I think it got that part wrong. From what I've seen, it's been love that causes most of the problems. So that's where I'll start: with love."

The old man clutched the coin tightly in his fist.

"We'll get to the killing soon enough."

ONE

The winter of 1881–82 found me clerking in a mercantile store in Argentine near Kansas City and living in a rented room with my wife of six months. Amity was a 19-year-old mulatto whore I smuggled out of a brothel at Hot Springs in Arkansas the previous summer.

It was not a life I was familiar with.

The job at Brown's on Strong Avenue was about the first straight job I had ever held, and it fit me like somebody else's clothes. I spent ten hours a day, six days a week, being sweetness and light to every manner of congenital idiot and unnatural fool that came through the door. I was also required to abstain from gambling, smoking, and drinking any spirit stronger than a cold cup of coffee.

I sold soap and pins and ribbons and lanterns and coal oil and everything else that modern folks require to run a house, all with a smile plastered on my face, and nobody ever troubled themselves to learn my name; at best, they would refer to me indirectly, as one would talk about a dog or a slow child.

"Come here and fetch that bucket from the shelf so's I can look at it," for example. Or, "That one-eyed feller says they're all out of carpet tacks."

And so forth.

The day (or at least the daylight) is short in winter, and I saw very little of it save for rippling glimpses of Strong Avenue through the undulating glass of the front windows. By the time I got home at night to the cold little room overlooking the Santa Fe yards it was full dark outside, but seldom could I see the moon or stars because of the constant smudge that issued from the smokestacks of the smelter which choked everything. The 18-acre smelter had been built a year or two before and ran around-the-clock smelting the ore that came to it by rail from as far away as South America. Every day, bricks of gold and silver were stacked on the docks, ready for armed guards to load them on the Wells Fargo wagons for the short journey to the Santa Fe depot. From there, the gold would mostly be sent to the federal government mint at Denver. Argentine, which had been built around the smelter, prospered. But there was a price to pay for such riches. The fumes from the smelter stung the eyes and scalded the lungs. Sometimes, when the weather was bad and the air hung close to the ground, the fumes were so bad that dogs and cats strangled to death in the street.

Most every day, the fumes shrouded the city like a blanket. Having spent most of my life out-of-doors, I longed for the sky. I missed the time that I had once spent in easy conversation with friends, the evenings of dice and cards and drinking whiskey, and the money that came with the rough life. The fiddle and the gun, the tools of my past life, were put away.

My father's fiddle hung from a peg in the rented room, collecting dust. The fiddle was already old when I was a boy, and the varnish was worn away on the back of the neck, where your palm slides up and down, and also where the body nestles against the crook of your arm. Nobody could play it except me, because it was strung left-handed—the coarse and fine strings were swapped, as if in a mirror image, and I held the fiddle in my right arm when I played it and bowed with my left. Even though it was old, it had a fine voice, and I spent many hours playing what had been my mother's favorite song, an old tune called "Star of the County Down."

The gun was a .36-caliber Manhattan revolver, a copy of the old percussion Colt navy. It was made by a New Jersey manufacturer that seized an opportunity when Col. Colt's patent on revolving firearms expired just before the war. At first glance, the two revolvers seem identical; both have a full trigger guard, a brass back strap, and blue frame and octagonal barrel. But if you look a bit closer, the Manhattan has an extra set of safety notches in the engraved cylinder. The engravings were of five scenes, three of which featured ships or boats. Another depicted cavalry attacking infantry, and the fifth was a curious scene of civilians firing revolvers at soldiers with rifles. Also, nearly all of the Manhattans used during the war carried five, instead of six, rounds.

My Manhattan came from a young guerrilla who was shot dead by Yankee troopers on our farm in Shelby County, Missouri. My mother carried the gun for a spell, then handed it to me. Not long after the war, I had a gunsmith convert the Manhattan to take cartridges, with a left-handed loading gate.

The converted Manhattan was kept loaded, but stuffed beneath the blue striped mattress upon which Amity and I slept. It was not needed to sell mercantile. Besides, I was afraid of what I might do if it were within easy reach during the working day, because of the demands made on me. Worst of all, they expected me to attend church every Sunday.

But to hell with that.

There's only so much a man can take. If salvation depended upon sitting in a hard pew while listening to some imbecile or fraud repeat fairy tales, then I decided to take my chances with perdition.

Every day, I thought about quitting. Not just of quitting, but of ripping off the hated white apron and throwing it upon the counter in disgust, of declaring in no uncertain terms just what I thought of Mr. Brown's operation, and of breaking a pane or two of that inconstant glass upon my escape into Strong Avenue.

Yet, I did not.

I stayed.

Swept the floors and retrieved the buckets and found more carpet tacks and refrained from cussing and smoking and drinking. Got up while it was still as dark as midnight outside and went home when it was the same. Smiled when I was called "that one-eyed feller" and thanked them for the nickels and dimes and dollars.

Why, you ask?

Because I was in love.

As near as I can tell, that condition is responsible

for most of the serious folly since the beginning of the world. I'm not talking about love in the general sense, such as loving one's neighbor, but being *in love*, which can undo a person faster than a fall from a wild horse. It lasts about a thousand days, in my experience, and I would as soon have a three-year case of dyspepsia; the effects are about the same. Your stomach hurts all the time, you sweat gallons, and you're so dizzy it's hard to form a straight thought.

Falling in love is a sucker's bet guaranteed to turn your life upside down and inside out. Happiness? Forget it. The best you can hope for is to simply survive. Think I'm fooling? Consider the great love stories, both real and imagined: Antony and Cleopatra (friendships and empires sundered, Antony dead by his own sword, Cleopatra a suicide by snakebite); Romeo and Juliet (families at war, friends killed, and self-made corpses both by the end of the play); and the insufferable Heathcliff, who plagues *Wuthering Heights* like an unscratchable itch and then dies miserable, just for spite.

The theme here is this: The wages of love are death. Your own death, the death of your beloved, and the death, perhaps, of anybody within shouting distance. It took me a long time to understand this, but it is as true as the rules of arithmetic taught in grade school. Show me a couple deeply in love, and I will show you a homicide waiting to happen. Ah, you will say, how wrong you are—where would we all be without love? How would we ever be born? The world itself depends upon love. But you confuse love with biology. Any union, regardless of passion, might produce offspring.

But it takes passion to truly muck things up.

And so it was with me and my beloved. The fleetest smile from Amity would send me to the cloud tops, while a scowl would dash my heart upon the rocks below. I set aside my nature, gave up both fiddle and gun, and donned a clerk's apron—all because I wanted to be a better person.

For her.

And she did the same *for me*.

What fools we were.

Two

I came to Hot Springs to rob the Arlington Hotel.

Long ago I had resolved never to rob a railroad or a bank. Those who specialize in such jobs either invite the attention of the Pinkertons or invoke the ire of the townsfolk, with equally bad results. Take Jesse James. A contemporary of mine who, like me, learned his trade as a youngster during the war and continued in some irregular way in and around Missouri for some years after, hitting both banks and trains.

To date, two things had distinguished Jesse's career: In 1873, the Pinkerton Detective Agency of Chicago, working on behalf of the Rock Island Railroad, threw a bomb into the family home at Liberty, killing a younger half-brother and blowing off his mother's left arm at the elbow; and in 1876, when the James-Younger gang tried to rob the bank at Northfield, Minnesota, the townspeople armed themselves with rifles and shotguns from the hardware stores and picked the gang to pieces, although Jesse and his brother Frank escaped.

I wanted no such adventures.

Being short on cash and long on warrants circulating in the St. Louis area, I decided to quit Missouri and move the operation to Arkansas. I arrived in Hot Springs in October of 1881, just as the trees were beginning to flame, and established myself at one of the lesser establishments on bathhouse row within the Reservation. It wasn't a reservation like you have out West, like the Indian reservations, but a reserve—a place set apart.

The Arlington is the biggest and highest-priced hotel in Hot Springs, three stories and 120 gas-lit rooms, and it's where the rich go to take the cure in the 143-degree water. If you couldn't afford the Arlington, there was a range of houses for every taste, all the way down to a public accommodation that was just a square of wooden benches set around a muddy hole. Rich or poor, finely educated or as dumb as a bag of hammers, bored of soul or dying in slow degrees from the syphilis, they all came to Hot Springs looking for the same thing—the balm of Gilead, in the form of the scalding iron and magnesia waters.

Hope springs infernal.

The Ozark Bathhouse was a white clapboard affair with gingerbread ornaments straddling the steaming spring. Like all of the institutions along Bathhouse Row, it had the stifling feel of a sanatorium. And it might as well have been. My neighbors on either side hacked and coughed as if they were bringing their lungs up, or they moaned and talked in their sleep, or they vomited their dinners into buckets beside their beds. About the only place I could tolerate in the Ozark was the pack room, where water nymphs frolicked naked across the stained-glass windows.

I did a lot of strolling, and invariably my strolls

would take me to the vicinity of the Arlington, where I would study the terrain and the routes of escape. Twice I ventured into the lobby to inquire about some trifling manner—a Little Rock newspaper, the railway schedule to Malvern—and, of course, to reconnoiter the front desk and environs. On my first visit, things were open and airy and had the atmosphere of a church social. None of the employees appeared armed, or even capable of using a gun if they could find one.

On my second visit to the Arlington, I was even more encouraged—the door behind the front desk had been left ajar, and I spied the heavy green Mosler hotel safe. I smiled as I took the railway schedule offered by the clerk. He was a slight young man of twenty with pale skin and sandy hair; I tipped him a half-dollar.

I wanted him to remember me.

"Thank you, sir," he said, slipping the coin into his vest pocket. "If there's anything else you need, just ask for Stuart. I'm here every day and on Saturday and Sunday nights, as well—until two o'clock in the morning."

"What a dedicated employee."

"It does keep me out of trouble," he said brightly.

Poor bastard, I thought. Better to put a ball in one's brain than to suffer that fate. But I nodded pleasantly.

"How kind of you," I said. "But I'm not a guest at the hotel. I'm just a simple country deacon from Yell County sent here to take delivery of a new pipe organ. I'm too poor to stay here, I'm afraid; my present rooms are in one of the lesser hotels down the row."

"No problem, sir," he said. "Perhaps your next trip, then."

"Perhaps," I said.

Then I turned to go, but paused.

"Stuart," I said, turning back. "There is something. The organ has been delayed for a few days, and I find myself at loose ends. When a man tires of soaking away his pin feathers in these boiling cauldrons, would there be a place to relax and, say, play a hand or two of cards?"

"Are you speaking of whist, or . . ."

"I mean bucking the tiger."

The boy smiled.

"The deacon is a faro player," he said. "Sir, you can find a card game or two at one of the joints run by Frank Flynn downtown. I would recommend the Hibernia."

He gave me directions.

"I'm not sure I got that," I said. "Could you repeat it, slowly?"

I wanted him to think I was a bit simple.

"You've played there yourself?" I asked.

The boy placed his elbows on the counter and leaned conspiratorially forward.

"Once or twice," he confided.

"And is it a square game?"

"As square as it gets," the boy said. "At least in this town."

"Thank you, Stuart," I said, touching the brim of my hat. "You've been very helpful."

The Hibernia was on the basement level just off Valley Street, behind an unlettered red door on which was a gilded painting of an Irish harp. It was not the kind of place I feel very comfortable—lots of dark wood and plush chairs and gas lights flickering in frosted globes. The backstop behind the bar had a lot of ornate carvings, faces of presidents and so forth, and there were some mirrors and a really big picture of a naked woman with a fat ass.

I bought a handful of checks and sat down with three other punters at the faro bank. The dealer was a large humorless man who seldom looked up from the board and who may have been mute, judging from his conversation skills; I found this unusual, because mostly when you're being cheated, the dealer is all smiles and fast jokes. For an alert player in a square game, the house has almost no advantage. That's why most houses cheat in some way, either by using a gaffed card box or a dealer gifted at sleight-of-hand.

The Hibernia relied on the former.

I tried to play the cards well enough not to lose much money and just badly enough not to attract much interest. It wasn't my intention to spend much time there; I just had to know the layout of the joint well enough so I could stitch a believable story together later. I had just lost fifty cents by flatting the ace when I felt a gentle hand upon my left shoulder.

"Buy a thirsty girl a drink, mister?"

She was on my blind side and I resisted the urge to grasp the hand and bend it back until the wrist snapped. Instead, I turned slowly and smiled, expecting to dismiss the whore with some puerile admonition about the dangers of strong spirits.

But I hesitated.

She was not yet twenty, a sylph with caramel skin and eyes the color of whiskey held to the light.

"What's your name?" she asked, brushing her dark hair from her face.

"Jacob," I said.

"Well, Jake," she said, her hand moving over my

shoulder in a well-practiced caress. "You are some-thing, ain't you? All done up in black and ready to preach in the morning."

"It's Jacob," I said. "Nobody calls me Jake."

"Are you in or out?" the dealer asked, impatient.

"So you can speak," I said. "And I had my doubts."

"In or out?" he growled.

"Out," I said. "Absolutely."

"Busted?" the girl asked.

"Only my pride," I said.

I pushed back from the faro table.

The girl grasped my elbow and pulled me toward a table in a dark corner. I let her. The seat of my pants had barely met the chair when the bartender was placing a couple of half-full glasses on the scarred table in front of us.

"Four bits," he said.

"Put it on my tab."

"You ain't got no tab here," he said.

"Right," I said, forking over fifty cents.

The bartender scooped up the money and went back to the bar. I watched him go, already nostalgic for the pair of quarter dollars. At this rate, I would soon be out of working capital. Still, I had my Double Eagle for insurance.

I lifted my glass and took a whiff. It smelled like benzene. I was fairly sure that what the girl had in her glass was room-temperature tea.

"What's your name?" I asked.

"Does it matter?"

"The truth matters," I said. "I don't lie and I cannot tolerate it in others."

"Call me Amity," she said.

"Sure."

"No, really," she said. "That's where I was born—Amity down in Clark County."

I remained skeptical.

"Doesn't matter if you believe me," she said, looking down at the table. She dipped a finger in her tea and slid it around the rim of the glass, making a quivering sound.

"Forget it."

"Buy me another drink."

"You haven't finished the tea you have."

Amity looked at me and smiled.

"My mother was Choctaw," she said. "My father was a black man, a slave owned by the family. A wealthy family, damned near as white as you are. When it became apparent that my mother was with child, they cast her out. No other family in the Choctaw Nation would have her, so she wandered across the line to Arkansas, begging food and sleeping in haylofts. She eventually made it to Amity, where she gave birth to me in a livery stable on the day Vicksburg fell. Then she took off all of her clothes and walked into the Caddo River without giving me a name."

I asked her how she survived.

"A Methodist minister by the name of Amariah Biggs found me squalling in the livery," she said. "Guess the old gent didn't have much of an imagination, because he named me after the town."

"Do you know what happened to your father?"

"He was worth too much to kill," Amity said. "They castrated him and then sold him to a white family somewhere near Little Rock. At least, that's what the letter said that my mother left behind in the pocket of her dress."

"So she was trying to walk to Little Rock to find him?"

"Yes," Amity said. "What a joke, huh?"

"I fail to see the humor."

"Well, you just aren't looking at it right."

She smiled and put a hand beneath her chin and cocked her head a bit.

"So, Jake, how did your parents name you?"

"I told you, nobody calls me Jake."

"Was it your father's name?"

"No," I said. "Named for the one in the Bible who wrestles with God in the desert, cheats his brother out of his birthright, and has a vision about a ladder to heaven."

"And do you wrestle with God and cheat?"

"Every god-damned day," I said.

"Any visions?"

"Not yet."

"How'd you lose that eye?"

"Careless," I said.

I sure as hell wasn't going to tell her that a murderous red-headed monster named Alf Bolin put it out with a rock during a fight when I was 13 years old in Taney County, Missouri. It would just lead to more questions. I'd have to explain about my mother and about how Bolin was the leader of a thieving gang I joined with, while not yet shaving, and how Bolin was killed when a Yankee trooper brought a sling blade down on his wicked head in 1863.

"Did it hurt?"

Amity reached out with her right hand to touch the

black eye patch, and I gently grasped her wrist. Her pulse ticked rapidly beneath the delicate skin, and I held on for a few seconds longer than I should have.

"Not at first," I said. "It didn't hurt at first."

"Tell me about your mother," she said.

"Her name was Eliza Gamble," I said. "She walked a bit like you and was fond of making deals with the devil. And she always kept her side of the bargain."

"You say the strangest things."

"Wait until you get to know me."

"Will I have the chance?"

I was becoming too fond of this girl, too quick. I was charmed in the worst way, anxious to gaze into her warm eyes and to breathe in her scent, which reminded me of vanilla extract. I had already revealed far too much about myself, and it was time to break it off. Her interest in me, I was sure, would end once she had squeezed from me all of the money she thought she could get. It wasn't that I resented her for this; on the contrary, I had some professional respect for how well she was playing the game.

"Jake," she said. "Will I have the chance?"

"Hardly, I think. We are a lonely man and a whore passing a few moments in idle converse. We may, after bargaining upon a price, share a brief and love-less encounter in one of the rooms upstairs, but after you have counted your money and given a percent-age to the house you'll be on to your next Johnny and never think of me again. Nor will I of you."

She smiled.

"I know what you're doing," she said. "I'd probably do the same, if I were you. But you've got me wrong."

"I seldom have people wrong."

"What do you do for a living?"

"Damn, but you are full of questions," I said.

"I'm curious," she said. "Don't see many of your type walking into the Hibernia."

"And just what type is mine?"

Her eyes narrowed.

"I don't know," she said. "But I know what you're not, and that is enough to make me curious. Buy me another drink, and we can sit here and work it out."

"I'll not pay four bits for another glass of coal oil for me and a few ounces of weak tea for you."

"Then what do you expect for a half dollar?"

"Old Crow," I said. "Old Grand Dad. Old Anything."

She smiled and called to the bartender.

"Jimmy," she said. "Bring us a couple of shots of the better stuff."

"I want to see his money first," the bartender said.

"Don't worry about it," Amity said. "I'm paying."

"Flynn ain't going to like that," Jimmy said.

"Just do it," she said.

Jimmy shook his head, but came out from behind the bar with two shot glasses clutched in one hand and a bottle of Old Crow in the other. He sat the glasses down with a clink and poured two fingers of whiskey in each.

Amity lifted her shot glass.

"Here's to us, Jake."

I picked up my shot, but paused.

"I've told you a couple times already," I said. "I don't let anybody call me Jake."

"I heard you," Amity said. "Thing is, I'm not just anybody."

She clinked her shot against mine.

THREE

Shortly before midnight on the next Sunday night, I walked briskly into the lobby of the Arlington Hotel, clutching a suitcase and a battered valise.

"Good to see you again, sir," the desk clerk said. "It has been a few days."

"Stuart," I said, placing the suitcase on the floor but keeping a tight hold on the valise. "Your advice was sterling. I did not have a chance to get to the faro tables until tonight, but what a night it was." I patted the valise for effect.

"You won?"

"The Lord was with me," I said.

I opened the valise and withdrew a $20 silver certificate. A bit clumsily, I placed it on the counter. As I did, I noted the time on the fancy clock over the desk. It was a quarter to midnight.

"There is your commission," I said.

"You are far too generous," he said.

"Nonsense," I said. "Take it, you've earned it."

He palmed the note and slipped it into his vest pocket.

"I can finally afford to stay in the Arlington tonight," I said. "Have you a room?"

"Of course," Stuart said.

"Excellent," I said. Then I looked at the valise, as if its possession were too weighty a responsibility.

"Sir?" Stuart asked.

"What shall I do with this?" I asked. "I would like to take the baths in the morning, but would be reluctant to leave this behind. If it were stolen, the church . . ."

"Yes, sir?"

"Well, since my good fortune comes from the Lord, it seems only right that I give my windfall to the church improvement fund. I can see it now—a magnificent new stained-glass window, showing Jesus forgiving the thief on the cross. It is my favorite passage. And yet, if the valise is stolen . . . tell me straight, how secure are your rooms?"

Stuart shook his head.

"Frankly, sir, I would not leave it in the room," he said in a near-whisper, then leaned forward. "Even the best door lock can be forced. And it has, sadly, happened here."

"I am grateful for your honesty," I said. "I will forego the baths, then."

I glanced at the clock. It was 11:47. I had to hurry this up.

"Not to worry," Stuart said. "I can put it in the hotel safe for you."

"Is it strong?"

"Very," Stuart said.

I hesitated.

"Could I see it?"

"We're not supposed to allow guests behind the counter," he said. "Especially not when we're alone."

"My mind would rest easy if only I could see the vault," I said, knowing that Stuart was anxious for another Stephen Decatur. "But I understand why it is not possible. You are a good employee, Stuart."

"There might be a way," he said. "That is, if you wouldn't mind being searched. . . ."

"Of course not," I said. "It would only be prudent."

Stuart stepped from behind the desk. I placed the valise on the floor and held out my arms awkwardly, allowing Stuart to inexpertly pat me down.

Then he beckoned me back. I picked up the valise and followed him to the door behind the desk. He unlocked it, then proudly showed me the squat green Mosler safe. It was shaped like a keg, but was made of solid steel, and the door was like a porthole on a battleship, but with a silver dial in the middle. It was bolted to an iron plate in the floor.

"Here's the monster," he said. "It weighs eight hundred pounds. Nobody is getting inside without the combination."

"Outstanding," I said. "You've convinced me, Stuart."

I opened the valise and reached inside with my left hand. I paused for a moment, knowing he was expecting me to produce another green banknote. Instead, I pulled out the converted Manhattan.

"You're no deacon," he said dejectedly.

I stepped into the room and closed the door behind me, but left it open a crack so that I could see the desk. I took a pair of handcuffs and a red bandana out of the valise, then threw the bag on the floor and motioned to the safe with the barrel of the gun.

"Open it," I said.

He sighed.

"If I do, I'll lose my job."

I cocked the Manhattan.

"If you don't," I said, "you'll lose your head."

Stuart spun the dials and dialed the combination, then worked the lever and swung the heavy door open. He stood back, so I could see the contents. I could see stacks of gold and silver coins, neat piles of greenbacks, and jewelry glittering in the light from the gas lamps.

I threw him the valise.

"Fill it," I said. "Do it quickly, please."

I glanced outside. The desk was still deserted.

Stuart used both hands to shovel the swag into the valise. It seemed to take him a long time. I heard footsteps outside, and through the crack in the door I could see a tired-looking man approach the desk. He paused, looked around for a moment, and then slapped the bell.

Stuart gave me a questioning look.

"Hellfire," I said.

"What do you want me to do?"

"Get rid of him," I whispered. "Quick, but natural. You're a nice kid, but if you so much as breathe a word of this, or try to run—"

"Bullet in the brain," Stuart said. "I understand."

He slipped outside. He retrieved the hotel key from one of the pigeonholes behind the desk, handing it over, and bade the man a good night as he walked toward the stairs.

"What time is it?" I asked.

"Eleven fifty-one," Stuart said.

Then I pulled Stuart back into the room with the safe and sat him down in a chair at a roll-top desk. I handcuffed his wrists to the chair, behind his back, and used the bandana to gag him, tying the ends behind his neck.

"Sorry," I said. "I know that tastes awful."

His eyes agreed.

Through the crack in the door, I saw Amity walking up to the desk. She was dressed respectable, down to the white gloves. She had a big hat with a lot of feathers.

"It's been a pleasure," I told Stuart. "You're right, you'll lose your job—but it is your choice to view this episode as a lesson learned or to fling yourself into the pit of despair. I advise the former. Use your newfound freedom to further your education. Travel. Read. Fall in love. Steal a bit, when you need money."

He tried to say something.

I nudged the bandana down with my thumb.

"But I have a wife and two kids."

"Steal big."

I replaced the bandana.

"Oh, almost forgot," I said, and took the $20 note from his vest pocket. Then I picked up the valise, and was reassured by its heft. I used my heel to swing the door shut as I left the room.

I carried the bag to the desk, and slid it across to Amity. She took it, opened the empty suitcase I had left on the floor, and placed the valise inside. Then she buckled the suitcase shut and stood.

"You're late," I said. "Trouble?"

"Nothing I couldn't handle," she said.

"Tell me."

"Thought I was being followed," she said. "But I crossed over a few blocks and backtracked, so I'm sure I lost them."

"Them?"

"Two men," she said. "In long coats, like drovers. Hats pulled low over their faces."

She leaned over the desk and we kissed.

"See you," she said, then turned.

She walked business-like toward the door. At that moment, I loved nothing so much as the way she held herself, high and proud. I marveled at the way her shoulders bobbed up and down, the tilt of her head, the grace in each step.

Four

I boarded the car just as the conductor hopped from the platform onto the train, a few cars back. The compact locomotive at the head of the eleven-car narrow gauge train began to growl and snort. Then there was a jolt as the drive wheels were engaged, and I grabbed a brass handhold until I regained my balance.

I made my way through the upholstered passenger car, searching for Amity. Mostly, the train was made up of freight cars, hauling eggs and milk and meat to the breakfast tables of Malvern and Little Rock. The few passengers aboard were salesmen and merchants, and they were sleeping in the plush upholstered seats. I went through one car, and then the next, searching for my new partner in crime.

Everywhere there was a diamond symbol, and beneath that the letters, JO. The railway had been built by an aging millionaire from Chicago, Diamond Jo Reynolds, because he was weary of the bumpy coach ride from Malvern to Hot Springs to take the cure for his rheumatism. Diamond Jo had made his fortune in steamboats on the upper Missouri and, as usual, his railroad was making money as well.

When I reached the end of the second car and still had not found her, my heart felt like it had dropped into my stomach. I had the growing feeling that I had been duped. After spending three days with her, I had been the one to suggest that she actually carry the loot out of the hotel, in a suitcase, in case I got pinched. But as I crossed into the third car, I was beginning to suspect that I had been played for a fool.

I shouldn't have.

Amity was sitting in the third car—the car for coloreds. The suitcase was on the seat beside her, her gloved hands clasped in her lap. There were three or four other blacks in the car, working people in drab uniforms. They watched without comment as I slid into the seat beside Amity and moved the suitcase to the floor.

"Hello, my love," she said.

"Any sign of the men in the dusters?"

"No," she said. "Any trouble at the hotel?"

"It was as quiet as the third of July," I said.

She smiled wickedly.

"I counted it."

"Risky."

"I couldn't help myself. I was alone here, and I couldn't resist. Just a quick count. Jake, we have twenty-three thousand dollars in cash. And that's not counting the jewelry."

She put a hand to her mouth to hide a giggle.

"We're rich," she said.

She was right. It wasn't the kind of money that would impress a Diamond Jo Reynolds, but it was enough that neither of us would have to work again, at least not for the next hundred years—though I doubted either of us would live to see 1981.

"This is your last job," she said. "You can retire."

"*We* can retire," I said.

"Buy a house."

"A farm," I said. "Someplace quiet and remote."

"Children?"

"Of course," I said. "Two, at least."

"But they would be—"

"We'll get married."

"That's not what I meant," she said. "They would be, you know . . . mixed blood."

"They would be ours," I said. "That's all that matters."

"Oh, Jake," she said. "I never wanted children before. The world seemed such an ugly place. But now, everything's different. How can things be so different so quickly? They say money can't buy happiness."

"No, but it comes damn close," I said.

We kissed again, then she rested her head on my shoulder.

"Well, ain't they a cute couple."

The gravelly voice with the Irish brogue came from behind us.

"Flynn," Amity said.

"Yes, my dear," Frank Flynn said, coming around to sit in the seat facing us. He was a man of thirty-five, with a ruddy face and hard brown eyes and a tangle of dark hair. He was wearing a striped three-piece suit, and the golden watch chain hanging from his vest gleamed in the lamp light.

"I'm assuming you've got a pistol on your person," Flynn said. "So keep your hands where I can see them."

Two of his gang took seats behind him, watching closely over their shoulders. They were big men in dusters and derby hats, and they kept their hands in their pockets, where they surely gripped revolvers.

"What are you doing to me, dear?" Flynn asked. "Don't you know you're breaking my heart, running away like this? Just what kind of Oscar have you found yourself? He's a runty little fellow, and doesn't seem capable of taking care of you at all."

I cocked my head to speak, but Flynn held up a finger.

"Hold your tongue, cousin," he said. "If you don't, I'll have the boys cut it out."

"Keep still, Jake," Amity said. "I've seen him do it before."

"Amity," Flynn said. "You're hurting my feelings. Don't you love me anymore, my dark little colleen?"

"I hate you."

"But you're my favorite whore," he said. "Hardly did I know you were an apprentice thief as well. You've made your skinny preacher a fine cully. How much did you steal?"

Amity shrugged.

"Now, the boys told me they watched you count it," he said. "So tell me, before I beat it out of your boyfriend here."

"Twenty-three thousand," she said.

"Brilliant," Flynn said.

Then he leaned back in the seat and crossed his arms.

"Here's my problem," he said. "You're my favorite

whore, but I can't stand the thought of you giving it away for free to this one-eyed bastard. It ruins, just ruins, the romance for me. Also, you helped him rob the richest hotel in Hot Springs and didn't say a word to me about it. It makes me look bad in front of my boys. If you were a man, my lovely Amity, I would have cut off your eggs and stuffed them in your throat. So, what to do?"

"You could let us go," she said.

"No, I don't think so," Flynn said.

"Then take me and let Jake go," she said. "I'm sorry, Francis, I didn't mean to hurt you. I will make it up to you, I promise."

Flynn smiled.

"I'm sure you will," he said.

"Take the money," she said.

"To hell with the money," Flynn said. "I piss that amount of money every morning before breakfast. It ain't about the money."

My left hand was resting on my pant leg, and I wanted to draw the Manhattan so badly that there seemed to be some magnetic attraction between my palm and the grip of the revolver. But the revolver was tucked into my waistband, beneath my coat, and there was little chance that I could draw it before one of Flynn's goons would kill me—or worse, miss me and kill Amity.

"You've decided against reaching for that gun," Flynn told me. "I can see it in your eyes. That's too bad, because I would liked to have seen the look in your eyes when my boys filled your guts with lead."

He said this last a bit too loudly. I heard some murmurs and rustling from the other passengers in the car. Flynn glanced over my shoulder, smiled reassuringly, and held up his hand.

"Don't worry, we're old friends," he said.

Then his eyes whipped back to me.

"I've seen your type before," he said in a low voice. "A broken-down, two-bit thief who skipped the last town just one step ahead of the law. You came to Hot Springs looking for some easy money, but you found something more—Amity. She conned you like she's conned a half-dozen others before you, giving them all some line about real love and how she never had the courage to leave until you came along. You were in way over your head, but you didn't know it until now."

I looked over at Amity. She glanced away.

"Tell him," Flynn said.

"Stop it," she said.

"Is it true?" I asked.

Amity began to cry, silently.

"Did she tell you that you make her feel like nobody ever has?" Flynn asked. "Did she tell you that nobody has ever induced in her such passion before? Does she still favor her right side, curling in that direction and panting like a dog when she spasms?"

I felt like somebody had reached up inside of me and was trying to jerk my lungs out. The blood rushed to my face and the night became unbearably hot. My vision became narrow and the gas lights in the car became hard and bright. Putting one thought after another became an impossible task.

"Boys," Flynn said. "Take his gun."

I reached for the Manhattan, but in my addled state I was a fraction of a second slow. One of Flynn's mules held his forearm across my throat while the other searched beneath my coat for the revolver. He found it, then handed it butt-first to Flynn.

"What a curious antique," Flynn said, looking at the converted Manhattan. "And left-handed to boot. Well, you had a surprise in you after all, didn't you?"

Flynn held the gun in his left hand and used his right thumb to open the gate. Then, one by one, he turned the cylinder and shook out the five .38 caliber cartridges onto the floor. He tossed the revolver to one of the goons, who shoved it back into my coat pocket.

"I expect you'll be wanting to kill me about now," Flynn said. "But you'd best forget about it. I have you beat in every way a man can be beat: I have more muscle, more guns, and more money. And, oh yes— I have your woman. You want to go home with me, don't you, dearest?"

"Yes," Amity said quietly. "Just don't hurt him."

"I promise," Flynn said. "But I've changed my mind about the money. Take it, boys."

One of the goons reached down and took the suitcase, then held it while Flynn examined it.

"Christ, what an ugly case," Flynn said as he unbuckled it. He opened the lid, then rummaged a bit inside. "Oh, you're a fiddle player too. Should have known. My old man was a fiddle player. I've never met a fiddle player yet that amounted to a damned thing. Where's the loot?"

"In the valise," Amity said.

"Ah," Flynn said, then handed the fiddle to one of the goons. Then he opened the valise and poured the contents inside the suitcase. I could hear coins and jewelry pouring into the bottom. "That's more like it."

He handed the valise to one of the goons.

"Stuff the fiddle in it and give it back," Flynn said. "But we'll be taking this ugly case off their hands."

The goon put the fiddle in the valise and handed it to Amity. She held it on her lap, her gloved hands folded over the top. She stared at Flynn, her face as hard as stone.

"Let's go home, Frank."

"Not this time," Flynn said. "I am tired of your games. My patience is exhausted and the thought of you rutting and plotting with this loathsome fiddle player upsets my digestion. It is time that you learned your lesson."

"Frank?"

"It's time to go, love."

"But there's no stop here," Amity said.

"None at all," Flynn said. "But get off, you must. Hold him, boys."

While the goons piled on me, Flynn jerked Amity to her feet.

"Leave the lady alone, Mister!" a black man called from the back of the car.

"She's no lady," Flynn said. "And unless you want me to have my boys cut off your nuts with a pair of rusty scissors, you'll shut the hell up and let me finish my business."

I struggled, but it was no use.

Flynn held Amity, with his left hand, by the back of the neck. She winced in pain as his thumb sank into her flesh, but did not try to fight. He dragged her to the door of the car. Then he reached beneath his jacket with his right hand, and brought out a gleaming pencil-thin knife.

"Run!" I shouted, before one of the goons slapped his sweaty hand over my mouth.

"Don't you hurt that woman!" the black man shouted.

"When I'm finished here," Flynn told the goons, "castrate that monkey."

"I'm getting the conductor," the man said.

"Do that," Flynn said. "And tell him Frank Flynn wants to see him."

"Let him go," Amity said. "You can do what you want with me, but let Jake go. Please, Frank."

"The problem, Amity, is that men are attracted to your pretty face before they realize your heart is as black as a gravedigger's arse," Flynn said. "Now, if only your face was as ugly as your soul. Let's fix that, shall we?"

He jammed the tip of the knife into her mouth and she gagged and screamed. She fought to get away. The muscles in Flynn's arm seemed like they would pop out of his left forearm as he struggled to keep his grip on the back of her neck, and his right elbow came up as he twisted the knife.

I could hear the blade scrape against her teeth.

The blade sliced into the corner of her mouth and then deep into her left cheek. She screamed while blood cascaded down the front of her dress. Then the knife came out of the side of her face, and he released her.

She stood there, swaying with the motion of the car, her eyes wide with terror and her white gloved hands pressed to her face. Blood welled in the spaces between the fingers.

I kicked and struggled like a man gone berserk,

but the goons had me pinned. I had nearly fought my
way free, but then one of them pressed his forearm
into my windpipe. It felt like I had swallowed my
Adam's apple. Unable to breathe, I was also unable
to fight. Then the other goon looked over his shoulder to see what had made me fight so hard.

"Jesus, Frank," he said.

Flynn grinned and wiped some of Amity's blood
from his face with the back of his hand.

"There," he said. "That ought to do it. Try to make
a living with a face like that, my dear. Hell, you'll
be unfit for anything but the two-dollar cribs."

Flynn sneered, dragged her onto the platform, and
threw her into the rushing darkness.

"Get rid of that fiddler trash as well."

Then Flynn jerked his head, and the goons dragged
me out onto the platform as well. They pitched me
head-first into the night, and threw the valise after.

FIVE

We survived the fall.

I carried Amity to a sharecropper's house by the side of the tracks, where I shouted for help and then kicked in the front door.

"What the hell?" the frightened father asked, stumbling out of a back room with his fists balled. But then the mother appeared behind him, holding a coal oil lantern. When she saw the blood dripping from Amity's hair onto the floor, she moved quickly toward the kitchen and motioned for me to follow.

I placed Amity on the kitchen table.

"Husband," the woman called. "Go fetch Granny Sifrah."

"She doesn't need a granny," I said. "She needs a surgeon."

The mother looked at me coldly.

"A white doctor would come, if it was you on that table," she said. "But this gal is yellow—high yellow, maybe, but still a nigrah."

"Find a doctor," I said.

"A white doctor will want money," she said. "You have money?"

I shook my head.

"Didn't think so," the woman said. "Now, Granny Sifrah will come no matter what your color, and whether you have money or not."

While we waited, the mother used many rags in an attempt to staunch the flow of blood. The rags came away from Amity's face heavy and bright, but soon after being thrown in a pile on the floor they became stiff and rust-colored.

After what seemed like a very long time, but which must have really been only a quarter of an hour or so, the husband returned with an old white-headed woman who clutched a carpet bag. She reached out one claw-like hand and turned Amity's face toward the lantern light, examined the wound with a practiced eye. Amity moaned and began to come around, but the woman took a brown bottle from the carpet bag, pulled the cork with her teeth, and coaxed Amity to take a swallow. Soon, Amity was quiet again.

The old woman glanced at me with cloudy eyes and said she would stitch her up as best she could, but that the scar would be hideous—the blade had severed the muscles in her cheek. As they knitted, the muscles in her cheeks would become rigid, pulling the left side of her mouth into a perpetual sneer.

"It takes a special kind of cruel to do something like that," she said.

"She'll live?"

"Of course," the old woman said.

"But there was so much blood."

"Seems that way with face hurts," she said. "But

nothing major was cut, except her vanity—which is worth considerable to a pretty young gal. Now, go on out onto the porch and let me tend to her. I'll be out directly."

I walked out onto the porch and sat in the darkness. The husband came out and sat with me. He rolled a quirly, expertly twisting and licking the smoke into a tight tube, then offered me the bag of tobacco. It was Duke of Durham, one of the cheaper brands.

"What?" he asked when I hesitated. "You're not one of those who prefer ready-mades, are you? I never trust those men. They seem somehow—well, I don't know how to explain it. Sissified."

"I'm not one of those," I said, taking the muslin sack of makings. "By habit, I smoke a pipe. But thanks, I need a smoke."

I took the makings and rolled one. The man held his out to me in his cupped hands and I lit mine. I drew the blue smoke into my lungs and let it out slow.

Dawn was just beginning to break pink in the east.

"This is the hardest part for men, ain't it?"

"What do you mean?"

"Sitting out here in the dark while our women are sick or giving birth, and there's nothing we can do but to smoke and wait," he said.

"I wouldn't know," I said.

"Well, I do," he said. "I got three children asleep inside, and waiting for each of them to be born always seemed like the longest night of my life. What's a white fellow like you doing with a colored gal like that?"

"Don't reckon that's any of your business."

"It is when you break down my door in the middle

of the night and carry her bleeding into my kitchen," he said. "Am I going to have any more trouble coming to this door because of you?"

"No," I said. "No more trouble. What's your name?"

He told me. I won't repeat it here, because I promised him no trouble would come to his family. It has been fifty years, but trouble has a way of hanging around.

"Thank you," I said.

Then Granny Sifrah came out onto the porch, and the husband got up and went inside. As the old woman eased herself into a rocking chair, she said Amity would be asleep for a spell—she had given her enough morphine to knock out a man twice her size.

I was leaning against a post, looking out over the blanket of fog that shrouded the cotton fields.

"Who did it?" she asked.

I remained silent.

"Not you, I think," she said. "Her pimp, probably. Are you the father?"

"What?"

"You don't know?" she asked. "She's with child."

I asked if she was sure.

"Boy, I've delivered a second-class city full of babies in my time," he said. "I can tell when a girl is in the family way. I'd say she's due early next year— March, maybe April. It'll be a male child."

"You can't know that," I said. "Nobody could."

"You'd be surprised at what I know," she said. "And you'd best be careful when it gets near her time. She's of a type that has difficulty with the first child. If she comes down with chills and a fever of a sudden, fetch the midwife."

The woman opened her carpet bag and took out a bottle of whiskey.

"Medicinal purposes?" I asked.

"If I ever saw anybody that needed a drink," she said, "it's you, boy."

I took the bottle, pulled the cork, and took a long swallow.

"You plotting revenge?" she asked.

"What's it to you?"

"Nothing," she said. "Except I just spent an hour stitching up a pretty little whore gal's face and I wouldn't want my work to count for nothing."

"How do you figure," I asked, "that your work is wasted if I put the sonuvabitch who did that to her in the ground?"

"She needs to heal," she said. "Oh, her face will knit quick enough, and she's going to have a wicked scar, but the far deeper hurt is the one you can't see. That wound will keep festering as long as that hate burns in your heart."

"Her face is ruined."

"It's her face," she said. "It's not her heart and it's not her soul. What we see in the mirror is just vanity. Only God sees our true selves."

I took another drink, then handed the bottle back.

"Might even be a blessing," she said.

She uncorked the bottle and took a nip.

"How do you reckon that?"

"This is a chance for her to stop whoring," she said. "And it's a chance for you to stop whatever the hell it is that you've been doing that passes for a living. Find an honest job. Take her and the baby far from here."

"And?" I asked.

"That's it," she said. "That's all there is, boy. Raise the child. Try to live without hurtin' anybody. Don't think too hard about anything that happened before. You can't change it. The only thing you can change is the future."

Three days later, Amity was well enough to travel, and we took our leave of the sharecropping family. By that time, I had retrieved the valise with the fiddle from the side of the tracks, and along with the Manhattan, it amounted to all the material wealth I had collected so far in thirty-two years of living. Being skilled in nothing but murder and robbery, I became an itinerant worker, a taker of odd jobs, a field hand. We moved from town to town, gradually edging our way north, to my home state of Missouri. Amity covered her face with a scarf and pretended that she didn't hear the gossip.

A month later, we crossed into Missouri.

I attempted to marry Amity at a Baptist church at Pierce City, but we were turned away because of the recent law against miscegenation. It was a crime for persons with at least one-eighth or more Negro blood (to be judged by a jury from the defendant's appearance) to marry white persons. The punishment was a hundred Yankee dollars and two years in the state penitentiary at Jefferson City.

So we skipped across the line into Kansas and at Fort Scott found a Universalist minister to conduct a quick ceremony in exchange for a sawbuck. Having discovered that there are more jobs where there are more people, we continued north, in the direction of Kansas City. When I finally got the job clerking at Brown's in Argentine, just outside of Kansas City, we stopped. We had found the place where we would make our stand, the former whore and the reformed outlaw.

And so it went.

At work, I swept the floors and retrieved the buckets and sold the carpet tacks. Despite the monotony of the job and my near-constant state of exhaustion, I was happy in a way; Amity seemed at peace with herself and trusting in my affection. The winter came, and so did New Year's, and Amity's stomach grew large.

Then came that last Sunday.

We were walking down Strong Avenue that morning and winter was whistling down from the north. But I had been caged all winter and was desperate to get some air, and after all it was my only morning off, so we bundled up and braved the cold for a walk around town.

I was on the street side, shielding Amity from the mud and traffic, and she was clutching my right arm in her gloved hand. The snow stung our faces and the cold made us numb. The fumes from the smelter hung close to the ground, like a fog, and the stench clawed at our throats. I could see Amity's watery and bloodshot eyes over her muffler.

I was miserably sorry that I had dragged her out.

"Let's go back," I said. "This yellow gas we are forced to breathe cannot pass for air."

"It's all right, Jake," she said. "It's not that bad. Let's walk a little farther."

So we did, navigating our way down the board sidewalks and the drunks sleeping off Saturday night. I looked up, hoping for a glimpse of the sun, but all I could see was sky the color of arsenic.

She stopped and squeezed my hand.

"What's wrong?" I asked.

"Dizzy," was all she said.

Then she slumped to the ground.

I called her name, but there was no response. She was as unconscious as if she'd downed a fifth of whiskey. I swept her up and carried her the rest of the way home, and up the stairs to our little room. I shouldered open the door and placed her on the bed.

Even though the room was cold, her forehead was beaded with sweat. Then she doubled over and retched fiercely into a bucket. While I cleaned up the mess, I told myself that she just had a touch of some common illness, something that would pass. But then she clutched my hand and stared at me through a fever haze.

"Get Granny Sifrah," she said weakly.

"She's four hundred miles away in Arkansas," I said, squeezing her hand. "But I will find someone here."

I started to rise, but Amity would not release my hand.

"Don't leave," she said.

"I'll be right back," I said. "You won't even miss me."

On my way out, I slipped the Manhattan in my coat pocket.

If it had been any day but Sunday, I would have gone to the store and asked old man Brown for help. But the store was locked up tight. The house was deserted because the landlord and all of the boarders were at church. So, I rushed down the stairs and into the street, where I began to grasp people by their sleeves and ask if they knew a midwife or a doctor. Mostly, I was sworn at for my trouble.

When I ran out of people on the street, I went to the nearest saloon, but found it deserted and the door locked because of some new damned law about being closed on Sundays. But through the window, I could see somebody throwing a pail of water on the floor to clean up a mess from the night before.

I tapped on the glass, but the man ignored me.

Then I rattled the glass with my fist, and he swore and gave me a one-fingered salute.

So I ran to the nearest church, a rich one, one of those Methodist jobs in white and green. Bounding up the steps, I swung open the big white doors and launched myself inside. I stumbled down the aisle while the startled congregation bent their necks to stare at me. The preacher was in the middle of a sermon about how the poor will always be with us, but he stopped in mid-sentence when he saw me.

"My wife is with child and bad sick," I said. "She needs a doctor."

The preacher glanced at a man in the second row.

"Doctor Quirk," he said.

The doctor turned to look at me. He was about forty, had shaggy hair, and the shoulders of his dark coat were frosted with dander. His skin was the color and consistency of wet dough and his bloodshot eyes were hard. His round wife and his two small round children were sitting on the pew next to him.

"Will you help her?" I asked.

He cleared his throat, but said nothing.

"Of course he will," his wife said.

"Please," I said.

The doctor sighed.

"All right," he said, grasping the back of the pew in front of him and pulling himself to his feet.

Now, I must tell you how much I hate doctors—they are a special fraternity of sadists and charlatans. They go to medical schools for a few months, learn the trade from other hacks and sawbones, and then inflict themselves on society. They killed about as many soldiers during the war as thrown lead. But because I knew damned little about women or childbirth, I was grateful to have found Quirk.

As we walked down the church steps, I asked hopefully if he was a surgeon.

"Nope," he said, pulling a cigar from his pocket. He bit off the end and spat it into the street. "But I'm plenty schooled. What's the trouble?"

I told him.

"How old is she?"

"Nineteen," I said.

"First child?"

"Yes," I said. "Is she in trouble?"

He chewed on the unlit cigar.

"Nine times out of ten, no."

"And the tenth?"

He didn't answer.

"There's something," I said as we approached my building. "About my wife."

"If she has a black eye, good," he said, looking at me conspiratorially. "Every woman needs to learn her place. They are grateful for the lesson."

"No," I said. "That's not it."

"Then what, man?"

"She's black."

He stopped.

"You mean, she's a—"

"Yes," I said. "One-half. The other half is Chero-kee. Have you a problem?"

"That poses no special risk," he said. "Medically speaking."

"And speaking socially?"

"It is a weakness," he said, "that is only a little above bestiality."

I choked down my rage and waited, my eyeballs burning from the cold and wind. Quirk pulled a match from his pocket and struck it against his heel. He cupped his hands around the flame and stoked the cigar, then threw the smoking match in the street.

"Is she pretty?" he asked.

"She has a comely body," I said.

"You have money?"

"Not much," I said.

"Why am I not surprised," Quirk said.

Even though I had worked for months, I hadn't managed to save a dime. Living was expensive and clerking paid little. Other than my lucky Double Eagle, I could lay my hands only on about five dollars.

Amity was unconscious by the time we got to the room. Her head was tilted back at an odd angle and her eyes were sunken. Her breathing was ragged. The doctor sat on the bed and touched her face and then felt her wrist for a pulse.

"Lord, you should have warned me about her face."

"Is she alive?"

"Barely," he said, taking off his jacket. "We must act quickly. How far along is she?"

"Eight months, perhaps."

He began rolling up his sleeves.

"What's wrong with her?" I asked.

"A condition that strikes young women, as if a bolt from the blue," he said. "I will require s butcher knife. Preferably, a sharp one."

"She needs an operation?" I asked.

"You don't understand," he said. "This woman is dying. There is only a chance now to save the child."

I blinked.

"Dying?"

"The knife," he said. "Quickly."

My head felt numb, as if somebody had struck me with a rock. By the time I fetched the knife, Amity wasn't breathing.

Quirk took the butcher knife and began cutting Amity's clothes away.

"What can I do?" I asked.

"Stay out of my way," he said.

"Save her."

"You don't understand," he said. "She's gone. I'm sorry, but she is as dead as Cleopatra. But there is a chance to save the child."

"She was breathing just a moment ago," I said. "You can do something. You must do something. Save her first."

He felt of her stomach with his hands, then plunged the butcher knife into her belly and split her from stem to sternum. Blood and water seeped out, and the skin parted to reveal layers of bright yellow fat. Now, I've seen plenty of blood and lights in my time, but always from men, and never had a scene so unnerved me—at least, not since my mother had died when I was a boy.

I pulled the Manhattan from my pocket and cocked it.

"You're killing her," I said. "Stop it!"

He glanced over his shoulder.

"Go outside," he said.

I didn't move.

"Shoot me, and you kill the child for certain," he said, the cigar still in the corner of his mouth. As he spoke, the tip bobbed and sloughed ashes into the wound. "Put that damned thing up and wait outside and let me do my work."

I thumbed the hammer down and put it in my pocket, then walked into the hallway. First, I just leaned against the wall, then I sort of slid down the wall to sit on the floor, and I folded my arms and rested my forehead on my arms. Then I jerked my head back and stared at the ceiling.

"Are you listening, you bloody old bastard?" I asked. "You've got me on my knees again, about to utter the most common of prayers—a prayer for the deliverance of a loved one. It is on a thousand lips at this very instant, being said earnestly and with clenched and clammy hands over the dimming lights of a thousand children, spouses, or lovers. Now there is one more voice to add to the chorus of pain, if not of praise. Spare her."

I wiped my eye with the back of my left hand.

"Take me," I said. "Or deduct a portion from my allotted years and give it to her. I swear I will go peaceably when my time comes early. Or, if you wish it, I will put a ball through my brain right now. Just give me the sign that you have heard my voice from among the thousands—show me that you have heard my plea alone among the millions uttered since day first dawned."

Then the door opened and the doctor came out, wiping his bloody hands on a rag and shaking his head. The cigar in the corner of his mouth was cold and dead.

"It was no use," he said. "The child was stillborn. I will send someone to help with the remains."

"She's dead?"

"And the child as well," he said.

He threw the bloody rag back into the room.

"Don't look so melancholy," Quirk said. "Soon enough, you'll find another little nigger bitch. It's a weakness. You can't help yourself."

I looked up at him.

"That'll be five dollars," he said.

"You're right," I said. "I can't help myself."

Then I drew the Manhattan from my pocket and cocked it, all in one motion. Quirk threw his hands up in front of his face. I pulled the trigger and sent a .38-caliber slug through the palm of his right hand—and right into the bridge of his nose. The round deflected downward and took part of his jaw with it.

My ears were shocked and ringing from the report. The hallway was thick with gun smoke, and its stench—something between rotten eggs and fireworks—stung my nostrils. There was also the coppery smell of the doctor's blood, which was dripping onto the floor from his shattered face.

"Christ, that was loud," Quirk mumbled.

Then he put his hand to his face, feeling of the broken parts, and the realization of what had happened began to manifest in his eyes.

"You sonuvabitch," Quirk said. "You'll hang for this."

"Oh, shut the muck up."

I put another round into the top of his forehead, spraying blood and brains down the hallway behind him and stinging my ears. The doctor dropped to his knees, swayed a bit, then fell over dead on his side.

On my way out, I took eighty-five dollars in paper money from his pocket.

SIX

Had it not been a Sunday morning, with all of the boarders at church, I would not be telling you this story now—I would have spent my days in some stinking prison. But luck, if you can call it that, was with me.

I walked into the room and stopped three feet from the bed, staring. Amity was in a mess of tangled bloody sheets, her belly split open from the ribcage down. In the crook of her arm the doctor had placed the child, a very blue and tiny boy.

There was nothing to say and no time to say it.

I walked across the room, took my father's fiddle and bow from the peg on the wall, and shoved it into the old valise. Then I walked out the door and right out of town until I came to the Santa Fe tracks, then began to follow them southwest.

It felt as natural as breathing.

As a boy during the war, I had walked alongside many miles of railroad tracks, the fiddle slung across my back from a piece of hemp. Now, a generation later, I was still walking, and still carrying the things that mattered—a fiddle and a gun.

The fiddle was light enough, but the gun felt like stones in my pocket.

The twin rails were the color of lead, and the ground was frozen as hard as flint. The trees were bare and dark on either side of the roadbed, the dull sky was close to the ground, but the wind had died and everything was deathly still. Each step seemed as loud as the breaking of glass, and my breath condensed and trailed over my shoulder.

By and by I heard a locomotive approaching from behind.

I was hiking up a curving grade, and moved over into the brush and crouched down to hide from the engineer in the cab. The locomotive was one of the newer Consolidateds, a demonic-looking machine in gleaming black with red and white pinstriping on the cowcatcher, the domes, and the cylinder headers. There was a big square headlight jutting out over the front of the boiler, and below that a red medallion with the number, 132. The wide funnel was panting dark smoke as the four white-rimmed drive wheels pulled the locomotive up the grade.

The locomotive rattled past, followed by the tender, an express car, and the first of seven passenger cars. The train slowed so on the grade that, by the time the last passenger car was approaching, it was an easy matter to run alongside and grab the railing and pull myself up unto the platform.

I brushed my clothes off the best I could, then tucked the valise under my arm and went through the door into the car proper, which was about a third full.

None of the passengers paid me much mind, thinking perhaps that I had been out on the platform all along. Without smiling, I picked a seat that was the furthest from everybody and sat down, placing the valise on the seat next to me.

Now, you might think at this point that I was overcome with grief, or that my mind was a torrent of dark thoughts, but it wasn't the case. I didn't feel anything. The world had kind of a hard bright edge to it, and I was curiously detached. I had as much emotion as if I was watching the mechanism ticking away in the guts of a watch. Amity and our child were dead and there wasn't a damned thing I could do about it. And Quirk? He deserved killing. The law might arrest me at the next stop—after all, how hard would it be to telegraph ahead to look out for a one-eyed killer?—but I still wouldn't regret sending that heartless bastard to hell.

This was just the way the world wound down.

Then the conductor came down the aisle, asking for tickets.

When he got to me I told him I didn't have one. He seemed to be used to this happening from time to time, because he didn't raise an eyebrow.

"Where're you headed?" he asked.

"Hell," I said.

"Topeka is the next stop and that will cost you 65 cents," he said. "Hell is a bit further on. It's at the end-of-track, a miserable place in Arizona Territory called Canyon Diablo."

Arizona, 1935

"You're killing me," Frankie said, slapping the pencil down on the sheaf of paper. "This isn't going to work at all. We'll never get the Hays Office to approve it for distribution."

"What the hell are you talking about?" the old man asked.

"It won't pass the production code. And if it doesn't pass the production code, it doesn't get the Hays Office seal of approval, and if it doesn't get the seal, no theater can show it—and RKO is fined $25,000 for promoting immorality."

"The goddamned Yankee government tells you what kind of stories you can tell?"

"The government and the Catholic Church," Frankie said. "We'll have to change a few things. Amity will have to be white, because we can't portray miscegenation. The bloody scene with the post-mortem cesarean section is a problem and will have to be implied, if it's included at all. And the murder of the doctor—why, that's just out of the question. You can't kill authority figures."

"Pity," Gamble said.

"Hollywood has changed since *Hellfire Canyon* was released," she said. "Sex and violence are out. Crime doesn't pay. Mother of mercy, it truly is the end of Rico. Huston couldn't even make the film now, at least not with that title—you can't say *hell*."

"You said people wanted my story," Gamble said.

"People are crazy for your story," Frankie said. "Jacob Gamble, the fiddling outlaw, was a sensation. The Robin Hood of the Ozarks. And we can tell the story, we just have to tinker with a few things."

"Tinker?"

"We'll have to make you sympathetic," Frankie

said. "A criminal working on the side of the law, maybe. Did you ever pin a badge on your chest?"

"I was working for a higher law."

"Now you're sounding like a Wobblie," she said. "That sort of thing doesn't play well."

Gamble shook his head.

"You don't understand."

Frankie chewed her lower lip.

"People want a happy ending," she said. "They want to know that everything will be okay. They're scared witless by real life and they want to be entertained and reassured. That's why they want westerns—they know that, in the past, things turned out all right."

"Then they are fools," Gamble said. "The past was one damned thing after another, and things never turned out right. The past was mostly about burying the people you love."

Frankie took a swig from a bottle of Coca-Cola and stared at the heat rising in waves from the asphalt on Route 66. A black 1932 Chevrolet sedan approached from the west, its engine sputtering. The car was caked in red dust, and the driver was peering through the crescent in the windshield that had been scooped out by the wiper blade. The Chevy swung into the service station driveway, and the brakes screeched as the car slowed, then stopped. A canvas bag of water swung heavily beneath the bumper.

Then the driver's door swung open, and the dust sloughed off to reveal neat white lettering: RKO PICTURES.

"Whole damn country is blowing away," Frankie said.

"Let it blow," Gamble said.

From behind the door of the Chevy the driver looked around, confused. He was a young man, and wore a white shirt and bow tie. He had a pair of sun goggles perched on the top of his head.

"Where is this?" he called.

"Two Guns," Frankie called.

"Then this is the place," he said. He turned his head and looked back down the road. In the distance, a caravan of cars and trucks was inching across the desert toward them.

"You from Los Angeles?" Frankie asked.

"Yeah," the young man said. "Film crew. Ran into a helluva dust storm this side of Needles. Golly, but this is gorgeous country. You the script writing girl? Heard you dress like a man."

"You heard right," she said.

"You do that as a gimmick or because you're funny?"

"What do you mean, funny?"

"You know," the man said. "Funny. That you don't like boys."

"I like boys just fine," Frankie said. "But I prefer men."

"Where's the railroad bridge?"

"Follow that gorge north," she said. "You can't miss it."

He stood on the running board to get a better view.

"There's a road on the east rim," Frankie said. "Go easy, or you'll bust an axle."

"Thanks," he said, pulling down the goggles. "See you around, brother."

The door slammed shut and the engine sputtered

to life. Then the Chevy wheeled around and made for the gorge.

Frankie shook a cigarette from a pack of Lucky Strikes. She put the cigarette between her lips and lit it with a Zippo lighter.

"How did it feel when you killed the doc?"

"Felt pretty good. About time for lunch, ain't it?"

"Not until we've done some real work," she said. "We've talked the morning away and we haven't gotten you to Canyon Diablo yet. And are we going to find out more about those creatures, those bloodthirsty little monsters, what did you call them—"

"*Los Sanguinarios.*"

"Yeah, those."

"We'll get to them by and by," Gamble said. "But like you said, we haven't gotten to Canyon Diablo yet."

SEVEN

Kansas whispered beneath the wheels of the train like the memory of a bad dream. Lost, I slumped in my seat and stared out the window as the train passed through the rolling hills and over the muddy rivers of eastern Kansas.

I paid for my fare with the money I had taken from the pockets of dead Quirk. Nobody asked about the blood-stained bills, and nowhere did detectives board the train, looking for a one-eyed murderer. Nobody cared, at least nobody with arrest powers. But had I robbed a bank or a railroad, I wouldn't have made it out of town.

We made a stop at Topeka, on the banks of the Kaw, and then continued on to Emporia, situated between the Neosho and Cottonwood rivers. There the train disgorged some passengers and took on others while boys with trays walked up and down the aisles, offering boxed lunches for fifty cents. I wasn't hungry, and I reckoned it would be a long time before I would be again—if ever.

The train continued on, following the route of the old Santa Fe Trail. We plunged into the heart of the prairie, a sea of tall grass broken by reefs of limestone, and the winter sky seemed to stretch forever. Around Newton the land began to change, to flatten, and the rivers became fewer and the trees sparse. The track became as straight as a rifle barrel, and the train shot along at fifty miles an hour. I watched my rippling shadow keeping pace along the roadbed. It occurred to me that not only was this the fastest I was ever likely to travel in my life, but that I was 500 miles from my birthplace in Shelby County, Missouri—as far from home as I had ever been.

It was an odd feeling.

Of course, I had not been back to the farm since the Yankees had burned us out in 1862. My father died in a federal prison. At thirteen years of age, I fell in with the thief and murderer Alf Bolin in Taney County and found my natural calling. My mother died a year after, in a guerrilla camp in north Texas, while giving birth to my bastard brother. The bastard lived, and I abandoned the infant there at Mineral Creek—but, if you've seen Mister Huston's film, you know all of this.

Night swallowed us up but still I did not sleep. Instead, I watched the stars glittering over the prairie. Every now and then a falling star would streak across the sky, burning brightly for a few moments and then fading into oblivion.

Then the sun came up behind us and cast long shadows on the land and on the far side of Dodge we encountered a knot of shaggy buffalo, standing dumbly alongside the tracks. There were only four or five of the beasts, watching the train pass with dull eyes, remnants of the great southern herd that just ten years before had so dominated the plains that they forced trains to stop while they surged across the tracks. Now they were all but gone, having been reduced to piles of bones. They had been killed for their hides and for their tails, which had been sent by the crateful back east for use as fly-swatters.

Now, all of my life I had lived in landscapes that were green, with just the right amount of hills and trees and a bit of water here and there in the form of proper rivers. But the farther west we went, the flatter and more alien the land became. There were few trees and damned little water and the horizon kept getting wider and wider. You'd think that when there was more land, the sky would get smaller, but that wasn't the case; as the land got bigger, so did the sky. Eventually it seemed the world was just going to swallow me up.

There was another stop at some town I forget the name of before passing into Colorado. At the next stop—La Junta, perhaps—we exchanged our prairie locomotive for a more robust model, and soon after the grade began to increase and the world changed again. Only this time the land had folded itself into rocks and mountains and there was lots of angry water in some places.

The sky narrowed to just a sliver.

Our pig of a locomotive chuffed and screamed and the cars jostled behind it and when the grade became too steep, a helper locomotive was coupled up behind to push us up Raton Pass. There was a tunnel at the top and somewhere in the blackness we crossed the Continental Divide. The tunnel was filled with smoke and sparks and the thunder of the locomotive and the clatter of the wheels. Just when it seemed like we would be in that hellish tunnel forever, we came out on the other side and were flowing toward the Pacific.

I slept, then.

EIGHT

"Welcome to hell."

The conductor was shaking my shoulder. I had been asleep, my head jammed against the window frame at an unnatural angle. I rose with a start and looked at the old man through bleary eyes.

"What?" I asked, rubbing my neck.

So much sunlight was coming through the windows it seemed like the car was on fire.

"Collect your crap and get off. I don't want to spend any more time here than I absolutely have to. And you wouldn't either, if you was smart—but the odds against that seem fairly long, considering you paid cash money to get here. You the new sheriff?"

"What?"

"They last a day or two before they're killed," the old man continued. "Hell, one of 'em only survived three hours. This is the roughest damned town I ever seen. Rougher than Dodge City at its worst, and that town was hell on wheels. They say Tombstone is a bad one too, but I don't know—ain't never been there because no rails go to it. Ever been to Tombstone?"

"No."

"Didn't figure you had. It's about three hundred and fifty miles south of us, damned near in Mexico. The Southern Pacific comes close to Tombstone, within twenty-five miles or so, to a whistlestop called Benson. Ain't never been there, neither, because it ain't on my line. God damn, boy, are you going to sit here all day? Get the muck off my train."

I grabbed the valise and headed for the doorway, blinking hard against the glare. My boots rang on the iron steps as I stepped off the car onto the roadbed.

The ground was hard and full of rocks, and everything was the color of rust or blood. Some of it was pinkish, like the color that water turns in a basin after cleaning a wound, and some of it was the dark, deep stain of old rust. About the only thing that wasn't red or brown were a few shrubby green plants and the sky, which was the color of faded denim.

Hard against the tracks was the yellow wooden depot. The Atlantic & Pacific locomotive had come to a hissing stop a little way beyond, beside a water tank. The spout had been lowered and water was being poured into the tender. Not far away, there were some freight docks, a warehouse, and a maze of stock pens where some cattle were shuffling about and making low sounds.

A railway crew was uncoupling some flatcars with some heavy ironwork strapped on top, all girders and angles. The train had pushed the flatcars ahead so that, once freed, the locomotive would be unfettered. The rest of the cars backed down the tracks all the way to Winslow. Some town men, judging from their appearance, were carrying crates of liquor and blocks of ice from the express car behind the locomotive and stacking them in the back of a wagon.

A weathered sign near the depot said WELCOME STRANGER TO CANYON DIABLO, ARIZONA TERRITORY. DITAT DEUS! The phrase was Latin and was the territory motto, meaning "God enriches."

"And impoverishes," I said to myself.

The town itself was thrown up a narrow strip that ran for maybe a mile along the north side of the tracks, and the buildings ranged from one- and two-story rock structures that were the same color as the ground to hastily-built wood-frame affairs, nearly all of which were unpainted. There were plenty of tents and tarpaper shacks thrown in for good measure, with wooden slats tacked up over the entrances announcing what could be found inside: A few offered rooms and grub, a couple proclaimed assorted games of chance, and several simply shouted WHISKEY!

There was only one street in town, and a big hand-lettered sign said it was HELL STREET. Near this sign was the largest building I could see, and about the only one that was painted—and it must have taken all of the labial pink paint in the territory to do it. The building looked like an opera house, but I couldn't imagine it did much of a business here at the end of the track.

If there were any homes in town, I didn't spot them.

Curious to see this hole in the ground that everybody had been talking about, I walked past the depot—which seemed to be deserted, despite a door that stood open—and followed the tracks to the west. Things were in a helluva mess, with tools and iron pieces and lumber all piled about, but nobody was working. When I neared the bridge, I left the tracks and veered to the north, finding a little jut of rock where I had a good view of things.

The canyon stretched from north to south from horizon to horizon, like a rip in the fabric of the earth, and the steep walls stair-stepped down to a little creek that glimmered at the bottom.

The span went about two-thirds of the way across.

Even though the bridge was unfinished, it was still the biggest human-made object I had ever seen. From my dizzying position on the east rim, the bridge looked like a cathedral of beams and braces, and the steel rails atop it blazed so with the afternoon sun that I had to shield my eyes.

"What now?" I asked.

There was no reply, just the sound of the creek far below.

I had managed to get as far west as fast as possible, and now that I was here, I didn't know what the hell I was going to do next. I was a stranger in a place that was alien to me as the surface of the moon, so I wasn't inclined to start planning my next job until I got a feel for things. I didn't want to spend any more time than I had to at the end of the Santa Fe tracks. I decided to find a dark and quiet spot to drink away the time until the next coach came along to take me someplace else.

I turned my back on the canyon and retraced my steps toward the center of town, my shadow preceding me. I was carrying the valise in my right hand, and my left swung easily at my side, near the Manhattan revolver in my pocket.

The men who had unloaded the liquor and the ice from the express car were gone, and so was the wagon. The rails were empty and the Atlantic & Pacific locomotive was just a dot of smoke at the end of the rails on the eastern horizon.

The only thing moving on Hell Street was a sand-colored dog. One eye was closed by an ugly scar, while the other was pale blue and constantly moving.

The dog was trotting in the shade of the buildings, something bloody in its teeth. As it came near me it growled and its lips curled back. I could see that the thing in its mouth was a jack rabbit, or what was left of one. The dog passed me, but kept his dark marble eye in my direction, then jumped up on the planks a few yards down and settled against the front door of a general store and began working over the dead rabbit.

The door swung open and a short man in an apron scurried out, wielding a broom.

"Scat!" the man said, sweeping the dog off the porch as he would so much dust. "Go away! I told you before, not to bring these dead things to me. Take it out in the desert, I will thank you."

The dog yelped and its hind legs seemed to be headed in a different direction than the rest of it as it scrambled to get off the porch. The man shook his head and took a couple of swipes after the dog as it slunk off, the dead critter still in its teeth.

"Didn't know *scat* works on dogs," I said.

"What doesn't work when you've got a broom in your hands?" the man asked with a shrug. "Oh, did you come from the train?"

"I sure as hell didn't walk," I said.

"Tough guy," the man said. "That's nice. We need more tough guys in this town. What, are you the new sheriff? My advice to you is to keep moving."

"I'm not the sheriff," I said.

"Would you like to be?" the man asked. "I'm on the hiring committee. We're taking applications."

"I thought you had already hired a sheriff," I said. "Why would you want to hire another?"

"Why not? We can't have a spare?"

"Thanks, but I'm not staying," I said. "A stagecoach must visit every once in a while. When can I expect the next?"

"What, you don't like our town?" the man said, leaning his broom against the porch railing and wiping the palms of his hands on his apron. "All right, all right, there will be one along by dark, maybe later. It's hard to tell. Depends on how much trouble they run into. Robbery is a diversion here in the territory."

"That's comforting."

"Don't you want to know where the stagecoach goes?"

"Not really," I said. "But where does it go?"

"Where doesn't it go?" he asked. "South, it goes south."

"That direction generally suits me," I said.

"Here is what I want to know," the man asked, coming down the steps. "What kind of man doesn't know or doesn't care where he's going? A thief, that's who. A criminal. A tough guy that just got off the train and has to ask where the stagecoach goes."

He reached out and motioned with his fingers.

"All right, let's have it."

"What do you mean?"

"What do I mean?" he asked, his eyes rolling upward. "Your shooting iron, your hog leg, your equalizer, the devil's right hand, your johnson, your mother dog and six pups. Whatever you call it, hand over the gun you have under that coat."

"Now, why should I do that?"

"Because it's the law," the man said. "Because I'm a good man and you're a smart man and neither of us wants trouble. Because you'll get it back before you get on the stagecoach."

I was getting ready to tell him to go straight to hell when the door behind him on the porch opened a crack. My hand went to the brass-and-walnut butt of the Manhattan in my pocket. I expected to see a slender rifle barrel or the snout of a double-barreled shotgun poking out from behind the door and the metallic *snick* of hammers being drawn to full cock.

"Mordechai?" a woman's voice called. "Is there trouble?"

"Trouble? No trouble," he said.

The woman took a step beyond the door, but kept a slender hand on the jamb. She was fair, with dark hair, and she wore a white blouse and a dark skirt. She seemed seven or eight years younger than me— twenty-six, maybe. She reminded me of Amity.

"No," I repeated. "No trouble."

Slowly, I pulled the Manhattan out of my coat. I turned it around in my hand and offered it, butt-first, to Mordechai. But he took it by the barrel, with two fingers, as if it were a rat, and dropped it into the pocket of his apron. Then he produced a tattered pasteboard playing card. It was the Queen of Spades.

"What's that?"

"Your receipt," he said, and tore the card in half.

I tucked my half in my vest pocket.

"No sidearms in the little bag?"

"No," I said. "A fiddle."

"Open it up," Mordechai said.

He peered in for a few moments, then gently reached inside and withdrew the fiddle. He held the instrument with one hand beneath the neck and the other at the tail, as one might a baby. His fingertips brushed the varnish, which was cracked and dark with age.

"It appears quite old," he said.

"My father's," I said.

"I am always surprised by how fragile they are," Mordechai said. "You wouldn't think something this delicate could produce such beautiful sounds, and in such quantity. I miss the sound of it. My father played as well."

He replaced the fiddle in the valise.

"It seems odd that you carry both a gun and a violin," Mordechai said.

"The gun belonged to my mother."

Mordechai laughed.

"I will keep this until your departure, if you like."

"Thanks just the same," I said, taking the bag. "But, no."

"Suit yourself."

"Tell me something," I said. "Where is everybody? I've never seen a town this dead in the middle of the afternoon. There are stores and other concerns lining the street, but you're the only shopkeeper I've seen."

"What can I tell you?" Mordechai said. "They are all drunk. In November, the railroad arrived and started building their bridge. Judge Rex declared a celebration."

"But November was six months ago," I said. "The whole town is still drunk?"

"Our people? No," he said. "But everyone else. The gentiles. The Indians. The Mexicans. Oh, they wake up an hour or so before sundown and start drinking again. By midnight, the town is fairly bursting at the seams. It stays that way until dawn. Judge Rex likes it that way."

"What kind of judge orders a town to drink?"

"A dangerous one," Mordechai said. "Take my advice, stay away from him. The smell alone!"

I asked whether he and his wife had any hot food in the general store.

"Astrid? No, we're not married. A hired girl. An orphan," he said. "And we have all of the uncooked bacon and beans or canned things you could want, but no meals. For that, you'll have to try at The Gilded Thing, that pink building across the street."

"The opera house?"

"Never had a performance," Mordechai said. "Judge Rex uses it as his headquarters because it has the biggest bar in town. But my advice is to stay away—it's a rough place. I'll sell you a can of peaches to stave off your hunger until the stage arrives. Say, two bits. That's cost."

"Thanks," I said, "But I'm hungry and I'll take my chances. This town doesn't look that tough to me."

NINE

I stepped through the open doorway into The Gilded Thing and let my eyes adjust to the gloom. There were a dozen or so men and a couple of snoring whores draped over the chairs and tables scattered about. One of the tables was tipped on its side, broken glass all around. There were a few faro and poker tables, and a single felt craps table in the middle. At the back of the building was the stage, empty except for an over-turned chair that somebody had thrown.

Off to the side of the stage was a circular staircase that spiraled up to the second floor. The staircase was made of iron and had been shipped in from some-where and bolted together. The staircase was painted black, just like the bridge over the gorge. A sign at the base of the staircase said PRIVATE!

The bar ran the length of the left wall and there was an impressive display of liquor behind it, along with a lithograph of "Custer's Last Rally" by the Irish artist John Mulvany. The painting was given away by the breweries and could be found in every saloon west of the Mississippi, although I thought it a poor piece of art—Custer held his pistol at an unnatural angle. Beneath the doomed general was a real bartender, carrying a bucket. He walked around the end of the bar and threw the bucket of sand over a bloodstain on the floor.

"What do you want?" the bartender asked, rubbing the sand into the wood without turning to look at me. He was twenty-five or so, with a head of curly unwashed hair and a perpetual sneer.

"A shot of whiskey," I said. "Some chow."

"The whiskey and a plate of beef and beans will cost you four bits," the bartender said, "if you want the cheap stuff. If you want something better, it varies. Personally, I wouldn't drink the cheap stuff with somebody else's gut."

"Then give me something middling," I said.

I found a table that seemed reasonably far from the nearest sleeping drunk and sat down. The bartender brought a bottle of bourbon over and placed a shot glass in front of me, but hesitated before pouring.

"Let me see your money."

I put some paper money on the table.

He poured the whiskey and I took a sip, thankful for the familiar smoky taste. The bartender picked up the dollar bill and rubbed it between his fingers.

"What is this, blood?" he asked.

"It's not yours," I said. "So don't worry about it."

Then he went through a door into a back room, and there was some banging of pots and some cursing. He came back with a spoon and a tin plate of food. He sat it in front of me and then put his forefinger in this mouth.

"Hope you're happy," he said. "I burned myself."

"How is that my fault?"

"You're the one who just had to eat," he said as he walked away.

I shook my head and began to eat. The beans were all right but the beef was rotten, and doctored with cayenne pepper so as to hide the taste. I spooned the beef to one side and ate the beans and drank the whiskey. Then I pushed the plate aside and asked for some coffee, which made the bartender roll his eyes like I had asked him to milk a coyote.

"Damn," he said. "Is there anything you don't want?"

Not long after I was brought a cup of coffee in name only, the one-eyed dog appeared in the doorway, sniffing the air for food. Its muzzle was dark with dried blood. The bartender snatched up a double-barreled ten gauge shotgun and let fly from behind the bar with both barrels, but the dog had jumped as soon as he saw the bartender's intent. The buckshot splintered a section of the door jamb and raised some dust in the street beyond.

"God damn dog," the bartender said, breaking open the shotgun and extracting the shells from the smoking chambers. "Every time that mutt comes around, there's trouble."

Some of the other patrons had stirred, lifting their heads to see what the fuss was about. Others remained as unconscious as the dead.

"Sonuvabitch," I said, shaking my head. "I'll never get used to that." A blue haze hung in the air and my ears rang so badly that at first I thought I might have suffered some permanent damage.

"Are you touched?" I asked.

"You saw the way he looked at me," the bartender said, sliding a couple of fresh shells into the guns and locking the breech. "He knows—he knows when there's going to be trouble, and he has his eye on me."

There was a shadow over the threshold, and the bartender again shouldered the shotgun.

"Don't shoot, you moron."

An ugly man with a bald head shaped like a bullet strode into the room and made for the bar. A quirt dangled from his right wrist.

The bartender lowered the gun.

"I'm sorry, Harlan," he stammered. "I've been trying to kill that damned dog—"

"Finley, you are a first-class moron," Harlan said, grasping the shotgun by the barrel and wrenching it out of the bartender's hands. He tossed the double on the bar top and then, with his left hand, grabbed the bartender by the front of his shirt and pulled him halfway across. Then he took the quirt in his right hand and began to whip the poor bartender across the head and shoulders.

"I told you not to bother about that dog," Harlan said between strokes.

"I'm sorry," Finley said, trying to shield his face with his hands.

"You'd better be," Harlan said, releasing him. "The next time I catch you doing something like that I'll give you a real beating."

The bartender shrank back, blood running from the corner of his mouth and, from a split ear, down the side of his neck. His eyes were watery with tears and snot dripped from one nostril. He wiped his face with the back of his hand.

Harlan released his grip on the quirt, and it hung limp from a leather strip around his right wrist. He put his hands on his hips and surveyed the bar, and eventually his gaze came to rest upon me.

"Who the hell are you?"

"Nobody," I said.

"I can see that," Harlan said. "But what was your name in the states?"

"Which state?" I asked.

Harlan laughed. It was a deep, rasping laugh, without a trace of mirth. Then the laughter stopped and he fixed me with his porcine eyes.

"What are you, some kind of one-eyed humorist?"

"Something like that," I said.

"Staying long?"

"Waiting for the next coach."

Harlan grunted his approval.

"That's good," he said. "Because I don't like the way you look. There's something vaguely Hebrew about you. What about it, stranger? Are you the wandering Jew?"

"I'm wandering, that's for damned sure," I said. "But I'm not an Israelite. And I didn't giggle or shoot dice while Christ was nailed to the cross."

Then I felt the building quiver and turned to see a very fat man descending the iron staircase. Only, this fat man didn't walk like most huge people do; instead of shuffling or waddling, he took quick and firm steps, and he swung his arms as he came. He hit the bottom as smoothly as some lighter man might step from a curb.

He wore a black string tie and a white suit that was stained with red dust, and he strode over to a large

round table near the stage. He sat down in a wooden
chair that was so large and ornate that it looked like a
throne, and Harlan came and sat in a smaller chair at
his right.

Finley rushed over with a tray, and placed a bottle
of whiskey and a clean glass in front of the fat man
and a mug of beer in front of Harlan.

"Anything else, Judge?"

"Steak," he said.

"Yes, your honor."

So, this fat bastard was Judge Rex and Harlan was
his chief thug. What a pair of deuces. One was a sadist
and the other probably hadn't seen his toes since Lee
surrendered at Appomattox. I began to relax, thinking that I would soon be shaking the dust of Canyon
Diablo from my boots.

"Who's that?" Judge Rex asked, looking at me.

"Nobody," Harlan said. "Some Hebrew waiting for
the stage."

"Why ain't he drinking?" Judge Rex asked. "We're
supposed to be celebrating."

"Don't know," Harlan said. "Maybe it's ag'in his religion."

"What do you say, boy?" Judge Rex asked, calling
to me. "Is it against your religion to drink?"

I smiled.

"Not at all," I said. "In fact, I'd say drinking *was* my
religion."

They laughed.

"Finley!" Judge Rex called. "Give this funny Jew
boy a shot of whatever he wants."

"Old Crow," I said.

While Finley fetched down the bottle from the

backboard, I passed a hand idly over the stubble on my chin. It had been days since I had washed or shaved.

"What's in the bag?" Judge Rex asked.

"Fiddle," I said.

"Saw us a little tune."

"I don't play anymore, I said.

"Shame."

"Indeed."

"You like our bridge?" Judge Rex asked.

"Biggest I ever saw," I said. "I hear the railroad has been working on it for six months. Is it ever going to be finished?"

Judge Rex shrugged.

"There were some mistakes," he said. "The railroad had the trusses and other parts made back East, and somebody must have measured once and cut twice. Some parts haven't fit exactly right."

I was having a hard time following what he was saying because I was studying his great huge face with its thick lips and heavy jowls which flapped as he spoke. I had, of course, seen fat people before, but his girth so exceeded anything I had ever seen that there is no word to describe it. To say that he was fat is like saying a steam whistle is loud.

"How much short was it?"

"Twelve feet," he said. "Things have kind of stopped out there in the middle, until they figure it out. I see that the train this afternoon was pushing some new trusses ahead of it. Maybe they will fit. If so, we'll have to make some adjustments of our own."

"How's that?"

"As long as this is the end-of-track," Judge Rex said, "this place is a going concern. Hell on wheels.

The train has to stop here, the stage stops here, there's whoring and gambling, and money fills my pockets. But as soon as the bridge is finished, the railroad moves on. This place becomes just another hard, hot, and dry spot along the track."

"And you aim to prevent that," I said.

"Accidents happen," Judge Rex said.

"And maybe the parts just won't fit again," I said.

I lifted the glass of whiskey Finley had just poured.

"Here's to American know-how," I said. "May the mechanical geniuses who gave us the wreck of the Sultana keep you in business until you've had your full measure of the wages of sin."

Judge Rex looked confused for a moment, but raised his whiskey as well. The glass was all but hidden in his huge paw. His fingers were like sausages and on one of the sausages a diamond ring glittered. Then he tilted his head back and threw the whiskey down his huge throat.

Then he pulled a card box out of his pocket, opened the flap, and took out a perfect tube of a cigarette. I had seen ready-mades before, but I had never seen a man smoke one. It was vaguely unsettling, like seeing a man wear a dress.

For the next hour or so I sat and drank a couple of glasses of whiskey. Judge Rex drank a couple of *bottles*. It got darker and Finley went around lighting the coal oil lamps, and men began drifting into the opera house. Most of them were rough characters who earned their livings with their hands or their backs, miners or railway workers or cowboys, and there was no joy in their eyes as they drank or played cards or shot dice.

"You know," Judge Rex said, his tongue lolling in

the corner of his great mouth, "one of the advantages to having money is having women, and my wife is the best-looking bitch in town."

"How fortunate for both of you," I said.

"I mean, she is a well-constructed piece. And thin. Like I've always said, the only fat I want to see in bed is mine."

"Who wouldn't?"

Judge Rex placed his head in his hands, and for a moment I thought he had gone to sleep. Then he roused and said, "Harlan! Go fetch Maude."

"Bring her here?"

"I want to show her off."

A few minutes after Harlan had left, an old fellow with graying hair and a hitch in his step came through the door into The Gilded Thing. He was wearing clean clothes and although his face was burned from the sun, he did not look the type who worked for a living. There was a tin star on his chest and a short-barreled Peacemaker in a low-slung holster on his right hip. A book was tucked beneath his left elbow.

Judge Rex laughed out loud.

"So the hiring committee is swearing in pensioners?" the fat man asked. "This is rich. Tell me, granddad, where did you get that limp? Shiloh? Buena Vista? Valley Forge?"

The gray man ignored Judge Rex and favored his right foot as he crossed to the bar, forcing patrons grudgingly aside as he went. He placed his book on the bar, and I could see that it was a well-thumbed Bible.

"Give him a drink, Finley," Judge Rex said.

The man smiled.

"Arbuckle's," he said.

"We don't serve nothing as weak as coffee," Finley said.

"All bars have coffee," the man said. "It's some kind of rule, I think, so the barkeep doesn't drink up all the stock. Besides, I can smell it."

"Get him some coffee," Judge Rex said.

Finley disappeared into the back room and there was more banging and cursing. He came back with a steaming ceramic cup.

"Obliged," the man said. "You would be the one they call Judge Rex."

"The same," the fat man said. "And you?"

"My name's not important," the man said. "But you can call me sheriff, if you like. And you're right about one thing—I did take a rebel ball in my foot, at Fredericksburg."

"A Yankee," Finley sneered. "We should beat him like an old rug."

Judge Rex held up a fleshy hand.

"Please excuse my hired man," Judge Rex said. "He was cuffed around some earlier and is looking for somebody to take it out on. Tell me, have you been in this line of work long?"

"Long enough," the man said. "Reckon I acquired a taste for it during the war. When I wasn't allowed to shoot at rebels anymore, I drifted to Kansas and took up the badge. I've been the law in nearly every cow town from Abilene to Baxter Springs. Was a peace officer in Denver. Of late was employed by the Atlantic and Pacific Railway to protect its interests in the territory. Now I work for the town committee."

"And that book," Judge Rex said. "I take you for a man of religious bent?"

The gray man smiled.

"You may take it any way you want," he said. "I need to start my rounds."

Then he finished his coffee and pushed away from the bar, tucking the book back under his elbow. Then he stopped and turned.

"The book is the law," he said.

"The law," Judge Rex said. "That book ain't the law. The law is a bitch with a heart of stone, a mother who would sell her own child for a shot of dope, a whore with a dose of clap and late with the rent. Justice may be blind, but she can damned sure hear the coins being dropped in the scales she holds."

As soon as the gray man left The Gilded Thing, he was forgotten. The drinking and the gambling resumed and the air was filled with cigar smoke and curses.

I kept hoping for the coach, but in vain.

Then Harlan came in, pushing a tall dark-headed woman.

"Get your claws off me," she shouted.

"Maude, my love!" Judge Rex cried. "Come to me."

"I told you," Harlan said. "Judge Rex wants you."

Maude shook her head but walked over and stood next to Judge Rex anyway. She was wearing a green dress that looked like a bag of cats when she walked. Her head, however, seemed too small for her body, and her face had a pinched and disagreeable look.

Judge Rex swung a big arm around her waist and kneaded one cheek of her behind with his fat fingers. Her expression, however, suggested she was neither pleased nor annoyed.

"See, what did I tell you?" Judge Rex asked. "What a beauty."

"Indeed," I said.

"Get up there on the stage," Judge Rex said.

"No, darling," Maude said, placing a small hand against his chest. "I don't want to dance, not tonight."

"I want everyone to see you," Judge Rex said. "They all want to see you. Get up there and give them an eyeful." Then he turned to the crowd. "You all want to see her, don't you?"

The men whistled and clapped and shouted.

"They can see me," Maude said. "I don't need to get up there."

"Show them what you show me," Judge Rex said, growing impatient.

"But I don't want to," she whispered.

"Come on, Maudie!" somebody shouted. "Show us something pink!"

She smiled nervously and put a hand to the base of her throat.

"You can't be serious."

"You were a whore when I married you," Judge Rex said. "You're a whore still, just on permanent assignment. Climb up there and show the boys what they're missing."

"No," she said.

"Do it."

"No," she said. "I'm scared."

"Then get out," he said.

"What?"

Judge Rex shoved her away.

"You are no wife of mine," he said. "You displease me. I divorce you, I divorce you, I divorce you!"

She stumbled backwards, then fell amid the crowd of men. Somebody snatched her up and kissed her, then handed her to the next man, who not only kissed her but groped her breasts as well. She managed to free herself, dodged a couple of grabs, then made for the door. But then a cowboy grabbed her wrist and pulled her back.

"Give me some spice!" he shouted as he pulled her toward him.

I came out of my chair, but I suppose now that Judge Rex just thought I was hoping to get in on the fun. But before I could help her, she turned and quick as a cat sank her teeth into the back of the cowboy's hand. He yelped and released his hold.

In an instant, she was gone.

"You want me to go after her?" Harlan asked.

"To hell with her," Judge Rex said. "I will choose a new wife. Bring me women! Harlan, gather your cousins and search the town for every unmarried woman under the age of thirty. Every maiden and whore and spinster. Bring them here, and we will survey their beauty, and I will choose one of them for my bride."

TEN

The girls were a sorry lot.

It didn't take Harlan's gang long to bring Judge Rex the unmarried women, and they ranged from the whores who worked the cribs along Hell Street to a few widows who had lost their men to sickness or the railroads or the Apaches. There were perhaps a dozen of them, and they were a rough lot. There was no talk of forcing them to shed their clothes—and I was glad, not wanting to be witness to rape—although a couple of the whores and one of the widows offered, but were met with disinterest. Plain women have few advantages in this life, but on this night it stood them in good stead.

"Let them go," Judge Rex said. "They displease me."

Then he breathed a heavy sigh and, defeated, put his chin down in his large hands. He closed his eyes and in a few moments I was relieved to hear snoring.

Then Harlan strode into the place, trailing a rope. The end of the six-foot rope was affixed to the tied hands of a struggling young woman whose dark hair covered her face.

"Come on," Harlan said, as if to an animal. He tugged on the rope and pulled the girl up onto the stage. She was dressed in her nightclothes, all white and ruffles, but there were so many layers that the only things that were really exposed were her bare arms.

"Wake up, boss," Harlan called. "See what I caught for you."

Judge Rex's eyes flapped open.

He stared for a moment at the stage, his head still on the table. Then he lifted his head and extended a hooked finger toward the stage.

"Her hair," he said. "Brush back her hair."

Harlan reached to do it, but the girl slapped him away with both tied hands.

"I'll do it," she said.

She brought her hands to her face and swept her dark hair back.

It was Astrid, the girl I had seen in the doorway of the general store earlier. My heart sank. She was so beautiful that Judge Rex was sure to desire her.

She was so beautiful, in fact, that I desired her as well—and it sparked a wildfire of emotion within me. And just when I thought that my capacity for feeling had forever been extinguished! Her brown eyes flickered in the glow of the footlights, her skin seemed to glow with some brilliance from within, and her curly hair fell about her shoulders like a veil. My attraction to her was not just physical, however; it also had to do with the way she comported herself, that although her hands were bound and she had been dragged like a slave before this obese monster, her shoulders were back, her chin was up, and her gaze remained steady.

"I've seen her before," Judge Rex said. "Where?"

"She is the Jew shopkeeper's hired girl, an orphan named Esther."

"Astrid," she said. "My name is Astrid. It means 'star.'"

"What does that filthy Jew do to you?" Harlan asked.

"Mordechai is a good man," she said, "and the cleanest man in Canyon Diablo. He has never treated me with anything but kindness. He has never bound my wrists, for example, or led me before a clamoring mob."

"Mordechai is a fool," Judge Rex said. "Remove your clothes, please."

The crowd hooted and whistled.

At this point, I was desperately wishing that I had not traded Mordechai the Manhattan for half of the Queen of Spades. All I had with me was the valise with the fiddle. But then I thought of the double behind the bar and the would-be dog killer Finley, and knew that even if I had a gun, it would make no difference.

"You heard him, sister," Harlan said, motioning with the quirt. "Take 'em off."

"I can't," she said, and held up her bound hands.

Harlan drew a knife from a sheath at his belt. He slipped the blade beneath her wrists and pulled the blade toward him. The leather parted with a *snap!*

"Proceed," Judge Rex said.

Astrid bit her lip. Then she lowered her head and brought her bound hands up and began unlacing her corset. Her hands moved surely, without a trace of hesitation, and when she was done she lifted her head and brushed the hair out of her eyes. She looked straight at Judge Rex—who, of course, was staring not at her face, but at her lovely breasts.

The room had gotten quiet all of a sudden.

"Yes," Judge Rex said. "Yes, you are exactly what I have been looking for. Oh, with you I am well pleased."

"No, no!"

Mordechai was shuffling behind the men crowding the stage, trying to find an opening.

"This can't be happening," he said. "Oh, Astrid, what are they doing to you? This is no place for a girl like you. Come down and go home with me."

Astrid covered her breasts by crossing her arms.

"Mordechai," she pleaded. "You mustn't—they will kill you."

"Get him out of here," Judge Rex said.

"With pleasure," Harlan said, and walked over and grabbed him by the back of the collar. He began dragging the man by his heels toward the door, and all the time Moredechai was shouting and flailing about, kicking over chairs and tables.

"No, no!" he shouted. "Get away! You mustn't do this!"

"Shut up, you Jew bastard," Harlan said, and with his free hand whipped him with the quirt. Mordechai put his hands up to protect his face, but his screaming continued.

"Leave her alone!" he screamed. "Astrid! Astrid!"

Harlan continued dragging Mordechai toward the door, but suddenly found his way blocked by the gray man. The gray man was standing with his legs apart, the book under his left arm, and his right hand resting on the butt of the Peacemaker.

"What in God's name is going on here?"

Harlan released his grip and Mordechai rolled away.

"Just having a little fun, sheriff," Harlan grinned in his pig-like way.

"Sheriff," Mordechai said, scrambling over to the gray man. He drew up on his knees and grasped the man's pant leg. "You must stop them—they have kidnapped Astrid and have made her disrobe before them. Rape will surely follow."

"Let her go," the gray man said.

The crowd hissed and grumbled.

"Stay out of this, old man," one of the cowboys said.

"Yeah," another said. "This ain't your business."

"You're all drunk," the sheriff said. "Go home and sober up."

The cowboy laughed.

"Stick around, sheriff," one of the miners called. "Even an old dog gets lucky every once in a while— after Judge Rex finishes with her, you might even get a poke at her yourself."

"Shut up!" the gray man shouted.

"Aw, don't be sore," the cowboy said. "If you don't like girls, we can probably find a boy for you. Bet we could even hold old Finley down long enough for you to have a go, if you've a mind."

"Stop that kind of talk right now," the bartender growled, "or I will show you what for, you left-handed bastard."

"Good lord," the gray man said. "Sodom and Gomorrah, that's what you have here. You are all an abomination. Let the girl go."

"Nobody's stopping her," Judge Rex said calmly. "She uncinched her own breasts. None of us have laid a hand upon her. Isn't that true, my dear Astrid?"

"That's a lie," Mordechai said.

"Shush," the sheriff said. "And let go of my leg. What about it, miss?"

Astrid shook her head.

"I was asleep," she said. "Harlan and two of his gang broke into my bedroom and dragged me here, on orders of Judge Rex. They told me that Judge Rex was looking for a new wife and that I had been summoned."

"That's all I need to hear," the gray man said, drawing the Peacemaker. "The fat man and this one with the quirt are under arrest. All of you others just back away or you'll find yourself sharing in the calaboose with these two."

The crowd muttered, but fell back.

"Sheriff," Harlan said, smiling. "You've got us all wrong."

Harlan showed the sheriff his palms, but took a few steps toward him.

"That's far enough," the man said, cocking the Peacemaker.

"How do you think you're going to take us in?" Harlan asked, stopping just beyond arm's length from the sheriff. "Look around you. There's a hundred of us here and only one of you. You won't make it out the door—not alive, anyway."

"Maybe not," the sheriff said. "But I'll have time to kill you and your master before I die."

"Harlan," Judge Rex said, as if addressing a willful child. "Cooperate with the good sheriff. This is simply a misunderstanding, and it will be cleared up quickly enough. If we have to spend a night in the sheriff's jail in the service of justice, then so be it."

"I want both of you to shut the hell up," the gray man said. He let the Bible drop from beneath his left elbow into his left hand, and without looking placed it slowly on the nearest table—in a puddle of beer.

"Dammit," the sheriff said as his fingers touched the wetness.

He glanced over and lifted the Bible from the table top. The book was dripping beer from its black cover. Still using just his left hand, he turned the book over and wiped the cover on his coat. Then the book slipped from his grasp, and he glanced down as he tried to catch it.

Harlan took one step toward the sheriff and shoved the Peacemaker skyward with his left hand while his right hand drove the hard woven leather handle of the quirt into the soft patch of skin at the base of his throat. The revolver barked and sent a ball into the ceiling while the sheriff took a step backward.

His mouth worked but no sound came out.

Harlan wrenched the Peacemaker from the sheriff's outstretched hand, recocked the gun, and placed the muzzle against his breast and pulled the trigger. The revolver bucked and left a smoking hole in the sheriff's shirt front.

The man fell to his knees. His right hand reached for the Bible on the floor.

Harlan cocked the gun again and sent another round into the sheriff's chest, then pulled the hammer back and fired another. The sheriff looked down at the crimson blossoms on his white shirt, then fell over dead.

Astrid screamed.

Harlan laughed and sent two more bullets into the gray man's back.

Mordechai, who was still kneeling on the floor, looked at the corpse beside him and glanced away, toward the Bible that had fallen from the gray man's grip. The book had landed on its spine and the pages had parted, revealing a .32-caliber Pocket Colt. The pages had carefully been cut away in the outline of the gun, so that it was carried securely within the Bible.

Mordechai stared at the gun for a moment, then snatched it up.

Harlan aimed the Peacemaker at Mordechai's head and pulled the trigger, but the hammer fell on a spent cylinder. He had shot the pistol dry while killing the sheriff and insulting the body.

Holding the Pocket pistol in a shaking hand, Mordechai rose to his feet.

"*May the apostates have no hope unless they return to the Torah,*" he recited, advancing on Harlan with the pistol extended in his left hand. Harlan began stepping backward, toward the bar. The crowd parted as they went. "*May the empire of pride be uprooted in our days. May the Nazarenes and the Minim perish in an instant. May they all be erased from the Book of Life, that they may not be counted among the righteous.*"

Then Mordechai squeezed the trigger, but nothing happened because he had not cocked the gun. He frowned and realized his mistake, then lowered the gun a bit and hooked his left thumb over the hammer and pulled it back to full cock. Shaking even more now, he pointed the gun again at Harlan.

"Mordechai," Astrid called. "You mustn't. Violence is not our way."

"I cannot leave you to these animals," Mordechai said.

He took another couple of steps forward—so as not to miss Harlan—and this brought him to the edge of my table. Out of the corner of my eye, I saw Finley coming up from behind the bar with the double in his hands.

I stood up and grabbed the Pocket Colt with my left hand, then drove my right fist into his jaw. Mordechai went sprawling backwards as I threw myself to the floor, knowing that Finley was bound to shoot.

He pulled both triggers and the ten gauge spat fire and lead from both barrels, but we were close enough to him that the buckshot didn't spread out to more than the size of a couple of dinner plates. The shot tore into the table where I had just been sitting, sending splinters into the air and collapsing the top right down the middle. My valise hit the floor, and I heard the strings of the fiddle go *plinck!* as the bridge collapsed.

"Sonuvabitch," the cowboy said who had done most of the goading earlier. He was looking down at his leg, where a shot had bounced off the tabletop and pierced the meat of his thigh. Blood was dribbling down his pant leg onto the floor. "You shot me, you dumb sonuvabtich."

The cowboy produced a Green River knife from a sheath in the back of his belt and made for the bar, but Finley dropped the shotgun and bolted for the back door. I heard pots and pans hitting the floor as the cowboy chased him through the kitchen, and then the screen door cracking back on its hinges as they ran out into the night.

Mordechai was out cold, sprawled on his back. Astrid had come down from the stage and was sitting beside Mordechai, holding his hand.

"Thank you," Astrid told me.

"Do you want to go home?" I asked.

"No," she said. "One man has already died for me tonight. That's too many, because I'm not worth it."

"Hand over that piece," Harlan said.

"Don't think so," I said.

I dropped the Pocket Colt into the nearest mug. The snout of the gun hit the bottom with a *clink* and the beer boiled over the top. Then I picked up my valise from the floor and inspected the outside, and was relieved to find there was only one neat round hole in a corner of the bag.

"Believe I'll wait outside for that coach," I said.

Harlan walked over and blocked my path, quirt in hand.

"You interfered," he said.

"Yes," I said. "I kept that man from putting a bullet in your brain."

"Maybe so," he said. "But you also kept Finley from killing that Jew boy. You interfered. So, now you are in for a beating."

"Expected as much."

"A proper beating," Judge Rex said. "Bloody and hurt."

Harlan smiled.

"You scared?" he asked.

"Not especially," I said. "There's only one person I'm scared of, and you ain't Him."

"Talk big, don't you?"

"Get to it," I said. "Or shut the muck up."

Harlan struck me across the face with the quirt and I went down to my hands and knees. There was the coppery taste of blood on my tongue. I drew the bank of my hand across the corner of my mouth, and my knuckles came back bloody. But I remained down, because there was no point in fighting back; Harlan was intent on giving me a beating, and nothing I could do would dissuade him. Besides, I had learned long ago that a beating was not to be feared, because fear made the pain worse, and in most cases it wasn't going to kill you. I have seen a number of men afraid of taking a beating, and disgrace themselves and their families in an attempt to get out of it.

"Why would you defend the Jews?" Judge Rex asked. "It seems strange for a true American and Christian. I have always believed the Hebrews to be an alien nationality, although possessing no country."

At that point Harlan kicked me in the ribs, and the blow took my breath and spun me over on my back.

"They obviously conspire against us, as evidenced by the closeness with which they cling together. The aid which they afford each other also, on all proper and sometimes improper occasions, the fact that nearly all of them pursue substantially the same employment, so far as I have known them—that of traders, merchants, and bankers," Judge Rex said. "The obedience to the prohibition against marriage to Gentiles, their faith, which looks forward to the time when they are to be gathered together in the former homeland, all serve to show a closer kindred than belongs to any other nation. It may also be remembered that when the savior undertook to choose twelve confidential friends from among that nation, he got one that was a thief and had the devil. And after Judas Iscariot betrayed our Savior to the priests, it was the Jews who crucified our Lord on that first Easter week."

Harlan was kicking me through all of this, and I was doubled up, with my knees toward my chest and my elbows protecting my ribs. I should have kept my mouth shut, but I couldn't.

"Nice speech," I wheezed. "But I've heard it before. It's from a letter published by Spoons Butler when he was stealing silverware as the military governor of New Orleans."

Then Harlan gave a good kick in my short ribs with the point of his cowboy boot, and there was a terrible-sounding crack. There was still a crowd in The Gilded Thing, and they all crowded around to watch, but none of them raised a hand to help me. Harlan knelt down and began pummeling my face with his fist. When he tired of that, he struck me with the back of his hand, and this time the blow loosened some of my teeth.

"Don't," Astrid said. "You'll kill him."

"So?" Harlan asked.

"Let's put out his other eye," Harlan suggested.

Astrid fixed Judge Rex with an iron stare.

"If you kill that stranger," she said, "I will make sure Judge Rex will never have me—not willingly, anyway. And every time he tries, I will remind him of the source of my reluctance."

Harlan had the butt of the quirt jammed in the socket of my good eye. He was starting to put his weight on it when Judge Rex called for him to stop.

"If I let him live," he asked, "you will be my wife?"

"Yes," Astrid said.

"A proper whore of a wife?"

"Yes," she said resignedly. "Let him live."

Judge Rex told Harlan to get off me. He did, and I rolled over on one side, coughed, and spat out some blood. I couldn't get up, but I wanted to remain conscious, so I kept my eyes open.

"Throw him and his bag on the stage when it comes," the fat man said. "Give him no whiskey or any other comfort. Harlan, go tell Mordechai's people to come gather him up. And get the body of the late sheriff out of here. I hate looking at it."

"He's about my size," Finley said. "I want his clothes."

The bartender crouched over the dead man's shins and pulled one boot off, then another. Then he undid the belt and pulled off his trousers, and when he got to the underwear he whistled.

"I'll be damned," Finley said. "Boss, you've got to look at this."

Harlan walked over and glanced down. He began to laugh.

"What is it?" Judge Rex demanded.

"He's cut," Harlan said.

"What do you mean, cut?" Judge Rex demanded. "Castrated?"

"No," Harlan said, "I mean he's been abbreviated. In a secret rite."

With a great effort, Judge Rex rose from his chair and lumbered over to look at the exposed body of the dead man.

"Betrayed," he said. "We have been betrayed."

"Filthy bastards," Harlan said.

"I want them all cleared out, tonight—men, women, children," Judge Rex said. "They can take whatever they can carry. But everything else, they must leave behind."

Astrid slipped up behind him.

"No," she said, placing a hand upon his arm. "Show some mercy."

"I will abide this infestation no longer," Judge Rex said.

"You must give them a little time." She smiled sweetly and placed her head against his arm. "Only a little time."

"How much time?" Judge Rex asked.

"Not long, my husband," she said. "Not long. Let providence decide. Cast the dice. What could be fairer?"

She gathered a pair of dice from the craps table and placed them in the palm of Judge Rex's right hand. He closed his big fingers around the dice and looked softly down at her.

Astrid stood on the tips of her toes to kiss his cheek.

Judge Rex laughed and flung the dice on the craps table. They bounced off the backstop and rolled to the middle of the table and came to rest. Three and two.

"Five," Rex said. "They have five weeks."

Harlan smiled.

"That's fitting," he said. "Come Easter, they must all be gone."

ELEVEN

Soon after Judge Rex left with Astrid to consummate the marriage, some middle-aged women in black came into The Gilded Thing. They moaned and cried over the body of the sheriff and ripped their clothes, and began using clean white cloths to mop up the blood around the body. A few of them lifted Mordechai to his feet and helped him out. Others came to me and dressed my wounds as best they could, stuffing cotton into my mouth to staunch the flow of blood from my lost teeth, and they took off my shirt and my coat and wrapped bandages tightly around my bruised ribs. I was on my side and watched as they wrung out the cloths they had used on the blood from the gray man.

"Why?" I mumbled through the cotton.

"It's our way," one of the women said. "We have to get every drop of spilled Jewish blood."

One of the younger women found a letter in the dead man's vest pocket and opened it.

"His name was Cohen," she said, glancing over the letter. "The address is General Delivery, Winslow.

It's his orders from the Atlantic and Pacific, to come here and take the job offered by the hiring committee and bring law to the town, so that the bridge can be finished."

She put the letter in her apron and turned to me.

"What are you called?"

I tried to rise up on one elbow and tried to speak, but couldn't because of the pain of my bruised ribs. So I lay back down with my back flat against the wooden floor and stared up at the purple ceiling.

"You'll heal," she said. "Nothing broken."

I tried to ask her to bring me my gun, but couldn't manage it. I winced and put a hand to the side of my mouth.

"That is nothing," she said. "Women loose a tooth for every child they bear. I have had three. And your tooth was on the side, it will not be noticed."

She cleaned my face with a damp rag.

"You are healthy," she said. "You will heal quickly. The worst will pass in a few days. But our misery will continue. In a week, we must leave our homes. The beast Harlan and his gang have already broken into the temple and taken the Book of Moses. They tied it to the back of a mule and drove it out of town, with our rabbi running behind."

I breathed a bit too deeply and grimaced with pain.

She withdrew a bottle of laudanum from her apron. She uncorked the small brown bottle and placed a hand beneath my head.

"Here," she said, pouring a couple of doses into my mouth. "This will dull the pain. The stage is here, and without this you will suffer with every lurch and shock of the road."

She replaced the cork and slipped the small brown bottle into my coat pocket. Then a couple of Harlan's men came into The Gilded Thing. One of them had a new Montana pinch hat and the other had an idiotic smile. They hauled me to my feet, and dragged me out to the waiting stage. The driver and the express messenger were already up in the box, ready to go. The driver was a young man and clean-shaven, with the reins in his gloved hands. The messenger was old and gray, and his beard was stained with tobacco. A double-barreled coach gun was nestled in the crook of his left arm.

"What have you there?" the messenger asked.

"A customer," the one with the Montana pinch said. "Judge Rex says he should get out of town and stay out."

"Can he pay?"

"Damned if I know," the Pinch said.

"Then he ain't boarding," the driver said. The team was spooky, and the coach rocked forward and back before the driver pulled back on the reins and stood on the brake lever.

"But Judge Rex says he should get out and stay out," the other thug, the one who always had the stupid grin, said. "If he comes back, he's a dead man."

"Looks like he's pretty close to that now," the express messenger said, then spat some tobacco over the side of the box.

"You're not putting him on this coach without paying the fare," the driver said. "Ten bucks, to the next stop."

"We ain't paying that," the Pinch said.

"But Judge Rex will kill us if we don't get him on that stage," the Smiling One said.

"You could send him freight," the express messenger said. "What's he weigh?"

"I dunno," the Pinch said, bouncing me against his arm. "A hundred and forty, maybe."

"Five bucks," the express messenger said. "To the end of the line."

The thugs argued for a bit, then the Smiling One took a half eagle from his pocket and tossed it to the messenger.

"Put him in the boot."

They dragged me around to the back of the coach, unbuckled a corner of the canvas that covered the rear boot, and shoved me in.

The Pinch threw the valise after me.

"So long, sucker!" the Smiling One said.

Then they closed the boot and the driver yelled *Ha*! and the coach jerked forward into the night.

TWELVE

I don't remember much about the stagecoach journey, because I spent most of it doped up on laudanum.

It was like being drunk, except I had no desire to poke or fight anybody, and, when I wasn't asleep, it was like I was in a sleeping dream. My broken ribs made it hard to breathe and about every inch of skin hurt. The stage rocked on its leather thoroughbraces and its spinning yellow wheels jolted and jarred against every damned rock and rut in the territory. If my senses hadn't been dampened by the mixture of opium and alcohol in my gut, I doubt that I could have stood it.

I spent that first night in the boot with the rest of the freight, but after the driver had pity on me and let me ride inside the coach when it wasn't more than half full of paying passengers. At stops, there was a running argument about whether I was allowed to eat or not; the driver was for it, saying as how it was only Christian, but the express messenger was against it, saying it was bad business to allow the freight to eat. I didn't have much of an appetite anyway, and confined myself to eating the scraps left by the other passengers. I never asked where we were going, because I just didn't care. Mostly, I spent the time sleeping.

After six days, the coach rolled to a stop, and the messenger came around to the boot and unbuckled the canvas and told me I had to get off because we had reached the end of the line. By that time, all of my laudanum was gone. When I stepped out of the coach onto the dusty street of a strange town, I felt like pan-fried hell.

"Where are we?" I asked.

"Tombstone," the driver replied.

My ribs hurt and the sunlight scalded my eye and I was none too steady on my feet. The ground was white and chalky and the town seemed to have been thrown up overnight, because everything was either the color of fresh lumber or gleamed of fresh paint. If you looked close in the alleys and between some buildings, however, you could see some charred boards sticking up out of the sand.

The town was laid out in the shape of a lozenge, and not quite square with the compass points, but a few degrees off kilter. The sort of north side seemed to be where the nicer homes were located, or at least where the Caucasians lived, while the Mexicans and the Chinese had their quarters on the west end. To the south, across a street called Toughnut, there were rows of shacks where the miners lived, and to the east were the whorehouses. In the center of this humanity was the business district, five or six blocks of saloons, churches, hotels, brothels, lumber yards, livery stables, cigar shops, general stores, gambling halls, and a newspaper called *The Epitaph*. On the southeast corner of town, an ice house and a new fire station were thrown in for good measure.

The mines were hard against the town's southern exposure, with hoists and derricks jutting into the air, and all manner of wooden buildings that served as offices and assay rooms, all painted Indian red. Some of the mines encroached on the city, so storefronts alternated with shafts, and all was a jumble of activity. On a hill not far away were a couple of bigger concerns, the Toughnut mine and the Contention, according to the signs. Piled about all of the mines were tailing piles of black earth.

Carrying the valise, I set off down the street, surveying the storefronts. There was a multitude of people on the street, and I found myself bobbing and weaving to avoid them, and every time one of them would bump up against me—which was often—pain would shoot from the top of my head down to my boots.

I wanted more dope. I needed a shot of whiskey, some grub, and a place to sleep.

There were also a lot of soldiers milling about, more soldiers, in fact, than I had seen since the war. They had sky-blue trousers and darker blue blouses, just like during the war. Some of the enlisted men wore kepis on their heads and others, black slouch hats. They seemed bored, and hung about in little knots, smoking and playing cards, and sometimes giving longing looks toward the saloons, which were forbidden to them.

Near the corner of Fifth and Allen Streets, I ducked into the first doorway that seemed promising. It was a gambler's hell called the Purgatory House and a sign said there were around-the-clock games downstairs and sleeping rooms upstairs.

Outside, the Purgatory was a typical frame building, cream-colored with baby blue trim and some silly pink flourishes, with overhanging eaves. There was an unusual amount of ornamentation in the form of spindles and knobs and so forth. The windows were frosted glass, so you couldn't see inside until you opened the door.

When you did, it was like opening a storybook.

Gas lights burned brilliantly from fixtures suspended from a tin ceiling. There was a fish pond sunk into the middle of the floor, stocked with goldfish. Benches were arranged around the pond, so you could sit and contemplate the life of the fish—or, more likely, to keep the drunks from staggering through the middle of it.

There were a dozen gaming tables, including poker and faro, a few Chuck-A-Luck cages, and a roulette wheel. The tables were doing a good business, with miners, cowboys, and other rough types rubbing elbows with swells in suits and top hats. A rodent with the face of a man was hovering near a lonely roulette table, waiting for suckers.

The bar was a monster, all mahogany and brass, with crystal glasses lining the backboard. There were almonds and pickled eggs and oranges on the bar top, along with a silver tray of oysters on ice. Old General Custer, forever about to meet his doom at the hands of Sitting Bull, looked down on me from an alcove beneath the bar's central canopy. I hated that painting. On either side of Custer were paintings of nymphs and satyrs.

I walked toward the bar, and as I passed the fish pond I dipped my hand in the water and splashed some on my face. A couple of cowboys down at the end of the bar laughed as I approached, and the bartender— a stern fellow in a dapper vest and a waxed mustache—watched me as if I was a mangy one-eyed dog that had just trotted in from the street.

"Get out of here," the bartender said. "We don't cater to bums."

I must have looked as I felt. I couldn't remember the last time I had shaved or had a bath, and my clothes were caked with road dust and dried blood.

"Let me see your money," the bartender said.

"Sure," I said. "Got a knife?"

"What are you, a wise ass?"

"Yeah," I said. "But I still need a knife."

The cowboys laughed.

"Come on, Felix," one urged. "Be a sport."

He grudgingly placed on the bar top a cheap knife that looked like it had been routinely used to open cans of fruit. I picked up the knife and ran my left thumb across the blade.

"Careful," one of the cowboys called, "you'll put your eye out."

They both guffawed and slapped each other on the back and spilled their beers. But when I slipped my eye patch over my head and began using the point of the knife to rip out the bottom stitches that held the cloth to the back of the leather, the cowboys and the bartender became attentive.

"What the hell is he doing?" one cowboy asked.

"Scat if I know," the other said.

I glanced over at him and smiled. Then I shook my lucky Double Eagle out of the slit in my eye patch.

The cowboys laughed again and spilled more beer.

"I'll be damned," the bartender said.

"You'll have company," I said. "Now, pour me that drink."

He filled half a shot glass with Old Crow. I took a sip and then another, and my head became a little clearer. I still had the Double Eagle in my hand, and I rubbed my thumb over the date.

"That'll be four bits."

When the bartender saw my reaction to the price of his whiskey, he shook his head.

"Mister, water costs three cents a gallon here," he said. "Don't you think everything else is going to be on the same scale? There's nothing here but silver—no trees, no grass, no nothin'. Everything has to be hauled in. Did you fall off the back of a wagon or something?"

"A stagecoach. I fell off the back of a stagecoach."

The bartender laughed.

"Why are there so many soldiers in town?" I asked. "I haven't seen this many Yankees since the occupation of Missouri."

"Injun jitters," the bartender said. "Geronimo has left the San Carlos Reservation and is holed up in the mountains in Old Mexico, making ready for war. We're only twenty-five miles from the border."

"The sign says rooms," I said. "How much?"

"Five dollars a night," he said.

"Any cheaper in town?"

"Some," he said. "Not many."

"How about in the next town?"

"Mister, there is no next town," the bartender said.

"Benson is about twenty miles north, and Mexico is about the same distance to the south. The rest is just mountains and desert."

"I understand now."

"You want a room or not?"

I finished the whiskey.

"How'd you like a ten-dollar tip for pouring the glass of whiskey?"

"What the hell are you talking about?"

"Let me run a tab," I said.

"I wouldn't let my own mother run a tab," the bartender said. "Everything is strictly on a cash basis when it comes to whiskey and women. I knew there was something wrong with you, mister, and know I know what it is—you're crazy."

"Maybe," I said. "But I'm going to take my lucky Double Eagle over to that roulette wheel and put it down. When I win, I'm going to give you ten dollars for just being a decent human being."

"And what happens when you lose?"

"Ah, that," I said, talking loud enough for the boss over at the roulette wheel to hear. "The way I figure it, that drink is paid for either way. If I lose, then the house has made twenty dollars and all it cost is a drink of whiskey and a spin of the roulette wheel. When you're gambling, whiskey is usually free because it dulls the wits and improves the margin for the house. If I win, then I pay for the drink with my own money and you get your ten-dollar tip. What do you say?"

The bartender looked over at the boss. I didn't turn to look, because I knew what the boss was going to do—he was going to shrug and then nod his head.

"All right," the bartender said. "But when you lose, I want you to walk right out that door. Listening to you talk makes my head hurt."

I walked over to the roulette wheel and stood opposite the rodent-faced boss. He was thin and bald and had a pair of eyeglasses perched on the bridge of his bony nose.

"Feeling lucky?" he asked.

The truth is that I had never felt less lucky in my life. I was trapped. I had enough money to run me for two or three days, and I was too stove up to pull even a small job or to work for a living. I couldn't take the suspense of waiting to see how it would all play out, to see which stinking alley I would die in, so I decided just to bet it all at once. Then, after I lost, I could truly declare that I had lost everything—my wife, my gun, all of my money, and my last bit of self-respect. Then I could go walk in front of a freight wagon with at least a bit of whiskey in my stomach.

But I couldn't stop playing the game.

"Luck," I told the rat-faced bastard, "is my middle name."

"Want change?"

"No."

"Then place your bet," the boss said.

The layout took every advantage for the house. Instead of just a single zero, it also had a double zero *and* an eagle, which made the odds of winning a straight-up bet 29 to 1.

I placed the gold piece down on the board, on top of the eagle. I kept my finger on it, however.

"What is today?" I asked.

"Tuesday," the boss said.

"No, the date."

"March the sixth," he said. "No, wait. It's the seventh."

I pushed the coin over to the seven and withdrew my hand. The boss nodded.

"Good luck," he said, but there wasn't a trace of good will in his voice.

He spun the roulette wheel fiercely in one direction, then sent the ball sailing in the other direction in the groove cut into the rim. I could feel the sounds of the wheel turning and the ball orbiting in the marrow of my bones. I closed my eyes and felt a strange sense of relief that the act was done and that the last play was finally, irrevocably, terribly in motion. I forgot about everything else for a moment, even my aching ribs.

Then the door to Purgatory burst open and broke the spell. One of the roughest-looking kids I had ever seen walked in. He was young, his skin was cracked and peeling from the sun, and his straight brown hair brushed his shoulders. He wore a yellow cloth headband, like an Apache, and a black neckerchief gathered at the throat by a silver conch. He wore a plain white shirt, and his blue denims were tucked into the tops of calf-length moccasins. He carried a bone-handled knife in a leather sheath at his belt.

His blue eyes were quick and somehow unsettling.

The racket of the ball bouncing from pocket to pocket drew my attention back to the roulette wheel. It was skipping wildly about, danced for a moment in the eleven slot, then jumped out and skidded across to number seven—and stayed there.

"Winner," the rat-faced boss announced. "We have a winner. Red seven."

He dug around in his bank and came up with an assortment of coin and paper and pushed them across the layout toward me.

"Sonuvabitch!" the kid with the bone-handled knife said, coming over to admire the mound of cash. He slapped me on the shoulder. "You have struck it rich, you sorry-looking geezer."

"Don't touch me," I said.

"Bastard!" the bartender called. "You've been told not to wear that knife in town. The marshal will have your hide. What have you been drinking?"

"Oh, leave me be," the kid said. "I ain't drunk."

Without touching the money yet, I counted it up in my head.

"You're twenty dollars short," I told the boss. "It should be five hundred and sixty."

"It is, with your Double Eagle."

"It should be five hundred and sixty without."

"He's right," the kid said. "Absolutely."

The rodent boss chewed his lip.

"Thanks, Bastard. My mistake," he said, grudgingly putting another twenty dollar note on the pile. "I'm sorry, sir. Accept my apologies. Would you care to let it ride?"

"No," I said, scooping up the money and filling my pockets. "Lightning never strikes in the same spot twice."

"Ha!" Bastard shouted. "You don't have a hair on your ass if you stop now. Sit down and let's play some cards."

"Sorry," I said, still shaky from the lack of dope. "Cards aren't my game."

"Let's shoot some dice, then."

I shook my head.

"Not today," I said. "But looks like there are plenty of fellows over at the craps table who would oblige you."

"Yeah," the kid said, and grinned, "but I *know* you got money."

The kid gave me an uneasy feeling, like a smiling dog you don't want to turn your back on. Wanting to leave things friendly, I asked the bartender to give the kid anything he wanted to drink. This seemed to brighten the kid up until the bartender said that no, he couldn't have one.

"Cully, you sonuvabitch," the kid said. "Just give me a beer."

"Bastard's banned from drinking in every joint in town," the bartender said. "Wildest drunk you ever seen. Last time, he ate a handful of our mucking goldfish, ran down the street screaming about being the meanest fish-eating sonuvabitch that Tombstone ever saw, and chased the whores from crib to crib on the other side of Sixth Street."

"I didn't hurt anybody," the kid said, moping.

"No, because you were too drunk to catch any of those whores," the bartender said. "But you did eat five dollars worth of goldfish, so no beer for you."

"Sorry, kid," I said.

His eyes clouded over.

"Don't call me that," he said. "I may be young, but I'm nobody's kid. Most folks just call me Bastard."

"Sure, no problem," I said.

The kid drifted over toward the craps table while I walked easy over to the bar. The bartender leaned close and asked if I wanted some advice.

"Be careful of that one," he said. "He represents one of the more dangerous species around Tombstone, along with the scorpion and the rattlesnake. He was raised by the Chiracahua Apache after they slaughtered his family in '71. He was a scout for the Army, but gave that up after the Cibicue Creek mutiny. Mainly he makes his living ambushing Mexican smugglers coming north on the Rio Sonora to buy liquor. He may be an unlettered fool, but he's mean as a snake and has the sharpest knife around. And he's good with it."

"Obliged," I said, pulling ten dollars in silver out of my pocket and placing it on the bar top. The bartender moved the tray of almonds over to where I could reach them and poured me another whiskey.

"This one's on me," he said.

Funny how money makes people treat you different.

"That bet was well-played," he said. "But if you don't mind my asking, how did you know you were going to win?"

"I told you it was my lucky Double Eagle," I said. "Will five hundred and sixty dollars last a month in this town?"

"Six months, if you're careful," he said.

"Then how about that room," I said, and took a pull of the whiskey.

"Sure," the bartender said. "Right away, sir."

"What's your name?"

"Culpepper," he said. "Felix Culpepper. But everybody calls me Cully."

"All right, Cully," I said, taking a handful of almonds. "I need a bath and a shave. I need my clothes washed. I need a new pair of boots."

"I'll arrange it."

I also asked for a pipe and some tobacco, a jar of liniment for my ribs, and a bottle of laudanum. The bartender gave me a knowing look as if to say, *so that's how it is*.

"And send for a woman," I said. "What's the selection?"

"It would be easier to name the types we can't get."

"A mulatto, then," I said. "A pretty one."

I swirled the whiskey around in the shot glass.

"And a redhead."

I emptied the whiskey and slammed the glass down.

"A redhead," I heard Bastard mutter to his companions at the craps table. "They tell me my mother had red hair and was of low character, but I don't know because I never met the bitch."

THIRTEEN

The window of my hotel room faced the west, and as the sun sank lower in the sky, a rectangle of sunlight crept across the floor toward the galvanized bathtub in which I reclined.

Ten minutes before, I had stepped careful and stiff into the water. My body had been a bag of aches, my eye was shuttered, and my soul was a shadow. Now, I rested my head against the rim of the tub and stared at the dust motes drifting in the shaft of sunlight. The gently swirling particles induced a profound sense of calm, and I became detached from the world. My mind was floating among those motes, free of logic, wrapped in a golden dream.

I reached out with my left hand and found the laudanum and took another pull.

The dream that I was a child again, sitting on the rough floor of our cabin in Missouri on a warm fall day, watching dust swirl in the sunlight that slanted in through the crack of the door. There was just a touch of woodsmoke on the air and across the field, an owl was calling. My mother was sitting at the table nearby with the book open before her, and every so often she would turn a page, and it would fall as gently as a leaf from a tree.

Then she glances at me and smiles.

"What do you see, Jacob?" she asks, brushing her red hair. My world dances in her hazel eyes. "What do you see?"

But I have no words for it. I have no words . . .

The banging at the door brought me back, like a hanged man reaching the end of the rope.

I sat up in the tub and rubbed my face with my hands.

"What, dammit?"

"The ladies, sir," a voice came. "They're here."

"It's unlocked," I said.

The door was swung open by a shiningly blond boy of twelve, wearing a pair of coveralls and holding a package in one hand. Behind him were the girls, both in their early or middle twenties. One was the color of butternut and had a warm, round face with dark hair, and the other was thin and pale and had a swath of freckles across the bridge of her nose and straight red hair. Both were dressed in high-collared dresses that were respectable enough for church, and the pale one carried my clean clothes wrapped in butcher paper.

The girls walked into the room business-like, and the red-headed one put the bundle down on the bed.

"Where do you want your tobacco and shaving things?" the boy asked.

"Place them near the basin," I said.

He did.

"Anything else, sir?" he asked.

"What's your name?"

"Sven."

"Sven, there's a silver dollar on the corner of the table to pay for those things." I had left ten dollars in coin out, and the rest of the loot I had stuffed in a pillow case and thrown in the closet, next to the valise.

"They weren't that much, mister. And I can't make change."

"Take the dollar," I said. "The change is your tip." The boy grabbed the dollar.

"Thanks, mister," he said, and was gone.

"I'm Anne and this is Charlotte," the red-headed girl said, removing her gloves.

"You dress damned well for whores," I said.

"That's because we're damned good whores," Charlotte said. "But first, we're going to be your barber and tailor, Mister Gamble. Annie has brought some clothes for you from the mercantile, but I reckon there will be some hemming needed."

In short order, both girls had stripped down to almost nothing.

Charlotte knelt beside me and ran a gentle hand through my hair.

"Lord, I think you have all the topsoil in the territory up there," she said. Then she glanced down and saw the purple bruises on my ribcage and made a clucking sound. "Somebody has been abusing you. I hope you gave as good as you got."

"Nope," I said. "It was pretty much one-sided."

"*Blessed are the peace-makers*," she recited. "*For they are the children of God.*"

"Well, I am a child of man," I said. "And the only Peacemaker I know of is made by Colonel Colt."

Anne unwrapped the straight-stemmed briar pipe and packed it with Lone Jack tobacco. She stuck the pipe in her mouth, lit a Lucifer by scraping it on the side of the tub, and held the match to the bowl, drawing fire into it. When she had it going proper, she placed it in my mouth.

I drew on the pipe and exhaled, and the blue smoke coiled in the air.

Charlotte used a bristle to whip up some shaving cream in a mug, then she lathered my cheeks and throat. Then she opened a straight razor and held it upright in her right hand.

"You've done this before," I said.

"What, cut a man's throat?" she asked. "Ear to ear, dozens of times."

"Charlie!" Anne said. "Stop that."

Charlotte smiled.

"Now, shift that pipe to the other side of your mouth," she said.

Then she put a finger under my chin, lifted my head, and began expertly scraping away the lather. Trusting her, I closed my eye. My once-aching muscles felt like they were going to slide right off my bones and pool in the bottom of the galvanized bathtub.

Anne, the red-headed one, was soaping my chest with a sponge and softly humming "Amazing Grace."

"Do you know Jesus?" Charlotte murmured.

"Are you of a religious bent?" I asked, taking the pipe from my mouth.

"I am saved, if that's what you mean," she said. "So is Annie, even though she was born a Roman Catholic. So tell me, Mister Gamble, do you love God?"

Even though I was being asked the question by a woman with a razor in her hand, I couldn't bring myself to lie.

"I don't love anyone," I said.

"That's a shame," Charlotte said. "Not anyone? Ever?"

Anne was still humming.

"Once or twice," I said. "In the past. I am now alone."

"No family?"

"Gone."

"Not a sister, or a sweetheart—"

"I said there was none."

"There must be something in that heart of yours," Charlotte said, pinching my nose between her fingers and lifting it up. "Don't talk just yet."

She shaved my upper lip and then shook the razor in the bathwater.

"Careful," I said.

"Well?" she asked. "What is in your heart?"

"Plenty," I said.

"But nothing good?"

"No."

"Not even for God?"

"That bloody bastard?" I asked. "No, nothing good."

"Then what?"

"Fear," I said.

Charlotte looked at me tenderly and smiled.

"*The fear of the Lord is clean*," she recited from Psalms, "*enduring forever.*"

The rectangle of sunlight on the floor had now crept all the way over to encompass the bathtub, and

me, and the whores kneeling on either side. I felt the
warmth of the sun on my face, and it was a blessing.

Arizona, 1935

"Why does it always come back to women with
you?" Frankie asked, lighting another Lucky Strike.
She was hiding from the sun by leaning against the
shadow side of an old rock wall.

"Jealous?" Gamble asked.

"You're eighty-five years old," she said, flicking the
ash from her cigarette. "I'm twenty-six. Should I be?"

"Don't mistake me for harmless," he said.

"That would be like assuming an antique gun can't
hurt you just because it's old," Frankie said.

They had hitched a ride on one of the production
vans that seemed to be constantly shuttling equipment and crew between the service station and lodge
at Two Guns and Canyon Diablo. It had been a ghost
town but, during the past week, had been turned into
a movie set. All that remained of the original town
was a few rock walls, some ruined rock buildings,
piles of weathered lumber, and outlines in the sand of
where the tents had been.

The RKO carpenters had thrown up a row of false
front buildings and had dressed them to look like
every other main street in every other western made—
blacksmith, livery, general store, saloon.

"Any of this look familiar?" Frankie asked.

Gamble walked toward her and reached out, and
Frankie thought for a moment he was going to touch
her face. She didn't flinch. Instead, his fingertips

brushed the surface of the rock wall beside her, feeling the surface of the stones.

"I know this wall," he said. "Used to be the end of the blind alley. The rest of it? It's just crap."

"We should get back to work," Frankie said. She threw the cigarette to the ground and brushed the bangs from her eyes. "Huston will be here the day after tomorrow. We're running out of time and we don't have a story we can use."

"Donovan," Gamble said. "You told me that you wanted to get things right. Now you're saying that all you need is a story you can use?"

Frankie bit her lower lip.

"Go ahead," she said. "I'm listening."

FOURTEEN

Three days later, I left Annie and Charlie sleeping and wrapped my aching ribs and climbed into my clean clothes and surveyed myself in the dresser mirror. The man staring back was thinner and a bit older than I recalled, but familiar nonetheless.

"Coffee," I told the image.

I left the hotel room and went downstairs and out onto Fifth Street. The sun had been up less than an hour, so the air was still cool, and I was glad I had worn my coat. Rubbing my hands together, I walked about a bit and passed more than a dozen restaurants. For no reason other than I liked the name, I stopped at the Pacific Chop House.

I had a breakfast of steak and eggs and then sat at a table by myself near the window, drinking coffee out of a white ceramic mug. I took the pipe from the pocket of my jacket, packed the bowl with tobacco, and dug in my vest pockets for a match.

Instead of a match, I found one-half of the Queen

of Spades. Creased and faded from having been washed with the vest, but intact.

"It seems you need a match," said a smartly dressed man of about thirty. He held a box of matches between his thumb and forefinger.

I slipped the half card back into my vest pocket and took the matches from the stranger, mumbling my thanks. I lit my pipe, threw the burnt match onto the floor, and handed the box back to him.

He removed his gray felt hat and held it to his chest.

"Pardon the intrusion," the man said, "but would you be the gentleman who beat the roulette wheel at the Purgatory?"

The man had a deep South accent and a perpetual smile. His skin was ashen, however, and his eyes were limned in red. He gave me a queer feeling.

"Are you the law?" I asked.

"No, it's not like that," he said. "I have acquaintances who are peace officers, but I myself am not."

"What, then?"

"A dentist by training, a gambler by profession, and a scoundrel by reputation," he said. "My name is John Holliday, but most folks call me Doc."

"You're up damned early for a professional gambler."

"I am not an early riser, sir," he said. "I have not yet visited my bed."

Then he cocked his head and smiled even broader. "By your speech, I take you for a native of Missourah. I, too, hail from the soil of the rebellion, and find myself largely a stranger among Yankees."

I used my boot to push out an empty chair from the table.

"Let me buy you breakfast," I said.

"No, thanks," he said. "No appetite these days, I'm afraid. I came out West for medical reasons, and while my own health has not improved, I'm afraid it has been decidedly detrimental for some of the natives."

He withdrew a handkerchief from his vest pocket and softly coughed into it.

"What do you mean?"

"I helped kill three miscreants in a fight last year at Harwood's lumber yard," he said. "It has created the worst kind of unpleasantness in town between my peace officer acquaintances and the friends of the deceased."

"That tends to happen."

"Indeed," Holliday said. "*Et in Arcadia ego.*"

"Yes," I said. "We must remember that we all will die."

"Ah, a literate man," he said. "Shame. It comes to nothing."

"What do you want to talk to me about?"

"Your luck at the wheel."

"I am not a cheat," I said.

"I have no doubt," the man said. "The only cheating done at the Purgatory is strictly confined to the house. What I'm trying to figure out, Missourah, is how you beat a rigged wheel."

"If I knew," I said, "I'd do it again."

"As would I," Holliday said, then sighed. "Who knows where luck comes from? As a professional, I know that everything evens out in the end, that what we call luck is just the swing of the statistical pendulum, that, given enough time, every game is true to the probabilities. And yet, when I have been the beneficiary of

those fortunate tides, I could swear there was something in my intent or being that was influencing the
cards. Tell me, has this been your experience?"

"No," I said. "It was my intent to lose."

"Remarkable," Holliday said.

"It is the easiest strategy in the world."

"I will have to try it sometime," he said. "Perhaps
you could come by the Occidental and show me how
it's done."

"I think you can work it out for yourself," I said.
"How'd you find me?"

"Your shiny black boots gave you away," he said.
"Your new friends at the Purgatory told me you had
stepped out, and that you were freshly shod."

"And yet my outfit is incomplete," I said. "Can
you recommend a firearms dealer?"

"Spangenberger's Gun Shop on Fourth Street," he
said. "But you must be warned that carrying or con-
cealing firearms within the city limits of Tombstone
is a crime."

"I have heard as much," I said.

"My peace officer associates are Republicans and,
as such, are humorless about such matters," Holliday
said. "They are also hardly better than the lot they are
sworn to combat. They are brothers and have had a
succession of jobs from across Missourah and Kansas
as officers of the law, yet fled from each just one step
ahead of a warrant for theft or malfeasance. One was
a pimp in Illinois, is married to one of his former
charges, and is conducting a very public affair with an
actress and badly soiled dove."

"I will attempt to avoid them," I said.

"They are a troublesome lot," he said, "but their favor confers certain advantages."

Holliday smiled and drew back his lapel to reveal the curved butt of a Colt Lightning double-action revolver sitting snugly in a shoulder holster.

"Are you planning a long stay?"

"Only as long as my luck holds," I said.

"Call upon me any time," Holliday said. "You can find me at the Occidental Saloon playing poker most nights. You must have a few dollars to spare, so why not try your luck?"

"I'm done with gambling," I said.

"Really?" Holliday asked. "Oh, well—you can always work in the mines. It's four dollars a day for those who work below ground, and three fifty for those above. The Dutch say there are little people down there called the kobolds who steal tools and use them to loosen the beams and timbers, hoping for cave-ins. Have you had much experience with either the pick or the shovel, Missourah?"

I did not smile.

"I fear that I have worn out my welcome," Holliday said. "Forgive my bad manners; I seem not to be able to help myself. I am grateful for your time. Good morning, and enjoy your days of leisure."

Holliday left, but the queer feeling remained.

At the gun shop I looked over the selection and reluctantly chose an 1873 model Colt single-action Army and a box of .45-caliber shells. The gun seemed big and awkward in my hand compared to the old Manhattan, but that one had been left behind at Canyon Diablo.

FIFTEEN

That afternoon, I lay on my back in the bed with the whores on either side. We had come in furious union and, now spent, lay in a tangle of arms and legs. I took Charlie's hand and placed it over my left eye, and then I took Annie's hand and placed hers over my dead socket.

"What are you doing?" Anne asked.

"Jesus healed blindness with his hands."

"He used spit and clay," Charlotte said. "And you're not blind."

"But I'm half-blind," I said.

"You're half-crazy, is what you are," Anne said, pulling her hand back. "Jesus was the son of God. We're whores and the daughters of whores. You need to lay off that little brown bottle."

Charlotte, who had left her hand on my good eye, kissed my forehead.

"Some of my favorite people were whores," I said.

"We're fond of you as well," Charlotte said. "But you are one of the strangest johnnies we've ever had."

"No," Anne said, "you're forgetting that little man from Tucson who would rub one out into our shoes and then make us walk in them. Now, that made me sick."

"It wasn't so bad," Charlotte said. "He didn't hurt anybody and he was very polite. He was a big tipper, too."

"Congress has made it a felony to take more than one wife because of the trouble with the Mormons, but there are yet places in the world that allow it. The Indian subcontinent. Damned near anywhere in Africa, I would think, or the unsettled parts of Central or South America."

"That's a pretty thought," Charlie said.

"Have you been to any of those places?" Annie asked.

"I've never seen an ocean," I said, "or been east of the Mississippi."

"It would be more practical for a woman to have two or more husbands," Charlie said thoughtfully. "A man is like a single-shot pistol—once he goes off, it takes a while to reload. But a woman is like a wheel gun, she can bust five or six caps in a row."

Annie laughed.

"Why, for that a woman doesn't need a man at all," she said.

"Then what *do* you need a man for?" I asked.

"Babies," Charlie said. "For most women, that seems important."

"Money," Annie said. "Always."

"Oh, don't look so hurt," Charlotte said, taking her hand away from my good eye. "You know it could never work with us."

"I know you'll only stay while the money lasts," I said, blinking against the light. "It's a comfort, really, to have things on a cash basis. That way, there are no misunderstandings."

"Don't be silly," Charlotte said. "We just couldn't court a man who doesn't go to church."

SIXTEEN

The cards slid across the green felt table and when all five had been dealt, I gathered them up in my left hand and took a look. It was another miserable hand—a pair of fives over nothing.

I'd been in Tombstone for a little over a week when I became bored enough to try my hand as a professional gambler. The girls were going through my money like the fire (which, I had been told, had started when a whiskey barrel exploded at the Occidental and destroyed the western half of the business district the previous June). The idea of clerking induced a profound sense of nausea, while the thought of going down in the mines with the kobolds resulted in a cold sweat. While I still had a little money, it seemed reasonable that I would try this new occupation.

"Are you in, Missourah?" Doc asked.

The bet had gone around the table and come to me. Doc and three others—a miner with a dirty face and two drunk cowboys—were proud of their cards; I had to throw down five dollars just to stay in the game, and I had learned from experience that it was a good way to lose half a sawbuck.

"Fold," I said, throwing my cards down.

"Sticking to your basic strategy, eh?" Doc asked.

The batwing doors of the Occidental banged open and Bastard stumbled in, carrying an orange cat by the scruff of the neck. The cat was hissing and screaming and windmilling all four legs, trying to get a tooth or a claw into the kid's hand.

"Bastard," Doc said calmly. "Stop molesting that pussy. Take it outside."

"Go to hell, Doc," the kid shouted. "There ain't any law about carrying a cat in town, is there? I know it's illegal to carry a weapon, and being a good citizen, I have left my knife elsewhere. But every man has the right to protect himself, doesn't he? I got to thinking—if you can't have a knife or a gun in your hand, what's the next best thing? Then I saw old scratch here and my problem was solved."

"That's the stupidest thing I ever heard," the miner at our table said.

"I do wish you hadn't said that," Doc said.

"Let's test it!" the kid yelled.

He lobbed the cat with an underhand toss and we watched it sail over the craps table, writhing and twisting in the air. It got its feet underneath it just before it landed in the middle or our table, scattering money and playing cards. Then its claws found purchase in the felt and it shot away toward the door, apparently none the worse for the adventure.

The kid roared with laughter, and so did the drunk cowboys.

"How impolite," Doc said, methodically picking out his last bet from the scattered coins.

"We ought to teach that little bastard a lesson," the miner said. His eyes burned in his blackened face, and his fists were clenched.

"Teach Bastard a lesson?" Doc asked. "Don't think it can be done. Besides, he will have carved you up like a Christmas goose before you can lay a hand on him."

"What do you know," the miner said. "You're a lunger—you couldn't go two minutes in a toe-to-toe fight."

"Be my guest," Holliday said.

The miner walked over to where the kid was leaning against the bar. The kid's back was to the room because he was asking the bartender for a beer. The bartender was refusing. But the kid must have seen the miner coming in the mirror, because just when it seemed that his fist was going to smack against the back of the kid's skull, he moved aside. The miner was off balance, and the kid grabbed a handful of hair on the top of the miner's head and bounced his face off the bar top.

The miner staggered back, blood pouring from his nose.

The kid laughed and walked down the bar to where a couple of patrons had abandoned their drinks, seeing the fight coming. He picked up one of the free range beers and gulped it down.

"Stop that," the bartender said.

"Come on," the kid said. "I have plenty of money. Sell me a drink."

The miner drew a hunting knife.

"I'll cut that smile off your face," he said.

Doc's hand went inside his jacket to the butt of his Lightning.

But the kid did not seem worried. As the miner advanced toward him with the knife, he took a couple of steps over to the billiard table. The kid picked up the cue ball and threw it. The white ball cracked against the miner's forehead as loudly if it were breaking a rack. The miner's eyes rolled up in his head and the knife fell from his hand. Then his knees buckled and he fell with such a thump that we could feel it through the soles of our boots.

"My God, he's killed him," one of the drunk cowboys said.

"I think not," Doc said. "But his head will ache so in the days to come that he will wish it *had* killed him."

One of the Earp brothers came in from the street. They all wore black and had elaborate mustaches, but I knew this was Virgil because his left arm was in a sling, having been crippled in an ambush three or four months before, as a result of hard feelings after the Harwood lumber fight. Also, his two brothers, Morgan and Wyatt, were younger.

"What in God's name is going on here?" Virgil asked.

"God has nothing to do with it," Doc said. "I would suspect the opposite authority, at best."

Virgil walked over to the miner on the floor.

"Has this man been shot?" he asked.

"With a billiard ball," Doc said. "The evidence is the ugly red welt in the middle of his forehead. The offending round has rolled over there, beneath the craps table."

"Who threw the ball?" Virgil asked.

"I did," the kid said cheerfully.

"Then you're under arrest," Virgil said.

"For assault with a cue ball?" the kid asked.

"I have to protest," Doc said. "While the young man's manners are atrocious, and he did fling a cat into the middle of our poker game, the miner was provoking the defendant with a rather wicked-looking hunting knife. Said knife is near our miner's right hand."

"Get out," Virgil told the kid.

"See you gents," the kid said. "Thanks for the beer."

As he walked out, the kid stepped in the middle of the unconscious man's chest.

SEVENTEEN

A week after the kid bounced a billiard ball off the miner's forehead, a stranger came into Tombstone asking questions. The stranger said his name was Candelario Montoya and that he was looking for a friend, a business acquaintance with whom he needed to settle a debt.

"What's the name of your friend?" I asked.

It was the middle of the afternoon and I was sitting on a bench outside the Purgatory, having given up gambling for the fourth time in as many days. Candelario sat down next to me and smiled. His clothes and his hair were covered in trail dust. He wore a gray jacket that was vaguely military in cut, a white shirt and black tie, and gray trousers tucked into gray cowboy boots. Instead of the great sombrero which most of his countrymen (and many whites in Tombstone) wore, he wore a short top hat. The band of the hat was the striking red-yellow-black-yellow hide of a coral snake.

"I am not sure what you know him by," Candelario said. "But he is a young man of nineteen or twenty *años*, and although he is a gringo, he wears a yellow headband and a black cloth around his neck, like an Apache. They tell me that he sometimes makes trouble in the taverns here. Have you seen him?"

"This debt," I said. "Does he owe you a lot of money?"

"No, it's not like that," Candelario said. "It is a small matter that I can quickly take care of once I find him. Do you know this young gringo, friend?"

He smiled broadly and, in supplication, showed me the palms of his hands.

"Where'd you say you were from?"

"I didn't," he said.

His hands went down, but his smile remained.

"I'm from Villa Bocoachi," he said. "Do you know it? No, I didn't think so."

"Ever been to Missouri? No? Then we're even."

He took off his hat and studied the snake band. Realizing that he would get no help, his tone changed.

"It is a very ancient place," Candelario said. "The name is not Spanish; it was already old when the Spanish arrived, four hundred years ago. The name comes from the very first people who lived there, and it means a kind of snake."

"A coral snake," I said.

"Perhaps," he said. "Bocoachi is small, but rich. We have many cattle. Our merchants travel north on the Rio Sonora to purchase goods here in Tombstone for sale back home. It is a dangerous journey and there are many *bandidos yanqui* along the way. Sometimes, the Yankee bandits kill to get what they want."

"So this debt you seek to repay this young man," I said. "It is a debt of blood?"

"You Anglos are always so dramatic," he said. "No, I am not an assassin. I am a member of the *guardia rurales* and have come to execute a warrant and bring this young man back for trial."

"That is a mite ambitious," I said, "considering you're not in Mexico. This is the states."

"Not quite," Candelario said. "Not yet. Arizona is a territory, not a state. I am within my rights under the Organic Act."

"Never cared much for laws," I said. "Don't know that one, but on principle I'll say I'm against it. I've also heard it said that the rurales are a lot like the Texas Rangers, only meaner. Don't care much for rangers or rurales or lawmen by any name."

Candelario shook his head.

"You Anglos," he said. "So wrong-headed. Your heroes are all criminals, like Jesse James. A killer and thief, but there has been an outpouring of grief at his death."

"James is dead?"

"You did not know?" he asked. "A week ago, in St. Joseph. Betrayed by a gang member and shot in the back of the head while his back was turned to straighten a painting in his home."

There was a pause while he studied my reaction.

"You knew this man?" he asked.

"No," I said. "But I feel a certain kinship."

"You are about the same age," he said.

"He was a bit older," I said. "Two years, I think."

"You are an outlaw."

"Not in Arizona Territory," I said.

Candelario donned his hat and stood.

"You know what happens to outlaws."

"We all have to die," I said.

"For some, it will be sooner than for others," he said. "You could do this young gringo a favor, senor. Convince him to surrender."

"How is that a favor?"

"It keeps him alive a little longer."

I stared beyond his shoulder.

"There is a reward," Candelario said. "I have money. Three hundred American dollars."

"How nice for you."

Candelario shrugged.

"Your loss," he said. "I will find this man. Perhaps not today, perhaps not tomorrow. But soon."

"Like some advice?" I asked.

He waited.

"I know this kid," I said. "You"ll need more rurales."

EIGHTEEN

I climbed the stairs to the room and found the shutters drawn and the girls in bed. I went over to the dressing table, uncorked the bottle of laudanum, and took a long pull. Then I sat down at the foot of the mattress and asked if they were asleep.

"Not now," Charlotte said.

"What is it?" Anne asked, stirring beneath the covers. "You want to have a go? I'm bleeding, but you could have Charlie."

"I'm bleeding, too," Charlotte said.

"My God, we've spent so much time together that we're on the same cycle," Anne said. "We're just one happy damn family, aren't we?"

"I don't want to muck," I said.

"Then why are you waking us up?" she asked, squinting. "It's not even dark yet."

"Let's get out of here," I said.

"Sure," Charlotte said. "You want steak or oysters tonight?"

"I don't mean out for dinner," I said. "I mean get

out of this town. Tonight. We could take the coach to Benson and catch the Southern Pacific there. We could be on the California side of Yuma by this time tomorrow."

"What's wrong with you, Jake?" Anne asked. "Are you wanting to marry both of us again? We've gone over that."

"Neither of you have to marry me," I said. "Let's just get out of here. We can cipher it all out later. I have this feeling that something horrible is going to happen."

"Brother, nothing's going to happen," Charlotte said.

"It's the dope," Anne said. "Makes you paranoid."

"Everything is okay," Charlie said sleepily. "You'll see. Let us sleep for another couple of hours, okay? Then we'll have a nice dinner."

That evening, the kid came into the Purgatory and sat down at a poker table with me and a cigar-smoking cowboy named Mike. The kid turned the chair around and was sitting in it backwards, which was annoying, and then he started yammering about how I never played poker with *him*.

"What's wrong?" the kid asked. "Do I smell or something?"

It pissed me off because I had five dollars in the pot. I also maybe was a little sorry I hadn't sold him out to the Rurale. I thought about telling him that the Mexican lawman was in town asking about him, but reckoned I'd done enough by just keeping my mouth shut. Also, I was feeling a little mean.

"Go take a bath," I told him, "and we'll discuss it."

Cowboy Mike laughed, the cigar still clamped in

his teeth. He was a Texan, and he was naturally a bit louder and bolder than most people.

"You stepped in that one," he told the kid.

The kid's face turned as red as a sugar beet. He didn't say anything, just turned and walked out. I figured he was going out to find a skunk or maybe a rattlesnake to bring back and throw in the middle of the table. It didn't matter anyway, because Cowboy Mike took my five dollars. He had a full house against my two pair.

"Another hand?" Cowboy Mike asked, shuffling the cards.

"Why not?" I asked, throwing my coins on the table. "After all, it's only money. It's not like I *need* it, or anything."

"Your luck is bound to change soon," Cowboy Mike said. "That's the problem with most people. They'll quit after they've lost a few hands, thinking they'll cut their losses. But if you keep playing, the law of averages says you are bound to start winning. Right?"

"Sure," I said. "Until you go bust."

The poker table was near the bar, under the Custer painting, and Cowboy Mike asked me why I kept glancing up at it.

"Because they never get the details right," I said. "Just look at the gunsmoke. Did you ever see smoke hang in perfect circles like that? No, it spreads like some jagged blossom. And the blood isn't right. Fresh blood is bright red, not the color of bricks."

"Never thought much about it," Cowboy Mike said. "How many cards you want?"

After I had lost another ten dollars, the kid came

back into the saloon. I braced myself, but he didn't appear to have anything in his hands. He walked over and asked if he could sit with us.

"Suits me," Cowboy Mike said. His cigar had gone out, but he kept it in the corner of his mouth. "If it suits my partner here."

"Sit down," I told the kid. "It will keep me from losing any more money."

He pulled out the chair and sat down, the right way.

"Want in?" Cowboy Mike asked.

"Nope," the kid said.

"Where you been?"

"Out looking at the stars," he said.

"You seem a mite moody," I said. "What's wrong?"

"Got the shakes," he said. "Haven't had a drink in three days, and it is wearing me down. Nobody in town will pour me so much as a beer."

"Play some cards," Cowboy Mike said. "It'll take your mind off it. You have money?"

"Yeah, I have money," the kid said, and pulled some Mexican pesos out of his pockets and put them on the table. "Deal me in, I reckon."

Cowboy Mike shuffled the cards and then dealt. The kid picked them up, one after another as they were dealt, and spread them out in his hand and stared at them dully.

I waited until all the cards were down before I scooped them up. When I looked at the faces, I was encouraged—I had a pair of aces and a pair of sevens.

The girls had come downstairs by now and were standing behind me. They both were dressed like they were going to church on a Sunday morning.

They said they were hungry and wanted to go down the street to the Russ House and have a steak.

"Go ahead," I said. "I'll be along directly."

"No," Charlotte said, placing her hand on my shoulder. "We want you to come with us."

"Yeah," Anne said. "It's a nice joint. They won't let us in without you."

"As soon as I finish this hand."

I drew one card and ended up with another seven, which made a full house. Feeling pretty good with myself, I raised by a couple of dollars but tried not to seem too confident.

That's when Candelario walked into Purgatory.

He went over, bought a shot of tequila from Cully, then sipped it as he turned and hooked one boot heel over the brass rail and rested his left elbow on the bar.

"Who's the fellow watching us?" Cowboy Mike asked.

The kid glanced over.

"Don't know," he said.

"If you're in, you're going to have to call," Cowboy Mike said.

The kid studied his cards.

"All right," he said, tossing his money in.

"Charlotte," I said. "Go get me a whiskey."

"Oh, Jake," she said. "I'm hungry."

"Do it," I said. "Make it a double. And bring back a drink for Cowboy Mike here as well."

"Naw," Cowboy Mike said. "I've achieved a state of equilibrium, where there is just enough alcohol in my blood to make me feel seven feet tall. If I had another, I would feel eight feet tall, and that would just be silly."

"Bring him another drink anyway," I said, giving Charlotte enough money. "Take Annie with you. Bring us both back two doubles each."

"Well, I suppose it wouldn't be friendly to turn it down," Cowboy Mike said. "Time to show what you got."

"Oh, you're going to sit here and get drunk?" Anne asked.

"I'll do what I damned please," I said, laying my cards down. "Do it."

All the kid had was a pair of tens, and Cowboy Mike had a full house, but with jacks high, so I won.

"Looks like your luck has changed," Cowboy Mike said as I drew in the pot.

"Something's about to change," I said.

The girls went over, bought the drinks, and tipped Cully about twice what would have been generous. Candelario touched his hand to the brim of his short top hat as they approached, then watched with detached interest as they carried the drinks back to the table.

"Now go get something to eat and leave me alone," I told them.

"What?" Annie protested.

"Just get out of here for a while."

"No problem," Charlotte said. "Let us know when you have that enormous bug that has crawled up your ass."

"Charlie!" Anne said, dragging her by the arm toward the door. "That's not very Christian. Come on, we'll find something in the Chinese quarter."

"That dark one is a bit of a pistol," Cowboy Mike

said, then reached for one of his drinks. I pulled it back.

"It's for the kid," I said.

"Really?" the kid said.

"Bastard can't drink in town," Cowboy Mike said. "It's a city ordinance."

"Trust me," I said, then inclined my head toward Candelario.

Cowboy Mike gave me a puzzled look.

I pushed the whiskey over to the kid, and he grabbed it and drank it down in about three seconds.

"Damn," the kid said, drawing another glass toward him. "That is the tonic of life, all right. Good for what ails you. Thanks for the drinks, you one-eyed sonuva-bitch!"

That drink was gone about as fast as the first.

"This might be a good time to leave," I told Cowboy Mike.

"Is that what I think it is over at the bar?" he asked.

"The same," I said.

I pushed both of my drinks across the table to Bastard.

"I haven't seen much fun in a spell," Cowboy Mike said, his blues eyes twinkling. He gave a cheerful little wave to Candelario, who gave a slight nod in return. "Reckon I'll stick around."

"Who the hell are you talking about?" the kid asked. "The greaser at the bar? Why, he ain't nothin'. Don't even know why they let him in. They have their own part of town, just like the Chinese."

"Finish your whiskey," I said.

"Mud in your eye!" the kid said, pouring another down his throat.

"What do you reckon he's waiting for?" Cowboy Mike asked.

"Thinks it'll be easier if the kid's drunk," he said. "Slows the reflexes, dulls the mind, erodes caution. Make it easier to kill him and have a legal excuse for doing so."

"What have I ever done to the sonuvabitch?" the kid asked.

Candelario unhooked his heel from the brass rail, put the empty shot glass down on the bar, and walked in our direction.

"You have a piece on you?" Cowboy Mike asked.

"Nope," the kid said. "No gun."

The kid had had eight shots of whiskey in a row, in less than five minutes, and I could tell the alcohol was beginning to hit him hard—his face was flushed and his eyes were red and watery.

"Sorry to interrupt your game," Candelario said. "But I have business with your young friend."

Candelario was still six feet away from the table, close enough to be assured of a clean shot if he had to draw his concealed piece, which I'm sure he had, but far enough away so that he was beyond arm's reach.

"Hell, I don't recall having any business with a greaser like you," the kid said.

"Let me refresh your memory," Candelario said, and withdrew a legal paper from his pocket. "On the night of March 3, 1882, a merchant from Villa Bocoachi was robbed and left for dead on the Rio Sonora about thirty miles south of here, in Mexico. His name was Emilio Ruiz and he was thirty-four years old. His stomach was split open by a knife and his guts spilled onto the ground. He left a widow and three children behind."

"So?" the kid asked. His face was flushed.

"Emilio Ruiz was found the next morning by a traveling *abogado*—how do you say, lawyer?"

"What's that got to do with me?" the kid asked, his voice nearly breaking.

"Emilio Ruiz was not yet dead," Candelario said. "He swore out a statement about what had happened, and gave a description of his killer. The description— a white man raised by the Apache, an Indian scout, a man of about *vente años* who carries a bone-handled knife with a peculiar black blade—is the description. Ruiz said the killer was known to him as *Bastardo*. That is how you are known here, is it not? The paper I have in my hand, amigo, is a warrant for your arrest."

The kid laughed.

"You're *loco*," he said.

"I am quite sane," Candelario said. "My job is to bring you back to Mexico. Here, you may read this warrant."

He held out the slip of official-looking paper, but the kid refused it.

"It won't make any sense," he said. "I can't read. Anyway, you've got the wrong man."

"I think not, señor," Candelario said. "I must take you back."

"Unarmed?" the kid asked. "You're joking, right?"

"The situation is without mirth," Candelario said.

"Well, I ain't afraid of you," the kid said. "I ain't afraid of nothing."

His flush had become more pronounced and was

spreading down the sides of his neck like a rash. His eyes were hard and wide, and his nostrils were flared. The whiskey was kicking in, and I reckon he felt about nine feet tall at the moment.

"You got the wrong man," the kid said. "My name is Ishmael."

Something funny seemed to happen to time at that moment—it didn't slow down exactly, but it seemed to expand and the spaces between everything got wider. I was acutely aware of the cards on the table, the empty glasses of whiskey in front of the kid, the stink of Cowboy Mike's cigar, and the smooth voice of the Rurale.

"Come peacefully," Candelario was saying. "It is best for all."

"Your name is Ishmael?" I asked.

"What of it?" the kid asked sternly.

"What's your last name?"

"Don't know," he said. "If I ever did, I've forgotten."

"Where were you born?"

"I beg your pardon," Candelario said. "But I am trying to execute a warrant upon a fugitive."

"It can wait," I said. "Kid, where were you born?"

"Texas," he said. "I don't know where, exactly, but they say my mother died in childbirth and that my brother abandoned me, but not before he gave me this ridiculous name—Ishmael. From the Bible or something. He's the real bastard. I only met the sonuvabitch once, on the day I was born. What kind of brother abandons you to strangers when you're just a baby? Oh, I used to daydream about him show-ing up one day and rescuing me from these families that took me in and treated me like a slave and then passed me on, but I didn't know anything about him, not even his name. As the years passed I grew to hate him, and the daydreams turned to killing. I swore I would kill the dirty sonuvabitch if I ever found him, and I mean it still."

"How do you know all this?"

"Because I heard it from every family that took me in," he said, "including the last family."

"What do you mean, 'last family'?"

"Their name was Oatman," he said. "Maybe you heard of them, because they were all killed by the Apaches that took me in. The mother, the father, the son and the two girls. Blood and brains across the floor of the wash. Well, I guess both girls, but I never saw the body of the youngest one. But I'm sure she's dead, because she ran off like a rabbit into the brush."

The kid was talking a blue streak, and his right hand was dropped down toward the top of his high moccasin.

"Everybody calls it the Oatman Massacre, but that ain't exactly right. It was more like a mistake, an accident created by a pack of morons, folks so stupid that they shouldn't have been allowed to have children of their own, or take other's children, either."

"Truly, I must insist," Candelario said. "Stop this."

"Shut up," me and the kid said together.

"I'd do it if I was you," Cowboy Mike said, grinning.

The kid turned his attention back to me.

"Now, why the muck do you want to know all this?"

Things got real quiet.

"Because I'm your brother," I said.

The kid pulled the bone-handled knife from the top of his moccasin boot and sprang across the table like a snake. I saw the black blade flashing toward me and jumped back, just in time to keep my throat from being slit.

If time had seemed big and drawn out before, it got short and hard now.

The table went over and glasses shattered on the floor and cards flew up in the air as the kid scrambled to get that blade on my flesh. Cowboy Mike had tipped over backwards in his chair and rolled away, and Candelario had pulled a .45-caliber Schofield revolver from beneath his coat.

"Fire in the hole!" Cowboy Mike yelled.

As soon as the kid saw the gun, he ducked—just as Candelario fired.

The bullet sailed over the kid's shoulder and across the bar and hit General Custer right between the eyes. The shot made my ears ring and filled the Purgatory with smoke.

Cowboy Mike shook his head and worked a finger in one ear.

"I'll never get used to the sound of a firearm going off indoors," he said. "Cully, you'd better go get the marshal. I think we're going to need one, and maybe a coroner, right quick."

The bartender ran for the door.

"Drop the knife," Candelario said, then brought the snout of the revolver to bear on the kid, who was crouching like some animal on the floor, looking for a way out.

"You're looking down the barrel of eternity, kid," Cowboy Mike said, getting to his feet and taking a few steps behind the Rurale, to be out of the line of fire. "Better drop that blade, or be prepared to explain to your maker the whats and why nots."

"I don't have to explain nothin' to nobody," the kid growled.

"Drop the knife," Candelario said.

"I'm going to kill this one-eyed sucker who left me to die when I was a howling infant," the kid raged. "I'm going to cut him up and drag him out into the desert and let the animals feed on him before he dies, so he knows what it feels like."

"This is your last warning," Candelario said, pointing the Schofield at the kid's chest. "Drop the knife."

"Make me," the kid said.

Then Candelario's eyes narrowed and I knew he was going to shoot. Just as I expected the Schofield to bark again, Cowboy Mike swung a chair down on top of the Rurale's head and shoulders. He fell to his knees, the gun still in his right hand, but Cowboy Mike reached out and snatched the Schofield.

"Can't let you do that," Cowboy Mike said. "These two need to fight it out, and then you can do what you can. If you don't like it, you can lump it."

Then Cowboy Mike tucked the Schofield in his waistband and gave Candelario a savage backhand, and the Rurale went down, the whites of his eyes showing between half-closed lids. His squat top hat with the coral snake band rolled across the floor and came to a rest against the bar.

The crowd, which had backed away when the gun went off, now crowded in. They were the usual lot of cowboys and miners, professional gamblers and working girls.

"Ten dollars on the Bastard!" a miner said.

"To kill or just to win?" one of the gamblers asked.

"Ten to win, twenty to kill," the miner said.

"I'll take a little of that action," Cowboy Mike said.

Then the kid sprang at me, teeth bared and knife in hand.

NINETEEN

I managed to grab the kid's right wrist before he connected the knife with my throat, and I had a real good look at the wicked thing. The blade was seven inches of dark steel, with a strange ripple pattern, and the handle was yellowed bone.

The kid was shouting and cussing and spitting all over my face.

He was pushing me backwards and eventually got me against the wall and put his full weight into the knife. I had my other hand on his wrist now, and was managing to keep the blade a few inches from my chin, but with his free hand he began punching me in the face.

Blood poured from my nose, and I tasted it in my mouth.

I increased the pressure and began to bend his right wrist backward, and he stopped punching me and used his free hand to support the back of his knife hand.

We remained like that for what seemed like hours,

but it really must have been only a minute or two, with our hands locked around the knife handle. We both were breathing like locomotives and my ribs, which had just about healed, began yelping from the strain of it all. Also, since it was *my* back to the wall, I knew I was losing.

I lifted my left foot and brought the heel of my new black boot down hard on the arch of his moccasined foot. He grimaced but kept his hold on the knife. I lifted my foot and did it again. His eyes squinted with pain and a little involuntary sound came from the back of his throat. He tried to bring his right knee up into my groin, but I knew he would try this, so I had twisted a little, so his knee just glanced off my thigh.

Then I lifted my left foot one more time and drove the heel downward.

He yelped and released the knife. As soon as I knew I had it, I flung it hard across the room, and it spun like a windmill and buried itself in a wood panel behind the bar.

He hit me once on the chin with his fist, but that's all—he wasn't used to facing a left-handed opponent. I jabbed, then connected with a right-left-right combination that sent him staggering backward, and he landed on his rump in the fish pond.

"That's not fair," he shouted.

"And trying to cut my throat is?" I asked. "You sonuvabitch. Whatever rules you're using, they aren't Marquis of Queensbury."

Cowboy Mike chuckled.

"Thanks," I said. "Bet for me next time, would you?"

The kid climbed dripping out of the fish pond and leaned against one of the benches for a moment, catching his breath. He was favoring the foot that I had stamped the hell out of, and blood was running from the corner of his mouth.

The crowd buzzed and the odds had apparently changed. It seemed I was the favorite to win, if not to kill.

"Truce," I said.

"Go to hell."

The kid picked up a chair and slammed it down on the nearest table, breaking the chair apart. He took the stoutest piece of wood and, holding it like a club, came toward me.

"What the hell is wrong with you?" I asked.

"You are," he said.

He cocked the piece of lumber behind his head, like a bat.

I was reaching for a stave from the wooden box near the pot-bellied stove when Wyatt, one of the Earp brothers, walked into the Purgatory. He apparently had been fetched form his bed, because he was wearing his dark long coat over a pair of red long johns. He had a long-barreled Colt Peacemaker in hand, muzzle pointed toward the sky.

"That'll do," he said quietly.

The kid dropped his piece of lumber.

"All bets are off," Cowboy Mike said. "The game has been called on account of the law."

Wyatt Earp walked in, shaking his head as he surveyed the mess we had made of the Purgatory.

"Damn it all," he said. "Somebody will have to pay for this. Who's the greaser on the floor?"

"Rurale," Cowboy Mike said. "Got a piece of paper he says is a Mexican warrant for Bastard's arrest. The charge is murder. He pulled this here Schofield pistol out of his pocket, and that was the beginning of the trouble."

"Is he dead?"

"No," Cowboy Mike said. "Just discouraged."

Just then a woman in her early twenties appeared in the doorway. She was in nightclothes, and her curly brown hair was piled atop her head. It was obvious she had just tumbled from the same bed Wyatt had come from.

"Wyatt, are you all right?"

"Go home, Josie," Wyatt said.

"I die a little every time you're called out," she said, resting her head tiredly on the doorframe. "I think of what happened to Virgil, and what could happen to you. The Clantons—"

"Dammit, I told you to go home."

Her eyes narrowed.

"I will," she said. "And you can go to your home and muck your wife."

Then she tossed her head and left.

Wyatt grimaced and made a sound deep in his throat, then kicked a chair over in frustration. Of course, I know now that the woman was Josephine Marcus, a Jewish dancer who had come to Tombstone with an acting troupe and stayed. Some years ago, I saw a photograph of a nude woman wrapped in some type of sheer garment who someone claimed was Marcus, but it was not the same woman I saw that night in Tombstone.

"Women," Wyatt muttered while standing near the

overturned chair. "They offer surpassing pleasure and constant trouble."

At that moment, the kid made for the nearest window. He hopped up on a table, gave a war whoop, and then dove through the glass and frame as smoothly as if he were diving into a river. Then he was out on the street, running into the darkness.

TWENTY

Wyatt Earp walked into the street swinging his long-barreled Colt, watching Bastard as he ran. He looked undecided for a moment, then holstered the revolver.

"Damn kid," he said.

"Aren't you going to shoot him?" Cowboy Mike asked, now in the street near Wyatt. "Hell, you shot down those fellows last year for less. You're supposed to be mighty handy with that big iron. Let's see that fancy gun work, you egg-sucking bastard."

While Cowboy Mike was delivering this tirade in memory of his dead friends, Virgil Earp was sliding down the sidewalk. I saw Virgil in the flicker of the gas lights, his ruined left arm hanging stiffly at his side, the dark solid shape of a gun in his right hand.

Virgil lifted the revolver and whacked the barrel against the back of Cowboy Mike's head. His knees folded and Cowboy Mike collapsed neatly in the dirt.

"Obliged," Wyatt said.

"What's the ruckus?" Virgil asked.

"Drunks," Wyatt said. "They've been fighting, tore the place all to hell. There's a greaser laid out on the floor in there that is supposed to be a Rurale with a Mexican murder warrant."

"To hell with Mexican law," Virgil said.

I was sitting on the floor of the Purgatory, a bloody mess, watching through the open door. The Earps came back inside and Wyatt grabbed me beneath one arm and hauled me to my feet.

"What's your story?" he asked.

"How much time you got?" I asked.

He cuffed my ear. It smarted.

"When I want jokes, you'll know because I'll be smiling," Wyatt said. "Do I look like I'm smiling?"

I glared at him. Maybe it was the taste of my own blood in my mouth, or maybe it was just because I hated the law, but I wasn't through yet. I spat out some red saliva.

"No, you're not smiling," I said. "But all cops are sadists. Maybe you only smile when—"

I wasn't going to say anything particularly witty, just something about his only smiling when beating women and children, but Wyatt hit me with his fist so hard that I couldn't get the rest of the sentence out. The blow sent me reeling against the bar, where I slid to the floor.

He walked over and took a pair of open handcuffs from the pocket of his coat and threw one of the cuffs over my left wrist. Then he ratcheted the manacle down tight.

"How's that feel, smartass?"

He grabbed me by the back of the neck and forced me down, his knee in the center of my back. I reckoned he was going to grab my other hand and bring it around to clamp the other half of the cuffs on, but instead he took my shackled left hand, stretched my arm out on the oak floor, and turned my palm face-up, so the back of my hand was against the heavy nickel-plated steel ring.

Virgil walked over and stood over me.

"You'll learn," he said, "that the Earps stick together. When you insult one of us, it is an insult to all, and we have long memories. You seem a bit slow, so we're going to give you something to help you remember this."

Then Virgil ground the heel of his boot into my palm and twisted it. My hand was wedged between his heel and the handcuff, which was on the oak floor; it had no give. In a moment—and with a bone-grinding sound—he scraped the flesh from the back of my hand.

"Bastards!" I yelled.

That was a mistake, because it got me a kick in the ribs.

Wyatt laughed, then wrenched my hand around and threw the other end of the cuffs around the brass rail that went along the bottom of the bar.

"Cool off there for a spell," Wyatt said.

Virgil walked over to Candelario on the floor and nudged him hard with the toe of his boot.

"How long do you think he's going to be out?"

"Hard to tell," Wyatt said.

"Well, I'm in no mood to drag him down to the jail," Virgil said, drawing a chair over and sitting. "I'll just wait here and smoke some and maybe drink some coffee until he wakes up, and can go to the calaboose under his own power. Why don't you go on over and play some billiards with Morgan?"

"I don't know, Virge," Wyatt said. "Maybe I should stay."

"Don't," Virgil said. "I'll be fine. Besides, in the mood you're in, you're a magnet for trouble. Somebody is liable to get killed."

"All right," Wyatt said.

"And put some clothes on," Virgil said. "You look unfinished in those red flannels."

Wyatt left, and Virgil took a cigar from his pocket and lit it. Then Cully brought him some coffee, and he sat there sipping it and dividing his attention between me and the unconscious Candelario.

"Where you from?" Virgil asked at length.

I wouldn't speak.

"Oh, don't be sore," he said. "If we didn't kick the shit out of people, our lives wouldn't be worth two cents. It comes with the job. Folks respect what they fear. Tell me where you're from."

"Missouri," I said.

"Which part?"

I told him.

"I know it," he said. "What's your name—your real name?"

I told him that, too.

"Never heard of you," he said.

"You don't sound like you're from Missouri."

"I'm not, at least not originally," he said. "Me and my brothers were born in Illinois."

"Yankees," I said in disgust. "All of you Yankee lawman are from Illinois, by way of Kansas. You and

Hickok and a dozen others like you. What were you doing in Missouri?"

"After the war, the old man moved the family to a sleepy little community in southwestern Missouri called Lamar," Virgil said. "That's where Wyatt got his first law job, as city constable. It didn't last. He stole some money from the court and then was accused in federal court of helping steal a couple of horses down in Indian Territory from a fellow."

"Damned serious charge," I said. "I never stole a horse in my life."

"You will, under the right circumstances," Virgil said. "And you won't hang if you don't get caught. You seem to be about Wyatt's age. How old are you?"

"Thirty-three," I said. "In the fall."

"Wyatt's a bit younger," he said.

"What happened to the horse thief indictment?"

"Wyatt made $500 bond and lit out for Kansas," he said. "For all we know, the warrant is still good. He never went back to find out, and nobody ever sent anybody to look for him. He became a buffalo hunter for a spell, then tried on a dozen other jobs for size, but the one he kept coming back to was peace officer, in Wichita and Dodge, mainly. The cow towns sorely needed 'em."

Virgil scratched his whiskers.

"You know, if Wyatt hadn't struck out from Missouri when he did, the roles might have been reversed— he could be sitting there on the floor all bloody and chained to the brass rail, and you could be down at Cambell and Hitch's Saloon, playing pool."

As I sat there hurting, it occurred to me that Virgil was right. The only thing that separated the Earps from common thugs (or an uncommon criminal, in my case) was the badge they wore.

It was close to 11 o'clock, and the wind had picked up outside.

"Going to storm," Virgil said.

Then we heard a sound like muffled thunder from across town, and Virgil sat up in alarm. He knew, like I did, that it was the sound of distant gunfire. There were shouts and cries, and in a moment Sven, the blond-headed boy, came running into the Purgatory.

"Marshal," he said, panting. "I've been sent to fetch you."

"What is it?" Virgil asked, on his feet now.

"Your brother, Morgan," the boy said, struggling for breath. "They shot him through the window of the saloon as he was playing pool. He's in bad shape, and Mister Wyatt says to come quick."

Virgil threw down his cigar and rushed out the door, along with the rest of the saloon. The only ones left behind were me and Candelario, who was still out cold.

I felt sorry for Virgil Earp for about ten seconds, until I realized that the cigar the one-armed sonuva-bitch had thrown down had rolled over into a pool of whiskey that had been spilled during my fight with Bastard. I watched as the cigar smoldered. For a moment, I thought I was safe, and then a pale blue flame rippled across the puddle of whiskey.

I jerked my left hand away hard, testing the stout-ness of both handcuff and brass rail, and both seemed as immovable as stone.

"Hey!" I yelled. "Anybody! A little help."

But everybody must have been occupied with the murder.

The flames had followed the puddle over to the end of the bar, where it ignited a stack of discarded *Epitaphs*. The fire was now orange and hot, and was blistering the finish on the near surface of the bar.

I fought my bonds again, to no avail. I started looking for anything within reach to pry the rail up or try to break the chain between the cuffs, but could find nothing.

"Hello!" I hollered. "Fire! Get the brigade."

The end of the bar was now burning, as was the floor behind. Then the flames hit some rags and other trash stored underneath. It flared and sent ugly black smoke to the ceiling.

"Not good," I told myself. "Not good at all."

I grasped the chain in both hands, put my feet against the bar, and pulled for all I was worth. I nearly pulled my shoulders out of their sockets, and still the damned rail would not budge.

"Help!" I screamed, and I'm not ashamed to admit it. "For God's sake, somebody help me!"

But there was no answer. I was in danger of being cooked alive if I didn't think of something fast. Already the tin ceiling was black was soot, the air was becoming thick, and the heat was making the sweat to trickle down my ribs.

Candelario, still face-down on the floor, coughed.

"Get up!" I shouted. "Get up, dammit, or we'll burn like the sinners we are!"

But the Mexican made no effort to rise.

The fire had now reached the rows of liquor stacked on the back bar and around that damned painting of Custer. The general bubbled up and then disappeared in a field of black. In a few moments first one bottle and then another exploded, showering flame and glass like bombs.

"Oh, muck."

Just then, the boy appeared in the doorway.

"Sven!" I called.

"I'll get help, Mister Gamble."

"No!" I shouted. "There's no time."

Three more whiskey bottles exploded, and the boy backed away.

"Don't!" I said. "Come back."

"I'm afraid," he said.

I spied a poker leaning against the pot-bellied stove in the corner of the room.

"Throw me that poker," I said. "Run and fetch it and you can throw it here, without coming close to the fire."

He looked unsure.

The heat now seemed to cook one side of my face.

"Do it, Sven!" I said.

"A dollar," he said.

"Done," I said. "Just do it."

Emboldened by money, the boy ran into the Purgatory, grabbed the poker, and raced halfway toward me. He threw it in my direction, then scurried out of the building to the safety of the street.

The poker slid across the floor, but stopped six inches from my reach.

"Really?" I asked, looking up, as if God would answer.

I scrunched over and pulled off one of my boots and lay on the floor. Knowing that the boot wasn't heavy enough to drag the poker to me, I paused, then realized if I turned it around I might be able to slide the poker inside the boot and then twist the boot to catch it and drag it toward me. My first couple of attempts were too timid. I couldn't get the poker inside the boot; I was afraid if I used too much force, I would just push it out of my reach.

Then an ember landed on my shoulder and burned a hole in my coat, and it prompted me to try the business again. Holding it by the heel, I gave the boot a right smart shove, and the poker went in. Then I twisted the boot and, with the poker jammed inside, pulled it toward me.

I took the poker and rammed it beneath the brass, got to my feet, and lifted with my all. There was a screeching sound as the screws which attached the rail to the bar began to come out of the wood. I tried again, and the screws began to pop out, one by one. But I found I couldn't get free because I would have to pry up the length of the rail to the end—about fifteen feet.

So, I took the poker and tried a new approach.

I jammed the pointed end into a link in the chain, shoved the end of the poker beneath my right arm, and put my weight on it. The link popped open and I fell backwards on the floor, free.

"Ha!" I laughed, throwing my head back.

I grabbed my boot and made for the stairs. Smoke was flowing up the stairwell, so I kept low and hid my face in the crook of my arm. I burst into my room and snatched the .45 Peacemaker and the shoulder rig from beneath the bed pillows. Then I went to the closet to grab the valise with the money and the fiddle, but it wasn't there. I looked around the inside of the closet, thinking it might have been knocked into a corner, but it was not to be found.

What I did find on the floor of the closet were a few splatters of blood. The blood dribbles went toward the open window, where the curtains blew inward on a gust of wind. I went to the window and looked out, but all I could see was the empty roof of the next building.

"Bastard," I said.

He had doubled back after running from Wyatt and had robbed me.

Cussing, I debated about whether I should venture out on the roof after him, but decided against it. I would rather risk the fire than jump from the roof to the alley.

I took the stairs two at a time back down to the Purgatory.

The fire was worse now. The bar was completely aflame and the heat was intense. The place where I had been chained to the brass rail now resembled the heart of a furnace. I had to shield my face as I passed through, and I didn't breathe for fear of inhaling smoke.

But when I had made it safely back to the street, I looked inside and could see the soles of the Mexican's boots. The flames were creeping closer to him, and although Candelario was coughing and moaning, he still wasn't rising.

"Oh, for God's sake," I said.

I sat my bundles down, ran back into the Purgatory, grabbed the Mexican by the ankles, and dragged him out the door and into the street. I could hear the bells of the fire brigade now and, because I didn't want to spend time in the city jail, knew it was time to leave Tombstone behind.

"Where's my money?" Sven asked. "A deal's a deal."

"You're right," I said.

I fished a dollar from my pocket and tossed it to him. He deftly caught it in one of his pudgy pink hands.

"Spend it well," I said, slipping out of my frock coat. "It is just about my last."

"I thought you was rich," Sven said.

"Things change," I said, donning the shoulder rig with the Peacemaker. "Don't tell anybody which direction I left."

"You bet," he said.

"Tell your friends Annie and Charlie that I didn't have time to say goodbye in person," I said, putting my jacket back on. "But tell them I will always remember them fondly and that, so far, I've liked their church best—but I'm still wrestling with God."

Then I walked away down Fifth Street. At the intersection with Fremont, I looked north and saw Bastard limping along, the valise under his arm. He turned to the northeast on First, and when the street ended he continued walking, into the desert.

I followed, determined to recover my father's fiddle—and my money.

Arizona, 1935

"That's more like it," Frankie said. "Violence plays."

She finished her notes with a flourish and slapped the pencil down on the top of the folding table. She and the old man were sitting beneath a tent pitched thirty yards from the Canyon Diablo bridge, and on the table between them were two water glasses and a fifth of Old Crow.

"Yes," the old man said. "It gets real interesting when the blood flows."

She picked up the bottle and put a couple of inches of whiskey in his glass, then added the same to hers. Then she took a swallow and closed her eyes.

"Is there anything in this world that whiskey cannot fix?"

"What's happened to you?" Gamble asked.

"What do you mean?"

"When we talked that night at the House of Lords bar in Joplin a year or so ago, you seemed like somebody I could trust with the truth," he said. "Now, you're smoking and drinking not for pleasure, but for relief. You're trying to twist the story to match some damned idea of what a western should be, rather than listening for what really happened. Has Hollywood done this to you?"

"No," Frankie said.

"Has Huston?" Gamble asked.

"Maybe," she said.

Gamble took a sip of whiskey.

"Nice breeze tonight," Gamble said, looking over the movie version of Canyon Diablo. It was nearly finished, and now that it was dusk and shadows had filled in the imperfections, it was almost possible to believe it was the real thing.

"You know, if I thought I was going to live long enough, I would write the damn thing myself," Gamble said. "Put it in a book, proper. Forget the talkies. Remember those ledger pages I gave you about my time with Alf Bolin and his gang? I think I could manage it. If I was going to live long enough, that is."

Frankie gave a dismissive wave.

"You're healthier than I am," she said.

Gamble was silent.

"You know something I don't?" she asked.

"I know when I'm going to die," he said.

"Scat," she said. "Nobody knows that."

He took another drink. He looked thoughtful for a moment and was about to say something when, as the Sante Fe Chief approached from Los Angeles, there was a great rumble from the west. The bridge sang as the massive locomotive crossed the gorge, pulling behind it a string of Pullman cars, its head-light piercing the gloom. The table between them shook as the Chief reached the eastern rim, then began to slow amid billows of steam and smoke.

"I didn't know the Santa Fe stopped here any-more," Gamble shouted.

"It doesn't," Frankie shouted. "It's Huston—he's arrived."

TWENTY-ONE

I was fairly beat up, but the weight of the Peacemaker in the shoulder rig gave me comfort. I followed Bastard into the desert, thinking that I would be able to get close enough to send a bullet into him and recover the valise. But I was a half mile outside of Tombstone before I had a glimpse of my prey, a shadow moving across the dark landscape.

I turned and looked behind me. The glow of the fire at the Purgatory was a smudge on the horizon. I knew that I had no hope of surviving for long in the desert, on foot and without provisions. But I thought that it couldn't hurt to trail Bastard for a mile or two. If only I could get closer than a hundred yards, I could pick him off with the Peacemaker—and never be in range of that damned knife of his.

So I went along for the next hour or so, encouraged by regular glimpses of Bastard's white shirt in the starlight. But no matter how hard I tried, I could never seem to catch up.

Along about two o'clock in the morning, I found

myself scrambling across a hard flat area surrounded by jagged rocks. I had glimpsed Bastard not far ahead, and this caused me to push a bit harder in hopes of getting a clear shot. Another forty yards ahead, as I was squeezing past one of those jagged rocks, Bastard jumped me.

He had been squatting atop the rock and, when I neared, he let out a scream of joy and his feet landed on my back. It drove me down on the rocks so hard that it drove the breath from my lungs and jarred the Peacemaker from the shoulder holster. It thudded in the sand about two feet from my head, but as I reached for it, Bastard stepped on the pistol with the sole of his moccasin.

Knowing what was coming next, I instinctively rolled over and brought my left hand up to my face. The black knife flashed downward. The blade glanced off the handcuff dangling from my wrist, then became caught in the fabric of my coat sleeve.

I jerked my left hand away, and the motion sent the knife into the darkness. Bastard tried to go after it, but I grabbed the waist of his denims and hauled him back.

"No, you don't!" I shouted, then backhanded him across the mouth.

He kicked and fought, but when I placed my left wrist against his throat and pressed the handcuff against his windpipe, he began gasping for breath.

"Why'd you steal my money?" I asked.

My nose was bleeding from the fight and big drops of blood splattered down on his face. He tried to speak, but couldn't. He motioned to his throat, and I eased up on the pressure a bit.

"What do you mean?" he rasped.

His breath smelled like stale cigar smoke and bad whiskey.

"You went up to my room and stole my money," I said. "You took the grip with the fiddle and you took my money from the closet. Where's my money?"

"You're crazy," he sputtered. "I took the fiddle because I wanted to take something of yours, but there wasn't any money in the closet. You can see for yourself—the bag is over there."

He made a tired motion with his hand.

I glanced over. The valise was on the ground, about twelve feet away.

"I can't," I said. It was hard to talk, because I was so winded. "If I let you up, you'll go for your knife."

"I don't even know where it is," he said. "Besides, why would I lie? I wish I had stolen your money—it would be something to be proud of."

Then I knew he was telling the truth. Anne and Charlotte had stolen the money, while I was playing cards with Cowboy Mike at the Purgatory. I had chased Bastard into the desert, when I should have stayed in Tombstone and tracked the whores down.

"Tell me, does that fiddle mean anything to you?"

"Some."

"Good," he said. "I'm glad I stole it."

We stayed like that for maybe a minute or two, both of us too exhausted to fight or even talk anymore. I was reluctant to give up the advantage, because as soon as I let him up, I knew he would try to murder me.

So, I decided I should just go ahead and kill him.

"Sorry," I said, "but I should have done this when you were born."

I leaned on the handcuff.

Bastard began to choke, then tried to pry my arm away. But I had my other hand against my forearm and the bracelet had him good and pinned. The windpipe is a fairly tender part of the anatomy, and it didn't take a whole lot of force to have Bastard dancing. His heels were digging into the ground and kicking away some loose rocks.

Then I felt something crawling up my right pants leg.

It was not a pleasant feeling.

Trying to identify an animal strictly by how it feels on your calf is an interesting challenge, and I was not good at it. The first thing that came into my mind was snake, and after that mental image of a coral snake or a rattler slithering up my trouser lodged itself in my brain, I could no longer maintain my control over Bastard.

I rolled off him and jerked up my pant leg, and tried to brush whatever it was away. As soon as I touched it, I knew it was a scorpion, and then a moment later I felt it sting my shin.

"Sonuvabitch!"

I brushed the scorpion off and ground it to pieces with the heel of my boot. Even before I was done, a burning sensation was spreading from the wound.

Bastard sat up, hacking and coughing.

"Just a scorpion," he said. "Won't kill you. Make you sick, maybe."

My head was swimming.

Bastard got to his feet and staggered over to where his knife had been slung. He searched on the ground a bit with his moccasin, then found it. I reckoned he was going to slit my throat, but he put the knife back in its sheath.

"You'll have to find your gun yourself," he said.

"Why aren't you going to kill me?" I asked.

"Can't," he said. "Not until the scorpion venom leaves your body. There is no power in killing an enemy on his sickbed. I cannot even touch you, or your weapons. It would be the reverse of counting coup. It would bring me dishonor and disappointment."

I lay on the ground, my chest heaving. It was difficult to concentrate.

"Besides," Bastard said. "I'm tired."

"All right," I said. "Leave the fiddle."

"No," he said. "I stole it fairly, it is mine. Would you expect me to return a horse that I had stolen from you? No, I think not. We will kill each other another day."

Then he picked up the valise and limped off.

I lay there for maybe a minute or an hour, then forced myself to my feet, leaning against one of the jagged rocks. It occurred to me that I was lost. Tombstone was no longer glowing behind me, and the night had clouded over, so I couldn't even see the stars to find my way.

The scorpion sting was burning, I was bleeding from maybe a dozen places, and my head was feeling like somebody had dipped a spoon in and scrambled things up. So I found a large flat stone and lay back, staring into the murky night sky. I asked God what kind of creator isn't satisfied at making something as wicked as a scorpion, but goes on and creates a human being.

TWENTY-TWO

A light rain came just after dawn.

It was no more than a mist, but it was enough to wake me. It was daylight sufficient for me to find the Peacemaker on the ground, and I stuffed it back into the shoulder holster. Then I found a rock overhang to protect me from the damp, and went back to sleep.

I had intended to nap for only an hour more, but I ended up sleeping the entire day. The scorpion sting had made me sick, but only as sick as a really bad hangover, but the fight had left me weak and bloody. It was easier to try and sleep things off than to get up and be in the world, and as long as I was sitting on a clean slab of rock, my fear of creeping things was kept to a minimum.

If I had dreams, I don't remember them.

About dark, the sound of something large moving through the scrub brought me around again. At first, I thought it was a horse, but there wasn't the clatter of hooves on the rocks. Whatever it was, it was tearing up a lot of scrub, and I could see the tops of the saguaros bending and breaking as it came my way. Then I thought it might be a bear, or a wild pig. We had varieties of both back in the Ozarks. But then the thing made an awful sound, which was like a cross between the bray of a donkey and the whistle of a steam locomotive, and it was a sound I had never heard before.

Apprehensive, I pulled the Peacemaker and held it in my lap.

Eventually, the thing lumbered into a clear spot. It was a dromedary, bristling with coarse red hair, and even from twenty yards the smell of the thing was noxious. The thing was gargantuan, six feet tall and nearly twice that from nose to tail. It had a chunk of brush in its mouth and was chewing it to pulp, its great tongue lolling to one side. Its eyes were large and wild, and if it saw me, it did not regard me as a threat. As it walked on its spindle legs, it turned its side to me. That's when I realized there was something strapped to its back.

It looked like a collection of white sticks wrapped in blue rags. As I looked more closely, I realized that the white sticks were long bones and that the rags had once been a Yankee uniform. A row of white ribs shone through a rent in the faded blue blouse, and the leather belt and boots were puckered and split.

The skull was missing.

I slapped myself, thinking that I must be dreaming.

The camel was still there, staring at me with disdain—and so was the ghostly rider. I picked up a fist-sized rock and chucked it near the thing. The camel stamped its feet, brayed, then it took off at a weird gate.

I knew now I hadn't been dreaming, but could not

accept that the camel and its headless rider were real. An animal that was foreign to this hemisphere, carrying the corpse of a Yankee. How could that be, I wondered? Yet I had seen—and smelled—the thing.

Not wanting to remain, for fear the beast would return, I started walking. The sky was still clouded over, so I didn't know where I was going, and the terrain was rough, so I only went a little ways—a mile, perhaps, then I settled down. I got cold so I got up and walked some more. Then the sun came up, and even though I had a relative idea of east and west, I was too damn tired to walk anymore, at least not until long about evening, when I set out again.

I was trying to trace my route back to Tombstone, but none of the terrain looked familiar. Instead of the alkali-colored sand that I remembered around Tombstone, this landscape was all dun and mauve colored.

Along about dark, I had to admit that I was absolutely—and hopelessly—lost.

TWENTY-THREE

Lost in the bowl of night, I found a rock outcropping and climbed up and sat down on the highest point. I was about thirty feet above the desert floor and had a good view in all directions.

There was a jagged bead of mountains on the horizon, and I'll be damned if I knew the names of any of them. It was also impossible to know how far away they were, because there was nothing to compare them to for scale. They might have been ten miles away or a hundred. There were perhaps half a dozen within my sight, and they seemed like islands floating just above the horizon. If, in the morning, they had drifted away and left the desert around me unfettered in all directions, I would not have been surprised.

I drew my knees up to my chin and watched the sunset glow die in the west. As the sky went from blue to indigo, the stars began to populate the sky, and the mountains began to fade into darkness. The moon was not yet up, and by the time it was full dark, the sky was clotted with stars; in some places, the stars were so numerous that they seemed like clouds. The Milky Way streaked overhead as if somebody had taken a brush dipped in stars and slung it arm's length across the night.

The sky was different than back home.

First off, there didn't seem to be that much of it in Missouri. Perhaps it's because of the trees and hills and other things which get in the way, but in the Ozarks things seem more compact. Also, the stars seem brighter out West, and there seem to be a helluva lot more of them.

I lay on my back on the rock to get a better view of the stars, and while I watched a shooting star blazed across the sky. It began as a brilliant white streak and then faded to an unearthly green. Childishly, I wasted a wish on it.

Then I realized how tired I was. The rock was warm, having absorbed the heat of the sun all day, and I became drowsy. Not even the roughness of the rock beneath my head could keep me awake. Then I remembered a passage from the book, about how Jacob went into the desert and at a certain place used a stone for his pillow. He had a dream of a ladder going up to heaven. He saw angels ascending and descending the ladder, and he knew that he had found the gate of heaven.

That made it hard to sleep.

If I did fall sleep, I was afraid I'd dream about ladders and angels and that didn't seem a restful prospect. So, I sat up again and clasped my hands around my legs and rested my chin on my knees.

Then I started to thinking about why the natural abode of God is the desert.

My first thought was that, at least for the Hebrew God which later became ours, that the folks who wrote about Him were all desert dwellers. It was just natural to place Him there, too. Then I tried to think of all the stories in which God appears or speaks in the book, and they all seemed to occur in the *remote* desert. They were plenty of cities in ancient times, but the Almighty doesn't seem to care much for town life. Seems to me He'd want to be where the people are, but no, the preference is for private meetings with prophets and other troublemakers who find themselves in the middle of an inhospitable place. The harder it is for a man to survive in such a place— if there's no water, say, or if there are ferocious beasts—the more the Lord seems to like it.

Off in the distance, a coyote called.

It sent a chill down my ribs.

Because I was feeling a bit anxious, I began staring harder into the darkness, but that makes the seeing worse. Look at something dead on during a really dark night, and it's going to disappear, but if you look a little off to one side, things seem brighter and clearer.

I was staring north, in the direction that Bastard had gone, trying to see the outlines of rocks and things, when of a sudden there appeared a dull glow. I thought I was imagining things at first, because staring into the dark will eventually make you see things, but by glancing at it and then away, I became convinced that there was really something out there. It was a yellow glow, as if cast by a lantern, and it seemed to bob and weave, but *that* may have been my imagination—look at any fixed point long enough and it will seem to move.

The coyotes began yipping back and forth now. Pretty soon they had a chorus going, and it made me feel a little less lonely. I wondered what the light might have been on the horizon, and briefly I considered trying to walk toward it to investigate. Surely it was a fire that Bastard had built as part of his camp. If there had been a moon out, I would have set off for the light, hoping to ambush him while he slept. But it was such a dark night, I reckoned that there was a good chance I would fall and break my neck, so I stayed put. When my eyes started dropping, I found a pebble and scratched a line on my rock, to mark the bearing of the light.

Eventually I fell asleep.

In my dreams, twenty years dropped away. I was a boy again, homeless, walking across Missouri during the war, with my father dead and my mother heavy with a bastard child. It was winter and I was hungry and cold, and I had my father's fiddle slung across my back. My mother wore a soldier's butternut coat with the .36-caliber Manhattan revolver tucked into the pocket. We fell in with a band of thieves around a place called Murder Rock in the Ozarks, and I learned to steal for a living. Then Alf Bolin, the red-headed giant who led the murderous lot, put out my right eye when he smashed a rock against my skull. Later we were at Mineral Creek in Texas, and my mother was dying in childbirth, and soon she was dead, and I was abandoning my half-brother with the doctor who had delivered him. And I was finally, completely, alone.

When I woke, I was freezing. The temperature had dropped during the night and my rock bed had cooled, and I was shivering. I sat up and rubbed my eye, and saw that dawn was brightening the sky over the mountains in the east. When there was enough light, I checked the line I had scratched in the rock, and lined it up with a snaggletooth peak. Then I climbed down and, before I resumed my journey north, I was distracted by some drawings on the side of my rock. The drawings were like the line I had scratched in the top of the rock, only much deeper, and shining white against the dark red surface.

There were horned stick animals that looked like deer or maybe antelopes, some wheels with radiating lines that could have been rays or spokes, some jagged lightning streaks, and a spiral that started small and got bigger and bigger. I touched the spiral with my fingertips, wondering who had made it—had it been ten years ago or a thousand? What was the human being like who scratched these drawings in the rock, and what was he thinking at the time? Had he, like me, spent the night atop the rock?

Had God talked to him?

I picked up a sharp stone, intent on making my own mark on the rock, but stopped. There wasn't anything for me to say. God had not talked to me. The only thing I could think of scratching into the rock was my initials, but that seemed like vandalizing a church.

I dropped the stone and trudged north.

TWENTY-FOUR

The sun came up and things began to warm a bit. The desert here was not as sparse as it was down around Tombstone, and the cactus ranged from the big saguaros, with arms like a man, to short barrel-shaped ones with red blossoms. There were a lot of scrubby plants, which made it difficult, in some places, to walk a straight line.

After I had walked a mile or two, the snaggletooth peak didn't seem any closer, but I was a damned sight warmer. I tried not to think about my hunger or my thirst. There was dew on the plants close to the ground, and I sopped some of this up with my bandana, but mostly it just left me wanting more. I saw a long-eared rabbit every so often, and thought about trying to kill one, but decided I couldn't afford to waste the time and let Bastard get even further ahead.

So I kept walking.

By and by I spied what looked like a pile of adobe bricks. As I got closer, I could see it was the ruins of an old mission church, something the Spanish had abandoned a couple of hundred years before. The roof of the church was gone and so were part of the walls, but the pillared entrance was intact and reminded me of drawings I had seen of the Alamo in Texas. Certainly, I thought, this is where the light had come from the night before. I approached cautiously, thinking Bastard might be hidden just behind one of those broken walls, waiting to spring out and slice me to pieces with the knife.

Then, a hundred yards away, I spied some weird movement beyond the adobe walls and flattened myself against the dirt. It was a shadow that looked almost human, flitting about. But I wasn't sure. So I lay there watching for a spell, and sure enough there was that funny motion again—it was like the quick movement of a coyote tearing away a chunk of meat and then trotting a few steps back. Only this time, the motion was accompanied by a pitiful human scream.

Ayúdeme, someone cried weakly. *Madre de Dios, ayúdeme.*

I got to my feet, shouting to try to scare the beasts away. I drew the Peacemaker and fired a couple of rounds into the air as I ran toward the mission. As I drew close, I could see a dozen men on the ground, some face-up, others not, a mix of white men and Indians, with guns or bows in or near their outstretched hands. Most were clearly dead, with brains spilling out of their skulls, great gunshot wounds in their chests, their throats slit, or prickly with arrows. There were also a cluster of dead horses on the far side of the mission, their bellies already beginning to swell with gas. The coyotes weren't bothering the bodies of the men or the horses, because they ordinarily shun dead things.

But there was a man slumped against one of the low walls, his head on his chest, his hands at his sides and his legs splayed. His guts were spilling out of his belly, and a coyote had a pink intestine hanging from his jaw.

I shouted, but the animal glared at me.

Coyotes are cowards, and are not known to eat human flesh, but this one was emboldened by something—the smell of warm blood, perhaps, or the taste of human flesh. Or maybe something else. Whatever it was, it sent a chill down my spine, as if I had confronted some ancient evil. I could not have been more revolted had I seen a man crouching there with a rope of human guts dangling from his mouth.

I pointed the Peacemaker and blew the coyote's mucking head asunder.

The other coyotes scattered into the scrub.

I knelt down beside the dying man, bunched up my coat, and placed it behind his head. He had brown skin and black hair and his hands were crusted in his own blood.

Gracias, he whispered. *Gracias, mis hermano. Aqua, por favor.*

"I don't know what you're asking," I said.

He blinked. Then, with great effort, he said:

"Water."

I shook my head.

"I have no water," I said. "Who did this to you?"

Los Sanguinarios.

"The cheerful?" I asked. "The ruddy? The optimistic?"

No, no. Matadors.

"I don't know what you mean," I said.

He grasped my sleeve with his ruddy hand.

Los Sanguinarios!

Then he threw his head back and clenched his teeth in pain.

Madre de Dios, matame.

I knew what I must do next, but still I hesitated. The man grimaced again in pain, and the look on his face was so pitiful, I could delay no longer. I pressed the muzzle of the revolver against his forehead and sent a bullet into his brain.

His body slumped in relief.

I replaced the Peacemaker in the shoulder rig and went from body to body, turning each over to make sure that I hadn't overlooked someone who was still alive. There were half a dozen white men, and judging from the poor manner in which they were dressed, they were all small-timers. The Indians were poorly provisioned as well; most did not have guns or even bows near them, but knives or clubs.

Then I heard a gurgling and choking sound, and realized that someone yet lived. I climbed over the far wall and found an old man sitting with his back against the trunk of a pinon tree in what had once been the mission's courtyard. He was dressed all in black, except for a white shirt beneath his vest, had a strange-looking black hat with no bill atop his head, and his unkempt gray beard was streaked with red. There was a terrible wound in his throat, and he was pressing his right hand against it, but blood was surging through his fingers. On the ground, where he had flung it, was a broken arrow.

It was a wicked-looking thing, and seemed shorter than it should be. The old man must have snapped the cedar shaft near the feathers and then pulled the other end through. The longer end had a finely flaked stone point and the shorter end, striped fletching made from what looked like turkey feathers.

Beside the old man was a wooden box, big enough to hold a carbine or sawed-off shotgun, upon which he rested the fingers of his left hand. The box appeared to be made of walnut, had brass furniture, and was fastened with two leather straps.

"He looks right queer, don't he?"

I turned my head to see Bastard crouching atop the ruined wall, the knife with the mottled blade held loosely in his right hand. The valise was beside him atop the wall. I was mindful not to reach for the butt of the Peacemaker, because Bastard was close enough to send that knife into the middle of my back before the gun had cleared the holster.

"He's in bad shape," I said.

"What's in the box?" Bastard asked.

"Not the faintest," I said.

Then I turned to the strange old man.

"Who did this?" I asked.

The old man blinked and glanced over at Bastard, then back to me. He tried to speak, but couldn't— the arrow had pierced his voice box, and he couldn't manage any sound more than a gurgle or a rasp.

"What's he trying to say?" Bastard asked.

"I wish I knew," I said. "Will you agree not to kill me while I minister to him?"

"He's a dead one soon," Bastard said. "He's lost too much blood. But at least you'll have company in the land of ghosts when I cut out your liver and eat it."

"You might get your blade in me, and it might be

a mortal wound, but you know I'll blow your brains all over the sand before I die," I said, my back still turned to him.

"Maybe," Bastard said. "But it will be worth it."

"Who did this?" I asked again.

The old man took his fingers from the box lid and, summoning an enormous effort, began tracing letters in the dust beside the box.

"What's he doing?" Bastard asked.

"Writing," I said.

The old man had written DEMONS in the dirt.

Displeasure clouded Bastard's face.

"What's it say?"

"Why should I tell you?" I asked. "You seem intent on us murdering each other. Read it yourself."

Bastard didn't say anything. But I could tell from the way his eyes shone that his curiosity had been aroused. Still, he couldn't bear to ask for my help.

"To hell with it," Bastard said. "Let him die. I don't care. Besides, I know who did this. Look at how the whites and the Indians fought together through the night against something. I've heard of this before."

"Who, then?"

Bastard shook his head.

"I won't say."

The old man gurgled to get my attention, then rapped his knuckles on the lid of the box. Then he scrawled a few more words: RETURN TORAH. Now I knew the man was a rabbi. REWARD—IN HEAVEN.

"It's about the box," I said.

"When he dies, and I kill you, I'll just take the box," Bastard said.

"Well, you'll have the box but not the reward," I said.

Bastard scratched his nose and looked away.

"What do you mean?"

"The old man says there a reward beyond our wildest dreams if we return the box," I said.

The old man heard this, and nodded. He brushed the words away and traced some more letters in the dirt.

"What's he writing now?"

"Not going to tell you," I said.

PLEASE, the rabbi wrote. DO THIS. LET ME DIE IN PEACE.

"God dammit," Bastard said, and the cussing drew a hard look from the dying rabbi. My half-brother looked guilty for a moment. "Okay, we can call a truce for a few minutes. Drop your gun."

"Why don't you drop the knife first?"

"At the same time, then," Bastard said.

Bastard came down from the wall, and we carefully placed our weapons on the ground. The he came over and knelt beside me as I explained, sort of, what the rabbi had written in the dust.

"Return it to where?" Bastard asked.

The old man didn't respond. His eyes were getting dull.

"Rabbi," I said. "Rabbi!"

He roused, and his eyes focused on my face.

"Return the box to where?"

He slowly drew more letters in the dirt.

TEMPLE.

"Where?" I asked. "What town?"

CANYON DIABLO.

My ribs ached at the thought. Then I had an image of Astrid in my mind's eye, and of somehow using the Torah to ransom her. She would be, well . . . grateful.

"Well?" Bastard asked. "Tell me."

"He wants us to return the box to its rightful owner," I said.

"Who's that?" Bastard asked.

"God," I said.

The rabbi reached out with his bloody right hand and grasped my collar, imploring me to agree.

"What's inside the box?" Bastard asked.

"Power," I said. "We are forbidden from opening it. But a treasure awaits us if we return it."

"How much treasure?"

"Beyond our dreams."

"My dreams are fairly tall," Bastard said.

I turned back to the rabbi.

"Tell me about the demons who did this."

But the rabbi slumped back against the pinon tree, dead.

"The ghost has flown," Bastard said. "And we're still here. Did you see what did this? Did you hear anything this morning?"

"No," I said. "I came up from a few miles south, from the picture rocks."

"I know," Bastard said. "I was watching, from a hundred paces away. If you hadn't slept on the rocks, you'd be dead now—I would have killed you while you slept. But the rocks are a forbidden place. Ghosts are there."

"Something's there, all right."

"Did any follow you?"

"Don't be stupid," I said.

"From the outside, every religion seems foolish," he said. "But you wouldn't think so if you could see what I see. All night long, the ghosts danced around the base of your rock. There was also a woman with long red hair up top with you. Who was she?"

"You're crazy," I said.

"Yes, I know," Bastard said. "But that doesn't mean I didn't see her."

"What do you think happened here?" I asked. "Who are these dead Indians?"

"They call themselves the River People," he said. "Pimas. Most of them, anyway. But the one on which the coyotes were dining, he was Yaqui. Probably escaped from slavery in the sugar and hemp plantations in Sonora."

"You think bandits killed them?"

"No," he said. "Not thieves. They didn't take anything. They all still have their weapons. But I can tell you this much—they died afraid. So much so that white and red fought together."

Bastard reached down and picked up the stone arrow point. He ran his fingers over the razor-sharp flint point.

"This is made the old way," he said. "Very old."

"How do you know?"

"The point has been flint-knapped," he said. "It takes time and much skill. Most tribes have used iron stone points for at least a generation now."

"So, who were they?"

"I can't say," Bastard said, and shrugged.

"You know more than you're telling," I said. "The Indian with his guts pulled out—he said something in Spanish, that sounded to me like the cheerful ones. I don't speak Spanish, but at least that's what I thought he said."

"You must have misunderstood."

"Maybe," I said. "I don't speak the lingo."

Bastard shrugged.

"Let's get out of here," I said.

"And get back to killing each other?"

"Maybe," I said. "Or we could call a truce. Just long enough for us to return this box and split the reward."

"And then we can kill each other?"

"Of course," I said.

"I don't know," Bastard said. "I was hoping to kill you now. Let's see what's in the box, then we can decide."

"We can't," I said. "It would dishonor a man's dying wish. Besides, the box does not contain an earthly treasure. It's something holy. Opening it would destroy the power."

Bastard fairly recoiled at the word, *power.*

"It belongs to God," I said.

"So where do we take it?" he asked.

"A temple," I said.

"A temple where?"

I hesitated.

"If I tell you," I said, "you'll kill me, return the box, and claim all of the reward for yourself. No, I think I'll keep that information in my back pocket for now."

"You're right, killing you would be the thing to do," Bastard said. "But if you don't tell me, how are you going to get that box to wherever it belongs? You're lost, amigo. You have no idea where you are. But I grew up in this desert and these mountains. Without me, you'd never get out alive."

TWENTY-FIVE

I told Bastard that we needed to head in the general direction of Coon Butte, and that as we got closer, I'd be more specific. Then we took what we needed from the pockets of the dead—a few cartridges, a couple of canteens, a hat, some tobacco.

"Let's get out of here," Bastard said. "They're going to stink soon."

"We can't leave them to the coyotes," I said.

"They weren't coyotes," Bastard said. "At least, not like you know coyotes. They were teasing the ghost out of that dying Indian. They crave the ghost in all of us, and they will tear us apart with the teeth to get at it. They carry the coyote sickness, and because you molested them, now you have the sickness, too."

"Bullshit," I said.

"They will come back at dark," he said. "By that time, we must be far away."

"What do you mean, 'they'? Who the hell are you talking about?"

But Bastard just shook his head.

Then Bastard suggested we cut up one of the dead horses and take the meat with us, but I told him I couldn't eat horse flesh. He asked me why, and I told him that for a white man, it was about the same as being a cannibal. The French ate horse meat, I pointed out.

"So does my tribe," he said.

He took his shooting star knife and carved up the flank of one of the horses, stuffing the meat in a haversack he had borrowed from one of the corpses. When he was finished, the sun was a couple of hands above the horizon, and already vultures were beginning to circle.

We left the mission and started walking north.

After two hours, it seemed like we hadn't gotten anywhere, because the terrain looked just like the area we left—a billiard table-flat desert with lots of scrub and, every so often, rocks jutting up out of the ground.

It was still early in the spring, but the temperature began to rise as the sun climbed higher in the sky. I started to sweat and pretty soon I was soaked, but it didn't seem to bother Bastard much. By 11 o'clock, judging from the sun, Bastard said it was time to sleep away the coming afternoon.

We found an overhanging ledge and settled ourselves beneath it, and Bastard sat with his back against the rock and his legs crossed and went right to sleep.

But I could find no position in which I was comfortable.

"Bastard," I said.

"I don't like that name," he said without stirring.

"Everybody in Tombstone calls you that," I said.

"Doesn't mean I like it," he said.

"Then what should I call you?"

"You shouldn't call me at all," he said, and went back to sleep.

Time squirmed. I hadn't had a drink or a slug of laudanum for three days, and most of the time I was engaged enough in the business of survival not to miss it. But now, with time to sit and do nothing, my hands began to tremble. My skin felt like it was about to crawl off on its own. At last, when the sun was a couple of hours away from disappearing, Bastard sat up.

"Why did you quit the army?" I asked, desperately wishing for some conversation to divert my mind from my misery.

"Why do you talk so?"

He made a little fire and cooked some of the horse meat on the ends of sticks and it smelled awful. He offered me some, but it turned my stomach and I shook my head.

"Suit yourself," he said. "It will be time to travel soon."

"I will be glad for the movement," I said. "The rest has made me ill."

"It is not the rest which has made you sick."

"You're one to talk," I said. "Every time I saw you in Tombstone you were begging for a drink. As I recall, you did not hold your liquor well."

"But I was not foolish enough to mix it with opium," he said.

"I'll be fine when we get moving," I said, wiping the sweat from my forehead with my sleeve. I had forgotten about the handcuff, however, and the metal bit into my brow.

"Damned thing," I muttered.

Bastard touched his throat.

"Hurts, doesn't it?"

Bastard finished his meal, wiped his fingers on his pants legs, and pulled the valise into his lap. He opened the bag and peered inside, looking closely at the fiddle but not touching it.

"You know I was raised from the age of eight by the Chiricahua," he said. "When my adopted family was killed in a dry wash, they called it the Oatman Massacre, but that is not the way it was. It was no more a massacre than a train wreck is a massacre."

He told me the story, which I have reproduced in the very first chapter of the book, and although I did not witness it, I am certain he was telling the truth. I had heard plenty of common lies, and a few uncommonly good ones, but the tale Bastard told was without ornamentation.

"Old Wolfskins, the warrior who slit the Oatman woman's throat after she blew her daughter's brains out, became my adopted Apache father," he said. "The Chiricahua way of life was harsh, but they treated me better than any of my white adopted families had. Soon I began to forget that I had been white at all."

"You forgot eight years of life?"

"I did not forget, exactly," he said. "But what I recalled of my white childhood was like trying to remember a dream the morning after. The feeling remains, but you cannot make sense of it. There wasn't much time for pondering the mystery, though, because we were at war—and had been at war for as long as anybody could remember. Even Old Wolfskins could not remember a time when the Chiricahua had been at peace.

As a younger man, he had been with Cochise when the great chief had waged war on the United States after he had been wrongly accused of kidnapping a white child, in 1861. Old Wolfskins had personally cut the throats of the Butterfield Stage employees Cochise had taken hostage—and he had used this knife."

"And he gave it to you."

"With his dying breath," he said. "We were with Cochise in the Dragoon Mountains—those mountains, there,' he said, pointing ahead of us, "when Old Wolfskins began having a fire in his belly. He could not hold down food and his scat was bloody and foul. He was afraid a witch had cast a spell on him, but the witch could not be found. Then an owl came to him one day to take his ghost to the underworld, and he knew his time had come. He said to me, 'I think I am going to die now. Here is my knife—it was forged by the whites from a shooting star that was found on the ground near the bowl-shaped canyon called Coon Butte, and it once had much power. The power may come back, if you can use it to cut out the white part of yourself.' I promised him that I would. And then he died, and we painted his face red, wrapped him in his favorite blanket, and took him to a secret cave and placed him inside it."

"Sounds like the Apache are a superstitious lot."

"Yes," Bastard said. "Much like the Christians."

"So, why aren't you still in those mountains raising hell?"

"Not long after Old Wolfskins died, our small band was captured by a squad of soldiers who were sent to take us to the San Carlos Reservation. We were weak and starving, and we had no fight left in us. But the soldiers recognized me as white. I was fifteen, too old to place with a family, so they put me in General Crook's army, as a scout. There were other Apache scouts, so at least I had some friends to talk to, and we believed we were doing right by convincing other Apaches to quit war and come into the rez. We could believe it as long as we did not look at how our people lived on the reservation—everybody was sick, and their spirits dragged the ground. Perhaps we should rest here a little while longer, because you are not looking so good."

"Don't worry about me," I said. "You haven't got to the part about why you quit."

"Cibicue Creek," he said. "Last August, the general at Fort Apache, which is halfway between here and Coon Butte, got scared of a medicine man at San Carlos Reservation by the name of Nokadelklinay. This man had started dancing and preaching that the whites would disappear and that the great chiefs would return. The more he danced, the more power he had. They said he started performing magic and that he had the power to raise the dead. Then he left San Carlos and led his followers back to his old village on Cibicue Creek. That was too much for General Carr, who sent two troops of cavalry and a company of Indian scouts to arrest him and bring him back to stand trial. I was one of the scouts, under the command of Lieutenant Cruse. But the scouts weren't sure that we were doing right. Dandy Jim and Deadshot were the most worried and were acting so strangely that before we reached Cibicue Creek, the lieutenant had all of us scouts unarmed.

"So, we arrested Nokadelklinay late one day and

started back the forty miles to Fort Apache with him. He was a strange man, frail and bird-like, and always talking to ghosts. Around his neck he wore a big bronze medal. He treated everyone, both Indian and white, as if we were children. We had only gotten a few miles back when it got dark and we made camp. The medicine man's followers, who had been trailing behind, caught up with us, and that made things worse. There must have been sixty or seventy of them. Also, the soldiers didn't trust us scouts, because some of us had been sneaking off to dance, and they ordered us to camp apart from the soldiers. But during the evening, one of the scouts, Mosby, got too close. The soldiers say he reached for a rifle, but I didn't see this. Of a sudden, there was a lot of shooting—the soldiers were shooting at the scouts, the followers were shooting into the soldiers, and we were in the middle. It was a real battle for maybe five minutes. Our friend Mosby was shot dead. Then eight or nine of us scouts decided to try to release the medicine man, because he had the power to raise the dead, so we ran into the soldier's camp. But a bugler saw us coming, pulled his .45 Colt, and— *blam, blam, blam!*—put three bullets into Nokadelklinay's head. He fell to the ground, his skull shattered.

"That stopped the fighting. Us scouts were arrested.

"There were nine dead soldiers, including the captain who had been commanding, and one dead medicine man. The lieutenant ordered a detail to bury the dead, and us prisoners were assigned to it. So, we began digging the graves, with Sergeant Jack Smith in charge of the squad. But while we were digging the graves, the medicine man's body began to move.

First one arm reached out, and then another, and he began to crawl along the ground. He lifted his head, staring at us with blind eyes, and with his brains dribbling out of his broken head. Then we knew that we had heard the truth, that he could raise the dead—he had done it with himself.

"Sergeant Smith jumped up, just as scared as we were, and he grabbed a hatchet that had been used to sharpen some stakes for the camp, and which had been left on the ground. He took the hatchet and attacked the corpse of Nokadelklinay. He had nearly chopped off the medicine man's head before the body finally lay still."

Bastard made slashing motions with his open hand.

"After Smith was finished, his face and arms were covered in the medicine man's blood," he said. "He flung away the hatchet and fell to his knees beside the corpse, and he tore away a silver medal that Nokadelklinay had worn around his neck. It had been given to him when a temporary peace was declared with Cochise, in 1871. It had a picture of President Grant, and Smith read the words on it: '*Let us have peace.*' He was laughing when he said it."

Bastard shook his head.

"That was enough for me, I knew that I was doing wrong as a scout and helping make war against my own people. They sent some of the scouts to prison for the mutiny and hanged three more. But I am white, so they couldn't hang me. And being white, I could not make war against the soldiers. So I decided that I would make war against the ancient enemy of my people, the Mexicans. Just the year before, they killed Victorio at Tres Castillo Peaks and made more than a hundred Apaches slaves for the copper mines."

I admitted to him that it made some strange kind of sense.

"But what about your promise to Old Wolfskins?" I asked. "How did you go about cutting away the white part?"

"By deciding I must kill you," he said. "But there is plenty of time for that, after we collect the reward for the holy box. Now, you must tell me a story." He tapped the valise in his lap. "Tell me about this fiddle."

"It was my father's," I said. "It was the only thing I saved from our cabin before the Yankees burned it. I carried it with me, slung across my back by a cord, when my mother and I walked across Missouri to the federal prison at Palmyra, where my rebel father was being held. He died of his wounds before my mother could obtain his release, but not before—"

I stopped. Was I going to tell him that my mother— no, *our* mother—had traded sex with the provost for the release of her husband? That his father was the provost, a wicked man named Strachan who had claimed my mother as a spoil of war?

"Not before what?" Bastard asked.

"Not before mother had bargained for his release," I said.

Bastard grunted.

"At least you knew your father," he said. "Do you play this thing?"

"Yes," I said.

"Show me."

"No," I said.

"Why not?"

"Don't feel like it," I said.

"So, you've dragged this thing with you all the way from Missouri and you don't feel like playing it?" he asked. "If it were my father's, I'd want to play it."

"I just don't want to play it right now," I said. "It doesn't mean I never want to play it."

"What do you like to play when you do?"

"Old songs, mostly," I said. "Songs that came across the Atlantic with our people. Mother had a favorite, an Irish tune called 'Star of the County Down.' I play that, sometimes."

"Don't know that I've heard it."

"You have," I said. "You just haven't had a name for it."

He closed the valise.

"What was she like?" he asked. "Was she young?"

"She was twenty-seven when she died," I said. Then I described her looks—the auburn hair, the eyes, the proud jaw. Her delicate hands. Her narrow waist.

"Was she a good woman?" he asked.

"She was a woman," I said.

No need to go into the details of her courageous, traitorous heart.

He looked off into the distance.

"Yes," I said. "She was sometimes a good woman."

"You carry this," he said, handing me the valise. "It's yours, not mine. Just as the memories are yours. I have nothing, nothing but the guilt of having killed her while clawing my way into the world."

TWENTY-SIX

We began walking, and I was glad for the movement—and the silence.

Our bearing continued to the northeast, and for an hour we walked across the desert. Bastard was hauling the haversack and the wooden box, and I was carrying the valise. The moon came up, and I began shivering and Bastard began giving me sidelong looks.

"The sickness is getting worse," he said.

"I'm all right," I said. "I just need a drink."

"We're a hundred miles away from the nearest whiskey."

We went on for another mile or so, and my shivering became more intense. I clenched my elbows against my ribs in an attempt to stop it, but it was no use—the more I tried to stop the shaking, the worse it got. And even though my body was cold, my head seemed like it was burning up.

Finally, I had to stop.

"Just give me a moment," I said, dropping to my knees in the sand. But stopping is a helluva lot easier than starting again, and once I stopped my legs became butter. My feet throbbed with bruises and blisters, and my skin felt like it had been cooked by the sun.

"Keep walking," Bastard said.

"I can't."

"Then I must leave you."

"Go on," I said. "I'll catch up."

"You won't," he said. "If you don't get up, you will die here, and we will never collect the treasure because I don't know which town this temple is in. You have the coyote sickness in your soul, and you must tell me now where to take the sacred box before you die."

It had become hard to think.

"Really, all I need is a shot of whiskey," I said. "Or a hit from the little brown bottle."

"There is nothing to drink," he said. "There is no dope. Get up."

I wanted to, but all I could do was shake. It was like my limbs were disconnected from the rest of me. I closed my eyes and asked him to leave me alone for a spell.

"Tell me where to take the magic box."

"And let you collect the reward while my bones are bleaching in the desert?" I asked. "Not a chance."

"As you wish," Bastard said. "You have your father's fiddle. I cannot leave you any food or water, because it would be wasted on a dead man. But you have that Colt's in its holster beneath your coat, and I will leave you with that because I know white men are cowards."

"You're as white as I am," I stammered.

"Only my skin," he said.

Then I had a terrific pain deep in my gut, and I

doubled over, my teeth clenched and my hands clawing the sand.

"I could kill you and spare you this humiliation," Bastard suggested. "I would gain no power from it, because of your weakened state, but it would be quick— I would slit your throat and you would bleed out quickly."

"Please," I said. "No favors."

Bastard shrugged.

"Farewell, Jacob Gamble," he said. "You left me alone at my birth, and now I leave you alone to your death. I'm glad I did not succeed in killing you earlier. This is much more satisfying."

Then he turned and walked to the northeast.

"Bastard!" I screamed.

He did not look back.

I lay on my back, writhing on the desert floor. Every so often I would cry out from the pain, but the knowledge that there was nobody to hear my cries made my distress worse. Never had I felt so alone— and I had been alone and in dire circumstances many times in my life. I cursed myself for the drinking and the laudanum, and I asked God to send me just a little to get me through, and then I would give it up forever. Now, I don't know how he would manage such a delivery when I was so remote from the nearest town, but logic wasn't a part of my thinking.

When relief was not forthcoming, and the pain was crashing over me in great waves, I became angry.

"Truly?" I screamed. "This is how I die? You've dealt me lifetimes of misery and taken every person I've ever loved, beginning with my father and my mother and right down through Amity, and you've done it ugly and for your own wicked pleasure."

I got to my knees and pulled the Colt from beneath my shoulder and pointed it skyward.

"I've hated you all my life," I screamed, and fired into the night sky. "Hated you, but was afraid of you. Was never afraid of a single thing on this earth, but I sure as hell have been afraid of you, waiting to see what else you were going to take from me. Well, you old sonuvabitch, I'm not going to let you have the last word. I am no longer afraid—I'm pissed."

I pressed the cold blue muzzle against my temple.

"My father in heaven," I muttered feverishly, "fallow be the name, the kingdom never comes, my will is never done, not on earth and surely not in heaven."

I pulled the hammer back to full cock.

"Don't give me this day my daily bread, or whiskey or dope, and don't forgive me a single trespass, just as I refuse to forgive those who trespass against me. You will no longer lead me into temptation and then refuse to deliver me from evil, for I end this now. Thine may be the kingdom and the power and the glory, but I will see it for never and never."

I took a breath.

"So fuck You."

I reckoned that was enough blasphemy to do send me where my mother and Amity had gone. Hell is for whores, right? Eternal damnation seemed a small price to pay to stop the earthly pain. And it was the least I deserved, after having abandoned my infant half-brother to die in some godforsaken town in north Texas.

Tears ran down my cheeks. There was a noise in

my head, like the sound the locomotive wheels make when an engineer locks the brake and steel grinds against iron, shooting sparks.

I was weak and shaking, and swaying on my knees. The world seemed to spin around me—the stars, the moon, the shadows of the mountains. In the distance, a coyote was barking.

Then I pulled the trigger.

Arizona, 1935

"Of course I was still alive—how else could I be telling you about it?" the old man asked, motioning for more whiskey. "But it would be some hours before I realized, with disappointment, that I had not sent my soul to hell."

"Yes," the tall man leaning against the wooden post intoned. "We have all shared that disappointment at one time or another, whether we will admit to it or not."

The man was wearing a tweed cap and a wrinkled jacket and on his left shoulder was a capuchin monkey. The man was not yet thirty, but his face was broad and deeply lined. His hands were thrust into his pockets.

Frankie reached across the camp table with a bottle of Old Crow in her hand and splashed some whiskey into the old man's water glass, then glanced at the tall man.

"John, you want a slug of this?"

"No, thank you," Huston said. "We shoot in the morning."

It was midnight, but the set was awash in light, to allow the crew to finish dressing the facades along

Hell Street. Bats fluttered overhead while generators hummed in the background.

Frankie closed her eyes.

"How can you start shooting?" she asked. "There's no script—no story."

"I know the story," Huston said. "It is an old story, the story of the man who shook his fist at God. Because I am an anarchist at heart, I am drawn to this story. And as far as the script—we only have to stay one scene ahead and remain curious about what comes next."

Frankie sighed and cradled her head in her hands.

Huston smiled and stroked the monkey on his shoulder.

"So, who's playing me in this talkie?" Jacob Gamble asked. "Don't tell me it's that kid from the last picture. He didn't look anything like me."

"No, not Tyrone Power," Huston said. "We have somebody new."

"Who?" Gamble asked. "That friar on your shoulder?"

"A stage actor," Huston said. "In his mid-thirties, so he's about the right age. He played a gangster named Duke Mantee in a Broadway play called *The Petrified Forest*. His name is Humphrey Bogart."

"Never heard of him," Gamble said.

"His voice rather sounds like yours, I think," Huston said. "Dry and wise. Now, let's hear the rest of your story. Tell us what fresh hell you landed in next."

TWENTY-SEVEN

Someone was cradling my head in her arms, and I was laying on a rough blanket on the floor of a wickiup. Naked, except for the damned handcuff around my left wrist. I knew it was daylight, because a column of sunlight slanted in through the smoke hole in the top of the dome-like structure. The framework was of curved cottonwood branches and the outside was covered with hides and grass. The whole thing wasn't more than seven or eight feet across, and about that high. There was a small fire in the middle of the floor.

"Where am I?"

The woman spoke to me in a mixture of Spanish and Apache, and, of course, I understood none of it. I did, however, understand the tone—it was soothing, as a loving wife might speak to her husband.

I rose on one elbow to look at the girl.

Her hair was long and black, her skin was a deep brown, and her eyes were like buckeyes. She was thin, but not skinny. She wore a loose buckskin shirt, gathered at the waist by an old army cartridge belt which held no rounds but did carry a knife and sheath. Beneath flowed a blue cotton skirt. I could not tell how old she was, but I do not think she could have been more than thirty.

"Who are you?"

Her tone became chiding, so I settled back down on the blanket.

"If you insist," I said. "But I have to tell you, I am somewhat alarmed at the theft of my clothes. They were perfectly good clothes, and as pleasant as it is to rest here now, I imagine that I may need them at some point in the future."

She pressed a finger to my lips in an attempt to silence me. Then she took a brown cake-like thing from a basket beside her and held it to my lips. I remember thinking of how beautiful the design of the basket was, with a sawtooth pattern woven in contrasting colors.

"Can't you tell me what you're called?" I asked, taking the food from her. I took a nibble of the cake—it was coarse and tasted something like a potato cake. I swallowed it, but could eat no more. Later, I was told the cakes were made by beating the crown of the century plant into a paste, and then roasting it.

"What's your name?" I asked. "You have me at a disadvantage . . ."

My stomach began to quiver.

"As I said, a disadvantage . . ."

I grasped my stomach with both hands and curled on my side in pain.

The girl brought a wooden bowl close to my head, and I was momentarily confused, until the column of vomit spewed from my throat. She expertly caught all of it in the bowl, then wiped my mouth with a damp cloth.

"Damn," I said, falling upon my back. "I feel like I puked my nuts up."

She made some soft sounds in her throat.

My head began to throb, and I touched my fingers to my forehead and discovered a bruise like an egg.

Then I noticed that she had a chain around her neck, and from it dangled some tin cone charms and a kind of metal tag. I reached out and turned the tag, and I could see some writing on it. It was a reservation identification tag. It said she belonged to the San Carlos reservation, and it gave her allotment number: 267.

But there was no name.

"I wish you could tell me your name," I said.

"Her name is Ashozen," Bastard said, ducking into the wickiup with the sacred box. He looked at me in disgust and threw the blanket over my thighs. "Keep your hands off of her, because the tribe can't afford to care for any of your bastard children."

"They took care of you."

"Not well," he said. "I damn near died of starvation before Old Wolfskins decided I had enough sand to be saved. You look like I should have left you out there on the playa."

"Why didn't you?"

"I became afraid to leave you to . . ."

"Why?" I asked.

"Beasts," he said. "So, I came back and saw you trying to screw the barrel of the Colt into your eye socket, so I picked up a rock and beaned you with it. The gun went off about that time."

"Explains the goose egg," I said. "How'd you get me here?"

"Carried you," he said. "Not all the way, though.

Some of my brothers from the tribe came along, and we put you in a blanket and brought you here."

"Apaches," I said.

"We don't like that word," he said. "That's the word the Spanish gave us, after hearing other tribes call us that. But that word means *enemy*. We call ourselves *Endeh*. It just means, the people."

"What does Ashozen mean?"

"The woman who must never lay with the wicked white stranger," he said.

"I'm not going to pollute her," I said. "Hell, I can barely hold my head up."

"But it has not stopped you from complaining," he said. "The woman's name means Stealer of Horses. Her husband went away with Victorio while fighting the Mexican army."

"Went away?" I asked. "You mean, died?"

Bastard looked away.

"We don't use that word here," he said. "It is bad luck, even to say it in English."

"In any language," I said.

Then Bastard said something to Ashozen in Apache. She left, taking the vomit bowl with her.

"What's on your mind?"

"This," he said, tapping the walnut box. "I want to know what is inside."

"Already told you," I said. "Power."

"Tell me exactly," he said. "I must know the right thing to do. I think you believe I am just a superstitious Indian. You are not telling me the truth about the box or what the old man said before he died."

"I told you the truth."

Bastard shook his head.

"Not all of it, I think."

He contemplated the box.

"What kind of power is it?" he asked. "Is it from *Ussen*, the creator? Or is it a more common type of animal power. Was the old man a witch? He was dressed strangely. I have seen some like him in Tombstone, but have not paid much attention to their ways. I did not think they were witches, however."

"Not a witch," I said. "More like a priest. Exactly like a priest, in fact."

"Christian, then."

"No, not Christian," I said. "But a priest of a faith older than Christ."

He blinked.

"What do they worship?"

"Some say they worship money, but that doesn't square with what I've seen. At least, they don't worship it any more than the average human animal. I know they admire learning. I don't know everything about what they believe, but I know they believe in one creator, whatever you call him, and that they reject Christ. They're waiting on somebody else."

"Who?"

"I don't know," I said. "A messiah."

"Like Nokadelklinay."

"Somebody stronger," I said. "They expect their savior to break some heads, I think. They've been pissed off for a very long time, and they are looking for some revenge."

"I like these people," Bastard said. "How long have they been waiting?"

"Very long," I said. "As old as history—four thousand years. Their homeland was taken, and they have been driven across the earth. They are mostly despised wherever they go."

"Why?"

"They are blamed for killing Christ."

"Did they?"

"Not the way I read the book," I said.

"Do you think their messiah will come?"

"I don't know. People believe many strange things. Some of the strange things are true. But many are not."

"So, what's in the box is connected to this messiah?"

"Yes, I think," I said.

"Then it must be a weapon. I thought that when I first saw the box. It is a sword or a gun."

"I don't think so."

"What, then?"

"It contains an object that is sacred to the old man's tribe, something that contains their power and wisdom. It's sacred to Christians, but in a different way."

"But I thought his tribe was hated for killing Jesus Christ. Why would the Christians believe in this object as well? Never mind, the superstitions of white people have always puzzled me. Let's open the box."

"We cannot touch it," I said. "It is not for us. Now, leave me be about this. I am tired of talking about it. If you want to open the box, take it far from here because I don't want any of the bad luck rubbing off on me."

Bastard flung up his hand.

"You are full of talk," he said. "I am sorry I saved you." He left the wickiup, taking the box with him.

TWENTY-EIGHT

I stayed in the wickiup with Ashozen for the next couple of days, regaining my strength and desperately wishing that she could speak English or that I could speak Spanish. She was always talking to me, and being unusually cheerful, even though I could understand none of it.

From Bastard, who was always interrupting us using one weak excuse or another, I learned that our camp was at the tip of the Dragoon Mountains, and that it was preparing for war—Geronimo had left the Sierra Madre in Old Mexico and was coming north once again to raid. When I asked Bastard how the tribe knew all this, he just shrugged and said he knew, that information was communicated in dreams just like the white man used the telegraph.

"You are lucky," Bastard told me on the afternoon of the third day. "The camp is about to engage in the Sunrise Dance for Ashozen's daughter, and the camp cannot refuse to offer hospitality to guests. There was much debate about whether you were a guest or an enemy, but it was finally decided that you are a guest, because you are kin—we are related by blood. So, once again, instead of getting what you deserve, you are getting what you want."

"How sorry for you," I said. "What's the Sunrise Dance?"

"It's when a girl becomes a woman."

"What's the daughter's name?"

"Lozen," he said. "She is named for her great-aunt, the sister of Victorio. I have heard the soldiers say that the people only rarely name girl children, but this is not true—it is a lie to make it seem we are uncivilized and that it is right to kill us, like the buffalo."

"From what I've seen, your adopted people are the equal of whites in every respect," I said. "You make war, you take slaves, you follow outrageous superstition. Put you in pews, and you could be Baptists."

"You turn everything into a joke," he said. "But you must show respect during the Sunrise Dance. You must not speak or touch any of the dancers or their masks. Do you understand?"

"Sure," I said. "It's church."

"I have your word, as worthless as it may be?"

"You don't touch the box, I don't touch the masks."

"After the ritual is concluded, on the morning of the fourth day, we will continue our journey," he said. "Ashozen will assist us. No, do not ask how. All will become clear then."

Ashozen returned my clothes to me—clean, no less, probably having been beaten in some mountain stream—and on the third day, I ventured outside. The camp was made of maybe sixty people, living in a score of wickiups, and people generally ignored me.

Their condition was generally poor, there were no old people, and the children were terrible thin, although they seemed happy enough. The infants were bound to cradleboards, and the children who were not yet ten ran about as naked as the day they were born.

The leader of the camp was a medicine man by the name of Kaskanashinay. He wore an antelope horn hat and walked about brooding all day long, just like the Baptist preachers I knew back home. I tried to engage him in conversation a couple of times, but he made it clear by his demeanor that he didn't have time for talk.

By watching, I figured out that Lozen was forbidden to see her mother in the days leading up to the ceremony, and was staying with relatives in another wickiup, preparing for the ceremony. In the morning, the whole camp turned out to see the girl, who looked to be fourteen or fifteen. She would kneel on a blanket and greet the sun, her arms outstretched and her palms facing outward. She was handsome, like her mother, and wore a spotless yellow buckskin dress. Her face was also covered in yellow clay.

The color, Bastard said, represented the sacred pollen and the girl was a stand-in for somebody called White Painted Woman.

Then the chanting and dancing began. Ordinarily, Bastard said, there would be a great bonfire in the middle of camp, but because the tribe was at war, the spirits had sent word that the fire wouldn't be necessary. Everybody seemed to have a helluva good time, what with the dancing and the chanting and the beating of drums, and along toward dark I figured everything was about to wrap up. Just then these four weird characters came waltzing down the mountain path.

They wore black hoods and had skirts of buckskin and red flannel and on their naked chests were painted stars and lightning streaks in white and yellow. They rattled as they danced because of all the abalone shells and tin things hanging from their costumes. On top of their heads were these large fan-like things made out of what could pass for pickets out of a fence.

Bastard told me that the four dancers were the *gan*, their name for the mountain spirits. He didn't say they represented the mountain spirits, but that they were literally the spirits themselves. They spun and wheeled like dervishes and generally acted possessed, and every so often, they would rush Lozen or somebody in the crowd and then break away at the last moment.

Behind the gan dancers came a naked young man painted in white from head to toe, and on top of his head he wore a wispy red feather, like flame sprouting from the top of his head. He was laughing and jumping up in the air and rolling in the dirt, only to come back up and do it all over again. Bastard said this was a clown character and could be either good or bad, depending on his mood.

After watching for a while, I could tell that the chants and actions weren't random, that they were acting out some kind of story that the crowd knew well, just like we stage *Hamlet* over and over, even though we know how it ends.

White Painted Woman was like Eve and the Virgin Mary, all wrapped up into one, Bastard told me. She was the first woman, and she survived the Great Flood by using an abalone shell like a raft, and then got stranded alone on a mountain when the waters receded. Sitting on her mountain, she is impregnated by the sun and soon gives birth to Killer of Enemies. Then the rain comes, and she is again with child, and she calls this one Son of Water.

But the world still wasn't safe for people to live in, Bastard said, at least not until the White Painted Woman's sons kill somebody called the Owl Man Giant.

Now, I don't know how this owl character enters the picture because as Bastard explained it, there was just White Painted Woman and her sons in the world. But, apparently, this giant owl man was a mean sonuvabitch and had been making the tribe miserable, at least until the woman's sons take their revenge. Bastard said the myth wasn't specific about how the sons kill old Owlbreath, but that the important thing is that they did it. After, the tribe lives in peace. Finally, when White Painted Woman is old and near death, she walks into the sunrise and is reborn young, again and again and again.

The dancing went on four days, with everybody playing their parts, and the girl staying mostly on the blanket and wearing the cracking yellow clay. On the night of the third day, Ashozen took me by the hand and pulled me into the wickiup. I reckoned that what would happen next would make Bastard howling mad, but I was wrong—instead of shucking her clothes, Ashozen began to talk really serious to me, being careful with every word, just as if I could understand. She might have been telling me of how it was for her when she became a woman, or how her husband who had fought with Victorio had made her feel, or whether she was worried about whether she would really be reborn as White Painted Woman when her time came. Whatever it was, I understood the tone, and with nothing to say, I simply placed my left hand over her heart.

She clasped my hand and held it in place for the longest time. Then she released it and we both slept. When we woke from our nap, Ashozen led me outside by the hand and had me kneel, with my left wrist over a flat rock. Then she picked up another rock, one about the size of a baseball, and held her free hand up to indicate that I should keep still. Before I had time to object and say that what we needed was a hacksaw, she had brought the rock down smartly on the edge of the bracelet. The cuff sprang open and my wrist felt light.

"Thank you," I said, rubbing my wrist. "I guess you learn all sorts of things being a reservation Indian."

At sunrise on the fourth day of the ritual, old brooding Kaskanashinay came up while the girl was on her blanket, with his hands upraised, and smacked her on the forehead with the heel of his right hand. There had been a red sun painted on his palm, and the symbol was transferred to the girl's forehead.

After that, the crowd thinned out in a hurry.

"Time to go," Bastard told me. He had a coil of knotted rope over his shoulder. He tossed me the Peacemaker in the shoulder rig, and I caught it in both hands. I strapped on the gun, shrugged my shoulder to test the fit, and then noticed that Bastard had the box with him, but not the valise.

"Where's the fiddle?" I asked.

"Kaskanashinay took a shine to it," he said. "He's

keeping it. He wanted to keep the sacred box, but I couldn't let him do that—there's treasure to be traded for it."

"He has the fiddle."

"Yeah."

"Can he play it?"

"How should I know?" Bastard asked. "What does it matter? All of a sudden, you're acting all bent."

"You didn't ask me."

"I figured you would see the logic in not letting him keep the box," Bastard said.

"Do I appear enamored of that thinking?"

I stamped off and found the medicine man sitting on a blanket in the sun, the valise beside him. His gnarled right hand was resting atop the bag. He was not altogether pleased to see that I aimed to talk.

"That's mine," I said, pointing at the bag.

He stared at the sky, as if he didn't hear me.

"Look, I know you can't understand a word I'm saying, but you damn well know my tone. That is my father's fiddle in that bag, and it means nothing to you but everything to me, and I aim to have it back if I have to kill you to get it."

"That would be a mistake," Bastard said, now beside me. "These folks have been friendly to you so far, but that's because of me. You shoot their beloved medicine man, and they will delight in hamstringing you and giving you over to the women to cut off your fingers and toes, a little bit at a time."

The medicine man looked at Bastard, then looked at me. Then he pointed at my shoulder.

"You're kidding."

"He's dead serious," Bastard said. "You better

decide which is more important to you, the gun or that fiddle."

"Dammit," I said, unstrapping the Peacemaker.

I handed over the piece and took the fiddle. The medicine man slid the gun out of the holster, admiringly. He smiled, knowing he had gotten the long end of the bargain.

"What are we supposed to do without a gun?" I asked.

"I'm fine without a gun," Bastard said. "You're the one who seems to feel lacking without a Colt's strapped to your leg."

"They say a man without a horse is not a man," I said. "Here I am, without horse or gun. What does that make me?"

"A pain in the ass," Bastard said.

Then he seemed to remember something.

"Did you lay with Ashozen?" he asked.

"We slept," I said. "That's all."

"I don't believe you."

"Bastard, you never believe me."

He winced.

"Why do you have to call me that?" he asked. "Why can't you call me by name? Why can't you call me—"

"Ishmael?" I asked.

"No," he said. "I hate that name. Damn you!"

"Tell me something I don't know. What's the rope for?"

He made fists of his hands and pounded his temples like somebody would beat a drum. His eyes were scrunched shut, and he had a terrible frown. Then he took a deep breath.

"No more jokes, please."

"Tell me why we need the rope."

"We're going down, out of the mountains. Only, we need to cross over a saddle about three miles to the northwest, and we need the rope when we get to the other side. It's a way the People hardly ever go."

"Why not?"

"Ghosts," he said. "On the other side of the saddle is a city of the dead."

"You mean a cemetery."

"No, I mean a city that died a long time ago," he said.

"You mean an Indian village."

"No, I mean a city," he said. "We don't know who built it. It's been deserted for as long as anybody can remember, and it's bad luck to cross it without the right kind of power. But we have the box."

TWENTY-NINE

That afternoon, we were threading our way down the mountain path toward the desert floor. Bastard was in the lead, and Ashozen was behind him, carrying God's box.

"Let me have that," I told her, reaching for the box.

"Leave her alone," Bastard called over his shoulder. "If you carry it for her, her feelings will be hurt; she'll think that you took it from her because she was carrying it badly."

Then we reached a ledge and Bastard paused and let the woman and me catch up to him. He knelt down, motioned for us to come close, and then in a voice just above a whisper he said, "The city of the dead is just below. It is important that we remain quiet and proceed single-file. Don't touch anything. We're going to drop down—"

Just then a pebble fell somewhere on the trail behind us, and Bastard sprang up and spun around like he'd been galvanized. He stared intently at the path we'd just come down, his eyes searching for something.

"You're not jumpy, are you?"

"You didn't see a shadow up there, did you?"

"What do you mean?"

"A shadow like a man, but not quite?"

"You mean like we saw at the old mission?" I asked. "No, I did not see that."

"Good."

"Why don't you tell me what killed the priest and the others? You know, don't you?"

"It's not good to talk about it."

"Tell me," I said. "Or I will make a joke about it."

"You wouldn't."

"Let me see what I can come up with," I said in my normal voice, and then got louder. "Knock, knock. Who's there? Lo. Lo who? Lo, the poor Indian who's had his guts pulled out—"

He clamped his hand over my mouth.

"Don't," he hissed.

He hesitated.

"They're called Los Sanguinarios."

He unclamped my mouth.

"*Los Sanguinarios*," Ashozen repeated reverently.

It was the same word the dying Indian at the mission had used.

"What's it mean?"

"The bloodthirsty," he said. "We don't know what they call themselves, because they don't speak any language we recognize—maybe they don't speak any human language at all, just an animal language. They were men once, but during a hard time long ago they became as animals."

"You mean they started killing for fun?" I asked. "Humans kill for fun. How are they different?"

"Because they kill for something else," he said. "Do you know how some animals will sometimes eat their own? Well, with the *Sanguinarios* it is the rule, rather than the exception."

"You mean, like Alferd Packer?"

Packer had been the rage of the newspapers a few years back, for having dispatched and then consumed some traveling companions while snowbound in the Rockies. Sentenced to die by a judge in Gunnison, he had since escaped and was still, for all anyone knew, eating his way through the West.

"I don't know who that is," Bastard said.

"Cannibal."

Bastard shushed me.

"These are beyond anything you ever heard of," he said. "They can turn into shadows at will, or take the form of coyotes. They use arrows, but not bows. They are a thousand winters old and are the only thing the People are afraid of. And this city was once their home."

"Is this story like the woman painted white?"

"It is not a myth," Bastard said. "Old Wolfskins told me he saw them once, and it was horrible. He said they were dark and hairy and smelled like rotting flesh."

Bastard led us to a fissure in the rocks and, one by one, we slid down it. We tried to be quiet, but our passage dislodged a few handfuls of dirt and gravel, which trickled down the face of the rock with a sound like rain. At the bottom of the fissure, beneath an overhang, we found ourselves in an adobe room with a single square window.

The room no longer had a roof, and the inside

walls were blackened from some fire long ago. In the corners of the room were piles of debris, including some broken pots, and the pots had an intricate saw-tooth design. There were also some bones, but I did not inspect them closely enough to tell if they were human or not. Everything was dusty and bone-dry and smelled of age.

We ducked through the low doorway and found ourselves on a terrace, with the city curving around us. There was row after row of buildings nestled up against the curving canyon wall, dotted with rooms with square windows and low doorways. I did not count the number of rooms, but for sheer size it was the equal of a few square blocks of downtown Kansas City or St. Louis—enough, say, for a few thousand residents.

I was unable to stifle my surprise.

"Sonuvabitch," I said.

Bastard turned and gave me a fierce stare.

I shrugged.

Now, I know what you're thinking—how did white men ever get across the Atlantic and build this city so long ago? Or, perhaps, it was the Egyptians. Or maybe even crazy old Joseph Smith was right and there was all sorts of traffic to the New World before it was properly discovered. At least, those were the thoughts that crossed my mind. But then I realized that the pattern on the shards of pottery was not all that much different from the pattern I had seen on Ashozen's woven basket. The name and fate of the city people may have been lost in time, but they were certainly some kind of relation to the Apache.

A lonely wind was blowing as we worked our way

down from terrace to terrace, and as we went I began to have the peculiar sensation that we were being watched. Bastard must have had it too, because he looked up at me and shook his head, as if to tell me to just keep going.

We had to stop every so often to take the box from Ashozen as she climbed down, or to scout out a way down to the next level. Finally, we came to the last level, and it was still thirty feet above the desert floor. Bastard unslung the knotted rope and tied off to a log jutting out of the side of one of the adobe walls. Then he tied the other end to one of the leather straps on the box and lowered it down.

He motioned for Ashozen to shinny down the rope, and then for me. Ashozen reached the bottom, and untied the box and moved it out of the way.

I jumped the last few feet to the ground.

Up top, Bastard got hold of the rope, swung out, and eased himself down. When we were finally eye level, I asked him how we were going to get the rope.

"We don't," he said. "Let's go, and don't look back."

The wind had picked up and was blowing through all of those square windows above us and was making a mournful chorus. How many lifetimes must have been lived in this valley? How long had it been since a human voice uttered the secret name of the city? A thousand years from now, would somebody come across the ruins of Kansas City and look up at the empty buildings and think the same thoughts? As we trudged away I could not help but take one last look. Glancing over my shoulder, I saw the end of the rope slithering up over the lip of the last terrace, toward a crouching shadow. Then sun went behind a cloud, and the city was lost in purple shadows.

Miles away, we found the coach road as it wended past the base of the mountain. We ate a few yucca cakes that Ashozen had brought along and drank some water from her canteen gourd.

"Do you think we were followed?" Bastard asked.

"We've not seen anybody."

"I think we were followed," he said. "I had the feeling all through the city of the dead that we were being watched, and now I'm sure we're being followed. Have you seen any shadows?"

"No."

"Good."

Then Bastard and I found comfortable spots, with our backs against the rock. Ashozen sat on a cotton-wood log a few yards away, staring patiently at the road.

"Done much of this kind of work?" Bastard asked. "Ambush, I mean."

"Some," I said. "A lot, actually. A long time ago."

"You don't mind killing soldiers, if we have to?"

"Not as long as they're wearing blue uniforms," I said. "But we won't have to kill anybody—at least not as long as they think we're ready to kill them. People are funny that way. So, act vicious."

"I *am* vicious," he fumed.

"No, we aren't," I said. "We have one funny-looking knife between us. If anything besides a padre on a burrow comes down that road, we're going to have a hard time pulling off an ambush with sheer force. So, we'd best come up with a plan."

Bastard nodded toward Ashozen.

"She's our plan," he said. "You'll see."

"She's a remarkable woman," I said. "You know, I think she is kind of soft on me. She spoke to me rather earnestly last night, and, although I couldn't understand a word, I think I got the tone."

Bastard smiled.

"You are a dumb sonuvabitch, aren't you?"

I accused him of just being jealous.

"The hell I am," Bastard said. "Look, her grandmother came to her in a dream and told her that one of us was going to die soon in battle, and she reckons it will be you. That's why she has been so nice to you."

"Why me?" I asked. "Why not you?"

"Because you're pale and weak."

"That's what she was trying to tell me?"

"No," he said. "She reckons you will see her goneaway husband in the next world soon, and she wants you to deliver a message. She wants you to tell him that her heart still beats for him and that she looks forward to the day when they will be united."

"Hellfire," I said. "Then why were you worried about me not sleeping with her?"

Bastard shook his head.

"I don't want to take care of your widow," he said. "If you lay with her, then you're married, and then when I kill you—or if somebody else beats me to it— then she is widowed again. Only this time, she will be my responsibility, because you're my brother. No matter how poor you are, or how many other wives you have, you automatically get another, whether you want one or not."

"Who cares for Ashozen now?"

"Nobody," Bastard said. "She has special status

because she has gifts. That's how she got her name. She also knows when the enemy is close and when somebody is going to die. How many wives do you have, by the way?"

"None," I said. "Well, I had one. But she's gone."

"You mean away, or—run off?"

"No, I mean gone in the sense of dead, no longer living, beneath the earth."

Bastard held up his hand.

"No more," he said. "You loved this woman?"

"I was a fool," I said. "But yes, I was in love."

"I have never been in love," Bastard said. "It would be better to be a fool than never to have been in love. Again, you discount the gifts you have been given. This is just one of the reasons why I hate you."

That put a blanket on the conversation, so we were left to our own thoughts for a spell. But patience was not one of Bastard's virtues, and he eventually asked:

"How long you think we've been here?"

"A while," I said. "An hour, maybe."

"I have a wretched sense of time," he said. "Minutes and hours are the same to me. I can count days, if I'm careful. I hate towns because everything seems to be happening at once. It makes me want to drink."

"You did seem a different person in Tombstone."

"Something has got to come along soon."

"Sooner or later, something always does," I said. "If not today, then certainly tomorrow. All we have to do is wait and see what the road brings us."

What the road brought was a prospector.

The prospector was at least sixty, wore a clean suit of clothes, and had a bushy head of white hair and a well-trimmed beard. He was riding one mule and leading another, which was laden with picks and shovels and so forth.

"Mules," Bastard said dismissively. "Damn near your padre on a burrow."

"You'd rather walk?" I asked.

Bastard spoke to Ashozen, and she nodded.

Ashozen walked out and stood in the middle of the road. As we watched from behind the rock, she undid the cartridge belt and dropped it in the sand. Then she stepped out of her blue cotton skirt and placed it beside the belt. She lithely pulled the buckskin shirt over her head, which left her unshucked except for her moccasins.

The prospector reined his mule to a stop, twenty yards away from what must have seemed an apparition. Ashozen shook her long black hair and placed her hands on her wide hips.

The prospector cleared his throat.

Ashozen stared unblinking at him.

"Miss," he said, finally. "Are you in some distress?"

She smiled.

The prospector patted the mule's neck.

"What do you think, George?" he asked. "What action befits a gentleman? Yes, I agree. But what if she is truly in need? No, we cannot leave her."

The prospector dropped the reins and swung down from the saddle. Then he took a striped blanket from the pack mule and approached Ashozen.

"If you don't like your clothes, perhaps you would prefer a blanket," the prospector said. Ashozen took the blanket and threw it like a cape around her shoulders.

Bastard came out from behind the boulder, the black knife in hand, with me following.

"Ah," the prospector said. "Now it makes sense."

"Shut up," Bastard said. He had slipped behind the prospector and had his right arm draped over his shoulder. The blade was against the prospector's throat.

"Where're your guns?" Bastard asked.

"I have none."

"Nobody travels without guns."

"Had enough of guns and killing," the prospector said. His eyes were staring down at the knife. "That's an interesting blade. If you would back off my throat a bit, I could see it better."

Ashozen was behind him, binding his hands with a bit of leather. Bastard stepped back, holding the knife in front of the prospector's face.

"Get a good look," Bastard said.

"That's celestial iron," the prospector said. "Beautiful. Did it come from around here? There's lots of the stuff up at Coon Butte."

"It is customary to kill you at this point," Bastard said.

"You're not going to kill me," the prospector said.

"How do you know?"

"Because I'm one lucky sonuvabitch," the prospector said. "I made a fortune in steamboats and then one in grain and made another by building a little narrow-gauge railroad in Arkansas. I don't expect my luck will run out now."

"You're Diamond Jo?" I asked. "I've been on your damned railroad. What are you doing out here by yourself?"

"Looking to make another fortune in mining," he said. "I work better alone. Gives me time to think and talk to God."

"Does He answer?" Bastard asked with a snort.

"Sometimes," Diamond Jo said. "If I listen hard enough."

"Don't believe everything the old sonuvabitch tells you."

Diamond Jo shook his head.

"If you've been listening to something that lies to you," Diamond Jo told me, "then it ain't Him talking."

"What are you boys after?" Diamond Jo asked.

"We're going to take your mules," I said.

"Check those packs," Bastard said. "There might be gold or silver."

"Sorry," the old man said. "All you'll find is a little copper. Take it if you want it, but you'll probably find the tent and other things of more use."

"Grub?"

"Plenty, if you like coffee and beans."

"Suits me," Bastard said.

"We'll leave you enough to get by for a spell," I said. "Ashozen here will keep you company until some Yankees come along. She doesn't speak any English, but she's a good listener."

"I'll get along fine by myself," Diamond Jo said. "Got a wife back in the states. Don't imagine she'd like the idea of me spending much time with this ripe young woman."

"You're a rare man," I said.

"And I would say you two are fairly unusual highwaymen."

"Hey," Bastard said, frowning. "I'm as mean as they come."

"I hope you remember our kindness when the

soldiers find you," I said. "Stealing a man's mount is a hanging offense."

"This ain't stealing," Diamond Jo said. "I prefer to think of it as loaning you my mules. Please, treat them well. They are good mules and deserve to be cared for."

"I understand," I said.

"The saddle mule answers to George Hearst," Diamond Jo said. "He's a bit nervous and dislikes dogs. The other one is John D. Rockefeller. They like to be sung to at night. Calms them down. Any lullaby will do."

THIRTY

Three days later, we reached Coon Butte. It was midafternoon and the sky was banked with clouds, creating a diffuse light, which brought out details in the terrain that would have been hidden in more harsh light. We sat atop our mules at the southwestern rim of the bowl-shaped valley, which was nearly a mile across.

"Strange, ain't it?" Bastard asked.

"It's the crater of an extinct volcano, which erupted eons ago," I said. "At least that's what the men who should know, the scientists, say. I've read it in the papers."

Bastard laughed.

"Then they are fools," he said. "The Apaches know that a star fell to earth and burned this hole in the ground."

I did not correct his superstition.

"We have arrived at Coon Butte," he said. "How far now?"

"Not far," I said.

"One day? Three days?"

"Less than a day," I said.

"Then tell me."

"In the morning," I said.

Then it began to snow, big flakes falling from the darkening sky. When I expressed my surprise, Bastard told me it was not unusual for early April.

We pitched the wedge tent from the pack and put the box and our bedrolls inside, out of the snow. Then we threw blankets over our shoulders and built a small fire, over which we started some coffee and boiled some beans.

"This is a strange country," I said, sipping coffee from a tin cup and watching the snow sprinkle the ground like powdered sugar. "This morning, we were sweating. Now we are hiding from the snow."

Bastard raked the stubble on his chin with his fingers.

"Will there be trouble?"

"There's always trouble," I said.

Then we ate the beans and slept, on either side of the small tent, with the mules hobbled nearby. In the middle of the night, I awoke and found that Bastard's bedroll was empty.

I lifted the tent flap.

It had stopped snowing. The moon was high above the caldera, making the thin layer of snow glisten. Bastard was sitting on a rock about twenty yards from the tent, and he had the sacred box in his lap. I didn't know if he had opened it or not.

I watched him for five or six minutes, and he sat there without moving a muscle. Then the mules shuffled a bit, and he began to sing to them in a reassuring voice.

"*Go to sleep my little baby*," he crooned. "*When you wake, you shall have all the pretty little horses.*"

I let the flap fall and went back to sleep.

By morning, all the snow had melted off. I didn't mention that I had heard Bastard sing or ask if he'd opened the box.

"All right," he said, packing the tent. "I've waited long enough. Which direction?"

"North by northwest," I said. "About twelve miles."

Bastard smiled sheepishly, as if he should have known the punchline to a joke.

"Canyon Diablo," he said.

THIRTY-ONE

There wasn't a human soul moving on Hell Street in Canyon Diablo. That damned one-eyed dog, however, was slinking along near the sidewalk, keeping pace, and making the mules nervous.

I patted George Hearst's neck.

"Easy," I told him.

"Do you think we've been followed?" Bastard asked. "I have the feeling we were followed."

"I've had that feeling for days," I said. "Didn't say anything because I thought it was foolish—haven't seen anything, just a shadow here and there."

At every fourth or fifth building, there was furniture piled in front or a wagon loaded with household things. The places already had a vacant look to them, with windows open and doors ajar. Inside, sad-looking women swept floors one last time while the men and children packed crates.

"Why are so many moving?" Bastard asked.

"They're Jews," I said. "They have been ordered to be out by Easter by the man who runs this town, or get burned out. It has been the same for them everywhere. Looks like they're getting out one step ahead of the torch."

We tied the mules to the rail outside the general store. The dog chose a spot in the street about twenty yards away, circled twice, then plopped down to watch, its tongue lolling from the side of its mouth.

"Where is everybody else?" Bastard asked.

"Drunk," I said.

"My kind of town," he said as he unstrapped the wooden box from behind John D. Rockefeller's saddle. "Let's collect our reward. I'm anxious to engage in some serious sin."

We stepped up onto the porch.

"This place doesn't look like much," Bastard said, looking over the storefront. "But if you had money in a town like this, you wouldn't advertise it, would you? Smart."

I made a fist and pounded on the door frame, then stepped back, waiting.

There was the sharp click of the latch and the door swung open on hinges that needed oil. Mordechai stood there, wiping his hands on his apron, his glasses on top of his head.

"Can't you see, I'm closed?" he asked. "What could be so important?"

"This," Bastard said, holding out the box in both hands.

Mordechai moved his glasses down to the bridge of his nose and peered at the box.

"Why are you standing there?" he asked, opening the door wide. "Come in, come in."

As we stepped inside and Mordechai closed the door

behind us, he kept up a steady stream of questions: Where did we find it? Where was the rabbi? Did anybody see us come into town with it? Had we opened it? Had we touched anything? And so on.

"Nope," Bastard said. "Didn't open it."

"Your rabbi is dead," I said. "Found him in the desert, where he and some Mexicans and some Apaches were killed by—by, well something."

"*Los Sanguinarios*," Bastard said.

"As he died, he asked us to return the box," I said.

Mordechai took the box, testing its heft, then placed it upright against his right shoulder. He stood there all somber while I told him about the demise of the rabbi and the adventure we had reaching Canyon Diablo.

"This is a mitzvah," Mordechai said. "I am filled with sadness for the death of Rabbi Weiss, but thankful for the return of the scrolls, because its worth is beyond measuring."

Then he asked me, "Don't I know you?"

"We've met," I said. "A few weeks back. I got off the train and was waiting for the coach, and I ran into some trouble."

"I remember now," Moredechai said. "I'm glad you survived."

"Why aren't you packed?" I asked, glancing around at the full shelves. "Aren't you leaving with the others?"

"Harlan will have to burn me out," he said. "And he'll probably use the matches and kerosene I've sold him. But I am too old to start over someplace else. I'm alone, and my back is killing me."

"You're alone?" I asked. "What of Astrid, your hired girl?"

"Aren't you going to check it?" Bastard interrupted, leaning against the counter and crossing his moccasins. "You know, make sure the little hand and everything is still in there."

He had looked.

"That is called the Yad,' Mordechai said. "It is a pointer used to follow the text. Please don't sit in the Torah's presence."

Without argument, Bastard stood up.

"I cannot open it here," Mordechai said. "But, I know its weight. It is complete."

"What is it?" Bastard asked.

"What do you mean?"

"I mean, what the hell is it?"

"Please," Mordechai said. "You have my thanks, but I thank you not to swear."

Bastard shrugged.

"What is it, you ask? This, my friend, is the law—the five books of Moses."

"I've heard of him," Bastard said. "Ten commandments and such."

"Not just ten commandments," Mordechai said. "There are six hundred and thirteen commandments in these books, all dictated to Moses on Mount Sinai. But it existed long before that—nine hundred and seventy-four generations before the world was made, and it is the design for all that is good on earth."

"Dandy," Bastard said. "Now, how about our reward?"

Mordechai stared at him.

Bastard stared back.

"What reward?" Mordechai asked.

"The reward the priest promised us before he died," he said.

Mordechai looked dumbly at me.

"The rabbi did promise a reward," I said slowly. "He couldn't talk—he wrote it out in the dust. Thing is, the reward he promised wasn't an earthly one."

"What?" Bastard asked.

"He didn't promise money," I said.

"You have restored our most sacred and valuable possession," Mordechai said. "Each Torah is made by hand, by a Torah scribe, and checked and re-checked for accuracy. It is a living thing. We cannot buy our books cheaply as the gentiles do, made on machines in the hundreds of thousands. It cost us everything to buy this one. We have little money left."

"How much?" Bastard asked.

"Doing good is its own reward, no?"

"You got that right," Bastard said. "Not only no, but hell no!" Then he turned on me. "Why did you lie?"

"I didn't lie, exactly," I said. "I let you believe—"

"Egg-sucking bastard!" he screamed. "You knew what you were doing!"

While we were arguing, Mordechai carried the scroll into the back room. Outside, the one-eyed dog was barking. The mules were braying.

Mordechai came back, carrying a handful of paper money.

"This would make you feel better, no?" he asked Bastard. "It is all I have today. Take it, take it. Please, no more shouting."

Bastard snatched the money from his hand.

"Forty-three dollars?" he asked. "That's it?"

"For now, yes," Mordechai said. "Later, before the others leave town, I could maybe take up a collection."

"Give the money back," I said.

Bastard stuffed the bills in his pocket.

"Make me," he said.

"Don't tempt me," I said.

The dog was barking like mad, and the mules had gone from braying to a sort of anxious whine. There were footsteps on the porch.

"Expecting someone?" I asked.

"No," Mordechai said.

"Where's Astrid?"

"With Judge Rex, of course," he said.

"You mean she stayed with him?"

"Isn't that what I just said?"

I must have done a poor job of hiding my disappointment.

"That's what this was about?" Bastard asked. "A girl? You dragged me over half the territory for a girl?"

"No, not really," I said. "Well, maybe. I don't know."

"You're lovesick," he said.

"I guess," I said. "For a dead girl."

There were more footsteps on the porch. Heavy ones.

"You're crazy as a pet coon," Bastard fumed. "This would have been good to know, early. But let's discuss your female trouble later. It looks like we're about to go into a fight, and all we have between us is the knife Old Wolfskins gave me."

I pulled the half of the Queen of Spades from my pocket and placed it on the counter.

"Mordechai," I said, "I think it's time to redeem my gun."

He went around the counter, rummaged in some

pigeonholes beneath a shelf, and came out with the Manhattan. I took the gun, flipped open the gate, and turned the cylinder. It was loaded.

Somebody started banging on the door.

"How many boxes of .38 rimfire cartridges do you have?"

Mordechai picked through the ammunition on the shelf.

"Three," he said.

"Give me two," I said. "One for each pocket."

The banging on the door became pounding.

"Mordechai, you filthy Jew!" Harlan shouted from the porch. "Open up!"

"You need more than a knife," I told Bastard.

"I'm not a great shot," he said.

"Then pick something loud and scary," I said.

"All guns are loud and scary," Bastard said, standing uncertainly in front of the rack of long guns.

While stuffing shells into my pockets, I went over and glanced at the guns. In the middle was a short-barreled shotgun in ten gauge.

"Take that Meteor coach gun," I said.

"Yeah, I like the sound of that," he said, picking it out of the rack.

"Open a box of shells," I said. "Buckshot. Start stuffing your pockets."

"I don't like this," Mordechai said. "Shouldn't we try talking first? We don't even know what they want."

"What do they ever want?" I asked. "They want to hurt somebody. You'd best hide and claim later you weren't here at all."

Mordechai crept up to the door and listened. He opened his mouth to say something, but then backed away when somebody started kicking the door hard enough to splinter the frame.

"Mordechai!" Harlan shouted. "What are you doing in there? We saw those strangers ride in with that scroll box. You know you ain't supposed to have that. This town ain't run by no Jew law. If you're in there hiding from us, we'll skin you alive and feed your hide to the dogs."

"Take your scroll and find the best hiding spot you can," I said. "Don't go out the back, because they're expecting that—I'm sure they've sent some men around to watch the back door. That's what I would do."

"You could stay here and hide."

"Nope," I said. "They'd burn us out. These things are very predictable. Then you'd lose your scroll and the store, and we'd all be dead. No, we'll have to go out the front."

"But they'll kill you," he said.

"If they don't kill him," Bastard said, breaking the shotgun and slipping in a couple of bright brass shells that were nearly the diameter of quarter dollars, "I will."

"I'm sorry to bring this kind of trouble."

"What, my people aren't used to it?" Mordechai said. "I still thank you for returning the scroll."

"Understood," I said. "Now, go. Hide it."

Mordechai disappeared into the back room.

The door was nearly out of the frame now.

"As soon as you see a face," I told Bastard, "you let go with both barrels. There will be a lot of smoke, so use the cover to drop down to the floor and reload. I'll jump out of the smoke and see if I can push 'em back, and when my pistol is dry, you come up and fire again and let me reload."

"What?" he asked.

"Shoot and reload," I said. "Keep low."

"Got it," he said. "What then? What do we do outside?"

"Hell," I said. "Don't worry about that. We'll probably be dead before we hit the street."

Bastard cocked both hammers on the Meteor.

Then the door fell inward and one of Harlan's henchman came in, holding a lever-action Winchester. He saw Bastard bring up the coach gun and managed to get one round off from the rifle, which zinged past us and broke a jug of molasses on a shelf behind us. Then Bastard pulled both triggers and unleashed hell. Most of the buckshot missed the man with the rifle but nearly cut in half a tough standing behind him. Some of the buck shattered the stock of the Winchester and some went into the man's thigh.

I rushed through the smoke and fired two rounds into the chest of the guy with the shattered rifle and stepped over him as he fell dead in the doorway. The man behind him was shockingly dead, because his guts were scattered across the porch. Harlan and a couple of his thugs were running like hell for the safety of the opposite sidewalk, and I snapped off two quick shots at the sonuvabitch, but missed both times.

"Reload!" I shouted behind me.

The one-eyed dog was barking furiously and the mules were fighting the post, shuffling away from the animal. Then I saw somebody coming up from behind, using the mules for cover, and I dropped down to one knee to try to see him beneath the belly of the beasts.

Then there was the flash of gunmetal as a rifle barrel came swinging down on me and I pointed the Manhattan and pulled the trigger, but the hammer fell on a dud cartridge.

The misfire should have cost my life.

I had no time to reload or even move for cover before I swallowed a round from the rifle. Then, quicker than I can tell it, George Hearst lashed out with a hind leg at the yapping dog but missed and put a hoof right in the man's face. There was a terrible pop as the man's skull caved and he fell backward, the rifle falling from his hands. The Winchester went off as the butt hit the ground, but the bullet went harmlessly into the air.

"Thanks, George," I said.

The mule brayed, as if in response.

Then Bastard came up and dropped to one knee beside me, the Meteor clutched in his hands. I had flipped open the gate and was punching out spent cartridges as fast as I could.

"What now?" he asked.

"Run," I said, digging into my pocket for more shells and jamming them one by one into the cylinder. Then Harlan and his boys opened up from across the street and slugs began digging into the planks around us; I felt one puff my sleeve without hitting meat. I closed the gate on the Manhattan and began running down the sidewalk, trying to present as hard a target as possible—and shooting sideways as I ran.

One of the mules screamed, and I glanced over my shoulder to see John D. Rockefeller falling to his knees, still hitched to the post. Then there was another volley and George Hearst fell beside him.

"They've killed the mules," Bastard said.

"We're next," I said.

There was damned little cover on the sidewalk—not a barrel, not a crate, not a water trough. As we ran, bullets were nipping at our heels, and we finally rounded the corner of the last building and dove into an alley, safe for the moment.

Problem was, it was a blind alley. A red rock wall, which enclosed the back yard of some whorehouse or gambler's hell, blocked our escape.

"You should have run in the opposite direction," I told Bastard as I jammed my back against the side of the building and reloaded the Manhattan. "This way, we're both going to die."

"You told me to run," he said. "You didn't say which way."

I closed the gate and cocked the Manhattan.

The buildings were close on either side, and the opening to the street was only about ten feet wide. Bastard started for the rock wall.

"Don't," I said. "Stay up here near the corners, because it'll make it harder for them to get us. Go down there and they have a lot more angles to pick you off."

"How high do you think this wall is?"

"I dunno," I said. "Twelve or fifteen feet."

"We can get up it," he said.

"How?"

"Jump up on my shoulders and you can reach the top," he said.

"Nuts to that," I said.

"No, really," he said. "Come on, you're lighter than I am. You go up first and pull me over."

I heard men running toward us in the street.

Bastard leaned the Meteor against the wall and hunched his shoulders.

"Let's go," he said. "We're out of time."

I poked my gun from around the corner and sent a couple of shots down the street, hoping to slow them down. Then I jammed the Manhattan in my pocket and took a run toward the wall. I hopped up on Bastard's shoulders and he stood up as I did it, and the momentum threw me up high enough that I could get a hand over the wall. I pulled myself up and then got a leg over the wall, then swiveled on my belly and reached down.

Our hands were separated by eighteen inches.

"Dammit," Bastard said. "Go on, it's no good."

I could see Harlan and two of his men out in the street, crouched down, approaching warily. I recognized the one with the Montana pinch hat and the other, who I had thought of as the Smiling One. Bastard snatched up the Meteor and fired one barrel, kicking up dust and scattering Harlan and the others, but doing no damage.

"Come on, jump," I said. "It's not that far."

Bastard fired the second barrel of the Meteor and then tossed the shotgun aside. He took a run and jumped, reaching out with his right hand toward my left. It was a helluva jump, as if he had springs in his moccasins, and he clamped his hand around my wrist.

"Got you," I said, and began pulling him up.

Bastard clawed at the wall with his other hand and then found some purchase on the wall with his right foot, and he was pushing himself up when I saw Harlan plant his feet in the red sand of the alley and use both hands to steady his Remington. The quirt was dangling from his wrist.

"Push," I said.

Harlan fired a single shot.

It struck Bastard in the back, low on one side, and the slug went through his body and ignited the 10-gauge shells in the pocket of his jeans. The pocket blew out in a flash of white light and smoke, spraying buckshot and blood.

Harlan laughed.

I increased my grip and pulled harder.

Bastard's eyes went wide in shock.

"Jacob," he said. "I am killed."

"You can make it," I said. "Just get over the wall."

"Let me go," he said.

"No!"

"It hurts," he said. "Let me go."

Then he sagged, and he started pulling me back over the wall into the alley. I fought, and in my struggle the Manhattan fell from my pocket to the ground on the gambler's hell side. The lower he sank, the less leverage I had, and by the time his feet touched the alley, I came tumbling down beside him.

My gun was on the other side of the wall. The Meteor was spent. Bastard was on his side, a bullet hole in his back and his stomach made a ruin from the explosion of the shells in his pocket. His blood was everywhere. There was nothing to do but to draw him to me and squeeze his hand.

"You didn't let go," he said.

"No, Ishmael," I said.

"I hate that name," he said, slurring his words.

"Couldn't you have thought of something else? Jack, maybe. I've always admired that name."

"Sure," I said. "That would have been better."

Blood dripped from the corner of his mouth.

"Did I ever tell you my Apache name?"

I shook my head.

"Good," he said. "You were a lousy brother, you know? But I'm glad that I did not kill you and eat your liver."

Then his eyes became dull. He took one last, ragged breath, and was gone. And I know this doesn't make any sense, but his body became *lighter* in my arms. How much does a human soul weigh? In Ishmael's case, it must have been heavy.

"You one-eyed sonuvabitch," Harlan said. "Three of my cousins are dead."

I couldn't look at him.

"Let go of that corpse and talk to me," Harlan said.

I didn't speak.

Harlan had his henchman lift me to my feet. But I kept hold of Ishmael's hand, and didn't let go until they pried my fingers away.

"You hurt bad?" Harlan asked.

I was bleeding from the side of the face, where some rock shards had splattered after the shotgun shells exploded. Harlan reached out and turned my face to get a look, and the quirt brushed my chest.

"No, it ain't deep," he said.

Harlan's cousin with the Montana pinch hat put this gun to my forehead.

"Let me blow his brains out," he said. "Then we can pick up the pieces of his broken skull and give them as a present to the boys' mother."

"What, and let him die easy?" Harlan said. "Let's skin him instead."

The Montana pinch reluctantly lowered the gun.

"You just had to bring the Jew law back, didn't you?" Harlan asked. "You should have learned your lesson the first time you came to town."

I spat in his face.

Harlan wiped his sleeve across his face.

"Cousin, what is today?"

"Friday," the Smiling One said. "Good Friday."

"That's what I thought," Harlan said.

He lashed me across the face with the quirt, then drew back for another strike. When I instinctively turned away from the next blow, he clubbed me in the head with the butt of his revolver.

THIRTY-TWO

When I came to, I was hanging two hundred and fifty feet above the Canyon Diablo gorge, lashed by my wrists to a wooden beam that was dangling from the end of the unfinished railway bridge.

The sun was the color of iron that had just been taken from a forge, and it was slipping beneath a bank of storm clouds that was coming in from the southwest. It had been about noon when Harlan killed Bastard in the blind alley, and now it was nearly dark, so I reckoned I had been hanging there for a few hours.

I looked up, but couldn't see the top of the bridge.

"Harlan!" I shouted. "You up there, you murderous sonuvabitch?"

There was no answer.

"If I get down from here, you're going to be one dead mouth-breathing, Jew-hating bastard." Then, softer: "If I get down from here. You know what you're doing, don't you?"

The hemp cut into my wrists and my arms felt like they were going to pull out of their sockets. My chest was tight and it was difficult to breathe. My ankles were bound, but free, and if I was careful I could get my feet on one of the steel members of the bridge and raise myself a bit to relieve the pressure on my arms and chest.

That lasted until the pain in my ankles became unbearable and my leg muscles began to shake, and then I had to let myself hang again from my wrists. The cycle repeated every five or six minutes, and became more painful each time.

I shouted for help, but none came.

Looking down, I could see the big girders of the bridge, spread out like a stepladder, and the little creek that meandered through the bottom of the canyon. Then a red-tailed hawk glided past, a hundred feet below me, and I realized how high I really was. From then on I tried not to look down, because it made me dizzy—and I couldn't help imagining what it would be like if the rope broke and I plunged to the bottom, tied to slab of lumber.

As the sun crawled toward the western rim and the shadows swept up from the floor of the canyon, I started reckoning how long it would be before I suffocated. An hour? Two? Maybe I would go mad first, I thought, but I couldn't decide if that would be better or not.

Then the thirst started.

My mouth was dry from the shouting, but soon it went from dry to burning. If only I could have a little water, I thought. I watched the storm clouds and wished them to hurry. The only thing worse than the thirst was the pain in my arms and chest.

I kept shifting around on the girder, trying to get

my feet beneath me, and shifting my arms around to where the pain was the least. But all of this was exhausting, and it wasn't long before my arms began to shake and then to spasm. It felt like somebody had stuck a hot poker beneath my shoulder blades, and I cried out in pain and anger.

"Harlan!" I screamed "This isn't done!"

Then my body went limp and my chin fell to my chest. I didn't pass out, but I wasn't exactly conscious, either. As my mind became dull, so did the pain. In my dream-like state, it seemed as if I were floating over the canyon. I was drifting on the wind, just like the dust motes that would dance in a shaft of sunlight back in the cabin in Missouri when I was a boy.

"What do you see, Jacob?" my mother asks, glancing up from the Bible, her eyes blazing. "What do you see?"

"Everything," I say.

The revelation hits me like a bolt of lightning. In an instant I see it all—the moment of my birth, my father's body carried out of the prison in Missouri, my mother's death during childbirth in Texas. The years unspool like a ball of twine that has been kicked across the floor. Now I am born, now I am thirteen, now I am thirty-two. Amity dies bloody in Argentine, I am killing the doctor, I am holding my brother as he dies.

Always and forever we cross the ocean of time, propelled forward by the beating of our hearts, battered by fear and desire, making for unknown shores.

"Forgive me, Lord, for I know not what I have done."

Then I was jerked upward.

I was being hauled up from the end of the bridge, and with each jerk of the rope, my arms felt like they were going to leave their sockets and I gasped in pain. Finally I reached the top, and was hauled over, and was held up by strong hands while the beam was cut free. The beam was then pitched over the bridge and sailed end over end into the darkness below.

Somebody handed me a cup of water, and I drank it down and asked for more. Then I looked at the faces around me and realized it was Mordechai and the women I had seen cleaning up the blood after the sheriff had been killed at the opera house.

"Thank you," I rasped.

Mordechai squeezed my shoulder.

"What, we would leave you hanging like a Christmas goose?"

"My brother?"

"Buried," he said. "At the gentile cemetery at the edge of town. I'm sorry, but we had to do it quickly, before the Sabbath."

"Harlan?"

"Dead drunk," he said. "Celebrating your crucifixion."

"He must die."

"How can you kill when you can't even stand?" Mordechai asked. "Come, it is nearly sundown. Rest tonight. Leave town tomorrow. Forget the killing."

THIRTY-THREE

At sunrise the next morning, I went to Bastard's grave at the edge of town. The ground was hard and dry, because it never did rain the night before. I sat cross-legged beside the mound of sand and rocks, wondering what Bastard would have thought about being put in the ground rather than tucked away in some cave.

I had the fiddle, because Mordechai had taken the valise from behind George Hearst's saddle before they hauled away the dead mules in front of his store. I also had Bastard's black knife in my pocket, because Mordechai had thought it was better somebody should have it than let it rust in a grave.

I held the fiddle close to my ear and turned the pegs, bringing the strings in tune. Then I took the bow in my left hand and stood.

"I'm not sure if you've even heard this tune," I said. "But I know our mother liked it and so I'm going to play it, because it seems like the right thing to do. At least, it will make me feel some better."

Then I went into a slow and mournful rendition of

"Star of the County Down." When I was finished, I tucked the fiddle under my arm and stood quiet for a moment.

"You were right," I said. "I was a lousy brother. I'm sorry, but there's not a damned thing I can do to make up for that now. If I had to do it again, I'd do it different, but time is a river that doesn't flow upstream. But I can guess what you'd want me to do, if you could talk, and I'm going to do it even though I reckon it's a mortal sin."

Then I walked back into town.

Mordechai had just opened his store, and I walked in and placed the fiddle on the counter.

"And what do you want me to do with this?" he asked.

"Put it someplace safe," I said.

"I can do that," he said. "But for why aren't you leaving town?"

"Things aren't done yet."

"No, Harlan has not finished killing you," he said. "There is still room beside your brother in the cemetery. Are you crazy? Get out of here."

When I didn't say anything, Mordechai shrugged.

"All right, it's your funeral," he said. "Everybody all of a sudden is changing their minds. After the Torah came back, the people have decided to stay."

THIRTY-FOUR

I took Mordechai's last box of .38 rimfires and slipped them into my pocket, then set out down Hell Street toward the opera house. The one-eyed dog fell in behind me, trotting as if he knew where I was going.

"What do you want?" I asked, turning.

He growled.

"Scat!" I shouted.

He barked once, then ran away.

"Smart dog," I said.

The doors of The Gilded Thing were wide open, just as I had left them. I walked in and planted my feet on the plank floor, feeling the red sand grind beneath my soles. The place was empty except for the bartender.

"What the hell do you want?" Finley asked.

"Out," I said, drawing the Manhattan. "Get out now. And don't reach for that scattergun beneath the bar, or they'll be picking your back teeth out of that wall behind you."

Finley showed me his palms, then ran out the back door.

"Astrid!" I shouted. "Come down!"

I could hear Judge Rex's footsteps above my head.

"What is it?" he roared, peeking from the top of the iron staircase. "Who's there?"

"Jacob Gamble," I said.

"Why, it's the humorist," Rex said, taking a couple of steps down. He had on a robe over his nightclothes and there was a machine-rolled cigarette in his hand. "I thought you would be dead by now."

"So did I."

"What do you want?"

"Astrid," I said.

He laughed.

"Of course you do," he said. "But you can't have her because she's mine. Like my clothes, or this building, or even this town. Mine. Understand?"

"Perfectly," I said. "Now, hand her over."

Just then the one-eyed dog barked outside, and I turned to see Harlan in the doorway, drawing his revolver. He fired, and the bullet sang past my ear and hit the staircase with a spark.

"Kill him, you idiot, not me," Judge Rex said, cringing.

I took a run and jumped over the bar. Harlan shot twice more, the slugs splintering the bar top.

"You all right, boss?" Harlan called.

"Less talk, more shooting," Rex called.

Harlan put a round through the bar, just a few inches from where I was sitting. I flattened myself on the floor and began crawling on my stomach toward the back door, the Manhattan still in my hand. Another couple of rounds came through, one at the far end and one just above my back.

Then I could hear the soft clicks and other metallic sounds of Harlan reloading, and I took my chance. I got my feet under me and then sprang up, pointing the revolver over the bar. Problem was, through the gunsmoke I could see the Montana pinch and the Smiling One now standing on either side of Harlan, guns in hand.

Both were a bit slow in reacting, however, and I put a bullet in the chest of the Smiling One before either could get their guns to bear. The Smiling One went down, a bloody froth on his lips, and this rattled the Montana pinch enough that he missed me by a foot as I ducked again behind the bar.

"Dammit," Harlan said. "Kill him."

"I thought we killed him yesterday," the Montana pinch said.

Bullets began coming through the bar again.

I saw the butt of the single-barreled shotgun and pulled it from the shelf. Putting the Manhattan in my pocket, I broke the breech and saw brass, then closed it back again. Then I put my back to the floor and held the scattergun with both hands over my chest.

"Truce," I shouted.

"Truce?" Harlan asked. "We have you outgunned! There's no truce, just dying."

My ears were ringing so that it was hard to make out the words.

"All right," I said "I give up."

I tensed, knowing that he would send Montana pinch creeping behind the bar.

"Throw your gun out," Harlan said.

"Okay, here it comes."

Just then I saw the peaked hat coming over the bar, and I fired the shotgun at it—and missed. The buckshot went into the ceiling and some dust and plaster came down, and a great cloud of gunsmoke hung over the bar. I made use of the cover to grab the Manhattan and run out the back door.

Now, I don't know what I expected when I walked into The Gilded Thing, other than to kill Harlan and maybe Rex and to free Astrid. And I might have done it, if the Smiling One and the Montana pinch hadn't heard the gunshots and come running.

In a few moments, Harlan and the Montana pinch were chasing me down Hell Street. Mordechai was standing in his doorway, and he watched as I passed.

"Why haven't I killed you yet?" Harlan called as he ran past.

"Nobody's perfect?" Mordechai asked.

"Your people have until morning," Harlan said. "Then, I burn you out."

Then they began shooting, and if they had stopped to take aim they would have killed me. As it was, they were kicking up the red dust around my heels.

Nearing the gorge, I left Hell Street and made for the Santa Fe tracks. There was more cover now, what with the rusting piles of equipment and the flatcars. I slipped between the flatcars with the great bridge pieces on them, just as I had last seen them seven weeks ago, and kept going south.

The terrain was so broken near the canyon that I couldn't go very fast, but at least there was cover. I reckoned Harlan and the Montana pinch would give up after a mile or so, but I was wrong. Every time I would stop, I would either hear them coming through the scrub, or they would get a glimpse and take a pot-shot at me.

This went on for three or four miles.

I kept looking for a spot to make a stand, but there was no high ground—things were flat as a flapjack until you got near the edge of the canyon, and then it turned into crevices and ravines.

So, I kept going south, picking my way over the rocks, and dodging the occasional bullet fired from behind. Then I came to a deeper ravine, and my only way across was a natural rock bridge of twenty or so feet. I was jumpy, because of being shot at, and tired. Also, I thought there were shadows moving in the scrub along the edge of the gorge.

I saw something dark out of the corner of my eye while crossing the rock bridge, and I paused a bit too long. Then I felt something slam into my right arm as I heard the gunshot, and I lost my footing and pitched into the ravine below.

I landed in the sand and rocks below.

The bullet had broken my arm just above the elbow. Blood was dripping down to my wrist and although it didn't hurt yet, it soon would. The walls of the ravine were too steep for me to climb out with just one arm.

A plume of red dust drifted in the air.

Behind it was a shadow where there was a deep cleft in the wall, and I thought it might be deep enough to hide in. I picked up the Manhattan and scrambled over to where some rock jutted out from the wall like the face of an old man.

I felt cool air on my face.

It was the cave, of course, that Bastard had told me about.

I slipped just deep enough inside the cave to be hidden by shadow, but still have a good view of the ravine. I held the Manhattan tightly in my left hand and waited. Soon, there was a cascade of rocks and red dust, and Harlan and the Montana pinch came sliding down.

"Look at the blood," the Montana pinch said. "Told you I got him."

"Be careful," Harlan said. "He might not be dead."

"Oh, he has to be somewhere down here," the Pinch said, peering over the rocks. "He's just crawled off a bit to die."

This was better than high ground. I could see their every move, but they couldn't see me. And once I killed one, the other—who would be struggling to climb up the ravine wall—would be just as easy.

I cocked the Manhattan and waited for the Pinch to come close to where I was hidden. When he did, I put a bullet right in his forehead.

He flew back, hands outstretched, dead.

If I thought gunplay indoors was loud, it was nothing compared to shooting from the mouth of a cave. My head felt like it was filled with tolling churchbells.

Then I tried to cock the revolver for another shot, but the hammer wouldn't come back. The cylinder had gotten jammed when I dropped it on the rocks when I fell, and I couldn't get another shot off.

Harlan had nearly climbed out of the ravine when he realized another shot wasn't coming. Slowly, he came back down, his Remington in hand.

"You've shot your pistol dry, haven't you?" Harlan called.

I backed deeper into the cave.

"You're deep in scat now, ain't you?" Harlan asked. "You're hurt real bad, and you're out of ammunition, and you got nowhere to go. I'm finally going to kill you, you filthy Jew-loving bastard."

I went deeper in the cave, remembering what Bastard had told me, keeping my good shoulder against the left wall. Harlan approached, taking each step slow, the bright barrel of the Remington leading the way.

Deeper I went.

"I can hear you," Harlan said.

He came farther still, and then he was lost in darkness, too.

Shutting my eyes and keeping my shoulder against the cold rock wall, I moved yet deeper into the cave. And every time I heard Harlan advance, the more distance I put between us. As long as I could keep him from bumping into me, I thought, I had a chance of surviving.

Then my boots found a tangle of twigs, and I froze—the crunching sound was so loud that Harlan would surely detect my location. I could not move in any direction, for fear of breaking more twigs and encouraging a bullet in the stomach.

Harlan laughed.

"I have you now," he said.

Then he lit a wooden match with his thumb. It sparked and caught, and he held the wavering orange flame over his head. He was about twenty feet away from me, and I could see him clearly, holding the Remington at gut-level.

I took the black knife from my pocket and flipped

away the sheath. I jammed the Manhattan beneath
my ruined arm and used the point of the knife to try
to free the cylinder.

"All jammed up, huh?"

Then his smile faded as he looked down at what my
boots were tangled in. It was a human ribcage. The
skull was not far away. Harlan turned, and the match
revealed more skeletons in various states of disarray.

"What the hell is this place?" he asked.

Then he saw a dark figure crouching at the edge of
his matchlight. Then it stood. It was human, but just
barely, and its eyes were wild and red-rimmed. It
wore nothing except a necklace of finger bones and
a filthy breachclout. It grinned, revealing a mouthful
of teeth that were sharp and yellow.

"Oh, Christ!" Harlan said.

Then the match burned down to his fingers and
Harlan dropped it. The Remington went off, and in
the flash of the gunshot I saw the *sanguinario* spring-
ing at Harlan like a mountain lion would pounce on
a lamb.

I also saw another one of the things coming at me.

Instinctively, I held the knife out and felt the blade
sink into the thing's chest. It let out a pitiful cry and
scurried back, and I could hear bones and skulls
being scattered as it went.

I stumbled toward the entrance, keeping my left
shoulder to the cave wall. I shoved the Manhattan in
my pocket but kept the knife out until I had made it
all the way back to the sunlight and rock that looked
like an old man.

The black blade was covered in blood.

Then I sat down on a rock on the far side of the

ravine from the cave, holding the knife tightly in my hand. I must have sat there for a couple of hours, bleeding and getting light-headed, but forcing myself to stay awake. If I went to sleep, whatever had gotten Harlan would try to eat me as well.

Finally, there were a skittering of pebbles from above.

"*¡Bastardo!*" someone called.

"He's dead."

"*¿Verdad?*"

It was Candelario, the Rurale who had tried to arrest Bastard in Tombstone. He came sliding down into the ravine.

"Yes, it's the truth," I said.

"That is too bad for me," he said.

"And for him."

"I have trailed you both for many days," he said. "I nearly had you at the ruined mission, where the massacre had occurred, but then I lost you in the Dragoon Mountains."

"Well, you have found me."

"What has happened to you?"

"Fell," I said. "Broke my arm."

"It looks like a gunshot wound," he said, removing his bandana to make me a sling. "Not to worry. I will help you get back on top, and then we will take you to the nearest town. It is not far away, where the railway bridge crosses the canyon."

I nodded.

"And you will show me where Bastard is buried, no?"

* * *

At Canyon Diablo, Mordechai cleaned my wound with whiskey and wrapped it with clean linen, but said they would have to send me back east to Winslow the next day so that a doctor could set it.

"I'd rather have a vet," I said.

Then I walked down the street to the opera house.

"Astrid!" I called from the bottom of the staircase.

"No need to shout," Judge Rex said from the top of the staircase.

"Harlan is dead," I said.

"So I've heard," Judge Rex said. "That kind of news travels fast."

"I want to talk to Astrid," I said. "You'd better not stand in the way, either."

"Of course not," the fat man said putting a store-bought cigarette in his mouth. "You are certainly free to speak to her. Astrid, my dear, the gentlemen in blood and black would like a word with you."

She slipped past him and came down the stairs. She was wearing a fine silk robe.

"It's over," I said. "Come with me."

"Why would I want to do that?" she asked, hugging her arms to her breasts.

"Because you're free now," I said. "Amity, you're free."

"Who's Amity?"

I closed my eyes. I was exhausted and had lost too much blood. My arm was hurting like a hell and what I needed was a shot of whiskey and a slug of laudanum.

"You look quite ill," she said.

"No," I said. "Come with me. You don't have to be with him anymore."

"Do you think I'm a piece of property to be handed over?"

"What?"

"That's how you spoke of me earlier. Didn't you think to ask me what I wanted?" she asked, her eyes hard and bright. "Look, I'm where I want to be. Rex is not so bad, at least not to me. And there's something to be said for a little money and power. All I was before this was a hired girl. At least now, I have some nice things and I get to encourage Rex to, you know, be kinder. The Jews can stay."

I was swaying a bit, so I put my hand on the staircase.

"Understand?" she asked.

"Sadly, yes."

I turned and made it halfway to the door.

"Humorist," Judge Rex called from the top of the staircase. "Don't go. I have a business proposition for you. It seems I am in need of a lieutenant. You have proven qualifications."

I paused, leaning against the bar for support.

"It's that easy for you?"

"I can make it worth your while."

"Go to hell," I said, lurching for the door.

"Alas," he said. "We are already there."

Arizona, 1935

"They shipped me back to Winslow, where I got my arm set by a vet and found a gunsmith to repair the Manhattan," the old man said. "They completed the bridge over Canyon Diablo a few months later, and then the town just dried up."

It was dawn, and the morning star was quickly fading.

Huston was sitting across from Jacob Gamble at the camp table, and the monkey was asleep in his lap. Frankie rubbed her eyes, then reviewed her notes.

"Jake," Frankie said, "Do you really expect us to believe that these *sanguinario* monsters killed Harlan?"

"There's an easy way to find out," Gamble said.

"What, go looking in the Apache death cave?" she asked. "No thanks—besides, they've hauled a lot of bones out of there over the years. They used them as props in those fake cliff dwellings, to impress the tourists. I don't think I'll learn anything by going down there and standing in the dark."

"You underestimate the dark," Gamble said.

Frankie shivered.

"What is today?" Gamble asked.

"Saturday," Frankie said. "No, Sunday. The four-teenth day of April. We have twenty days left to make this movie. John, are you ready to shoot?"

"We have to, Bogart has a six o'clock call," Huston said.

"Is he here yet?"

"The studio promised he would be."

"Do we have a scene?"

"You mean one that'll pass the production code?"

Frankie put the pencil in her mouth and leafed through her pages.

"What about the crucifixion?" Huston asked.

Frankie mumbled.

"Take the pencil out of your mouth."

"Yeah, it might work," Frankie said. "He's alone.

But the next train is at eight thirty-five—can we finish by then?"

"If we can't," Huston said, "then we'll stay on Bogart's face while the train rumbles overhead. That should introduce an authentic element of anguish."

"You can't torture the poor man," Frankie said.

"Of course I can," Huston said. "He's an *actor*."

"Are you finished with me?" Gamble asked.

"Yes," Huston said. "Until we need to know what comes next."

The black 1934 Chevrolet with RKO on the sides pulled to a stop in the middle of Hell Street. The man in the goggles got out and strode over to the table, holding an envelope tightly in his hand.

"Mister Huston," he said. "I tried finding you last night, but you weren't at the motel up on Route 66. This cable came for you."

Huston opened the envelope and unfolded the Western Union telegram. He read the message, then laughed so loudly that he woke the monkey.

"What is it?" Frankie asked.

He handed her the telegram.

MR JOHN HUSTON CANYON DIABLO ARIZ =
BOGART UNAVAILABLE =
WARNER BROS MAKING 'PETRIFIED FOREST' =
RELEASE PRODUCTION TO CHARLES VIDOR FOR
'THE ARIZONIAN'

"That's it then," Frankie said. "It's over."

"For now," Huston said.

"Us, too?" she asked quietly.

"That as well," Huston said.

He rose from the table and put the monkey on his shoulder.

"Good day," Huston said, and tipped his cap before walking away.

Frankie slumped in her chair.

"So, what are you going to do now?" Gamble asked.

"What I've always done," Frankie said. "Shift for myself, mainly. Steer clear of trouble, when I can. And you?"

"Mexico," he said. "Or further south. There are still wild places down there, I hear. Places where a man can live like a man—and die like a man, if he has to."

Frankie smiled.

"Come with me," Gamble said. "Make an old man happy."

"I've had enough of making men happy," Frankie said. "I don't want to live in some banana republic waiting for you to die like a man. That's a scene I'd rather not witness in real life."

Gamble smiled.

"You're okay, kid," he said, rising.

Gamble stood.

"Jake," she said. "You really know when you're going to die?"

"Yes," he said.

"Does it scare you?"

"No," he said. "Kind of a relief, actually."

"Then tell me," she said. "It's not Mexico, is it? Are you still shaking your fist at God? Is there gunplay? Is a woman involved? Just give me a hint."

"Can't," Gamble said, fixing his cuffs and testing the weight of the .45 automatic in his coat pocket.

"Why not?"

"Because," he said, leaning down and kissing her on the forehead. "It would spoil what comes next."

In a land of legends the Loner has nothing to prove.
That's usually when violence finds its way to him . . .

VENGEANCE WILL BE MINE

For a posse chasing a murderous band of outlaws, a
quiet kid with a lightning-fast gun is good company.
And when the outlaws turn around and attack the posse,
the Loner doesn't have a choice: he's now caught up in
a running gun battle across West Texas. The Loner
knows the men he's fighting are bad to the bone—led
by a merciless killer named Warren Latch. But what
about the guys on his side? As men on both sides of
the fight bite the dust, the Loner has fewer allies and
no way out. That's when a beautiful bounty hunter
appears on the scene—to lead the way into another
vendetta, another betrayal, and one final bloody
fight to the death. . . .

The Loner: BRUTAL VENGEANCE

USA Today Bestselling Author
J. A. Johnstone

On sale now, wherever Pinnacle Books are sold!

THE GREATEST WESTERN WRITER
OF THE 21ST CENTURY

*In the harsh, unforgiving American frontier, in the
vast wilderness that is Wyoming a ruthless gang of
cutthroats is cutting a bloody swath of death and
destruction through the territory. No one can
stop them . . . no one, that is, except for a legendary
mountain man named Matt Jensen.*

Massacre at Powder River

The year is 1884. A 10-year-old British boy has come
to visit his uncle's Wyoming spread . . . just as the
vicious Yellow Kerchief Gang has the ranch under
siege. Outgunned and outmatched, a British rancher is
willing to pay $5,000 for help. That is more than
enough money to bring Matt Jensen into the fray.
A huge, bloody gunfight, fueled by betrayal, erupts
at the Powder River. But Matt has to shoot carefully.
The Yellow Kerchief Gang has a hostage—the British
lad, whose name is Winnie. And Matt has history on his
hands, because Winston Churchill must survive. . . .
Fifty years later, Winston Churchill will fight
a war of his own—carrying a Matt Jensen .44 shell
in his pocket and a gunfighter's spirit in his soul.

MATT JENSEN, THE LAST MOUNTAIN MAN:
Massacre at Powder River

A Bold Epic Series by the *USA Today* Bestselling Author
WILLIAM W. JOHNSTONE
with J. A. Johnstone

On sale now, wherever Pinnacle Books are sold!